PRAISE FOR THE STAGE DIVE SERIES

"The stuff my rock-star dreams are made of. A thrill ride. I felt every stomach-dip in the process. And I want to turn right around and ride it again. Every girl who's ever had a rock-star crush, this would be the ultimate fantasy."

—*Maryse's Book Blog*

"This book rocked my world!! *Lick* is an addictive blend of heartwarming passion and lighthearted fun. It's a story you can lose yourself in. The perfect rock-star romance!"

—*Aestas Book Blog*

"An engrossing, sexy, and emotional read."   —*Dear Author*

"Scrumptious and delicious. Firmly in my top ten best books this year!"   —*The Book Pushers*

"Pure rocker perfection in every single way . . . *Play* is a splendid marriage of romance and comedy, and I would recommend it to anyone who likes their love stories with a side of giggles."

—*Natasha is a Book Junkie*

"Kylie Scott is quickly becoming one of my favorite authors at combining funny with sexy, and I can't wait to read more from her. *Play* is a definite must-read!"   —*Smut Book Club*

"*Lick* is a breath of fresh air with a unique story line, think *Hangover* meets Contemporary Romance."

—*The Rock Stars of Romance*

ALSO BY KYLIE SCOTT

Lick

Play

Kylie Scott

 ST. MARTIN'S GRIFFIN ⚐ NEW YORK

PLAY. Copyright © 2014 by Kylie Scott. All rights reserved. Printed in the United States of America. For information, address St. Martin's Press, 175 Fifth Avenue, New York, N.Y. 10010.

www.stmartins.com

Designed by Steven Seighman

The Library of Congress Cataloging-in-Publication Data
is available upon request.

ISBN 978-1-250-05237-7 (trade paperback)
ISBN 978-1-4668-5423-9 (e-book)

St. Martin's Griffin books may be purchased for educational, business, or promotional use. For information on bulk purchases, please contact Macmillan Corporate and Premium Sales Department at 1-800-221-7945, extension 5442, or write specialmarkets@macmillan.com.

First published as an e-book in April 2014 by St. Martin's Griffin

First St. Martin's Griffin Paperback Edition: September 2014

10 9 8 7 6 5 4 3 2 1

For Hugh. Always and ever and all the rest.

ACKNOWLEDGMENTS

Any lyrics come courtesy of Soviet X-Ray Record Club. You can learn more about the band here: www.sovietxrayrecordclub.com.

Many thanks to my awesome agent, Amy Tannenbaum; my beyond wonderful editor, Rose Hilliard at St. Martin's Press; Cate, Haylee, Danielle, and everyone at Macmillan Australia (you rock); everyone at Macmillan UK; and to Joel, Mark, and Tara at Momentum. Also, thank you to Chas and everyone at Rockstar PR and Literary Services for all your hard work.

Big thanks to my beta and crit queens: Jo (you're not quite as bad as I make you out to be, mostly), Sali Benbow-Powers, Kendall Ryan, and Hang Le. The time you spend and care you invest in giving me your honest opinion is always appreciated.

Thanks to my friends, Joanna Wylde, Kim Karr, Katy Evans, Kim Jones, and Renee Carlino for being the wealth of sanity and support that they are.

Thank you to all the bloggers and readers, especially to Dear Author, Jen and Gitte from Totally Booked, Aestas, Natasha is a Book Junkie, Maryse, The Rock Stars of Romance, Smut Book Club, Shh Mom's Reading, Up All Night Book Blog, Smexy Books, The Book Pushers, Twinsie Talk, Book Chatter Cath, Katrina, Dawn, Under the Covers, Kaetrin, Amber, Angie, Lori, and all of my Groupie Girls. Without a doubt I've forgotten important people who have been kind and supportive. My apologies and thank you very much. I wish I could give you all your own rock star for Christmas.

Play

CHAPTER ONE

Something was wrong. I knew it the moment I walked in the door. With one hand I flicked on the light, dumping my purse onto the couch with the other. After the dimly lit hallway, the sudden glare was dazzling. Little lights flashed before my eyes. When they cleared all I saw were spaces . . . spaces where, just this morning, things had been.

Like the couch.

My purse hit the floor and everything came tumbling out, tampons, loose coins, pens and makeup. A stick of deodorant rolled into the corner. The now empty corner since both the TV and its cabinet were gone. My thrift-store retro table and chairs remained, same with my overflowing bookcase. But the bulk of the room lay bare.

"Skye?"

No answer.

"What the hell?" A stupid question, what had happened here was obvious. Across from me, my roommate's door stood wide open. Nothing but darkness and dust bunnies in there. No point in denying it.

Skye had bailed on me.

My shoulders slumped as the weight of two months' worth of back rent, food and utilities came crushing down upon me. Even my throat closed tight. So this is what it felt like to have a friend fuck you over. I could barely breathe.

"Anne, can I borrow your velvet coat? I promise I'll . . ." Lauren, my neighbor from the apartment next door, strode in (knocking never had been her style). Then, like me, she stopped dead. "Where's your couch?"

I took a deep breath and let it out slow. It didn't help. "I guess Skye took it."

"Skye's gone?"

My mouth opened, but really, what was there to say?

"She's gone and you didn't know she was leaving?" Lauren cocked her head, making her mass of long dark hair swing to and fro. I'd always envied her that hair. Mine was strawberry blond and fine. Anything past shoulder length and it hung limp like I'd stuck my head in a bucket of grease. It's why I didn't tend to let it grow longer than jaw length.

Not that hair mattered.

Making rent mattered.

Having food to eat mattered.

Hair styles? Not so much.

My eyes burned, betrayal stung like a bitch. Skye and I had been friends for years. I'd trusted her. We'd trash-talked boys and shared secrets, cried on each other's shoulders. It just didn't make sense.

Except it did.

It so very painfully did.

"No." My voice sounded strange. I swallowed hard, clearing my throat. "No, I didn't know she was leaving."

"Weird. You two always seemed to get along great."

"Yeah."

"Why would she take off like that?"

"She owed me money," I admitted, kneeling to collect the

contents of my purse. Not to pray to God. I'd given up on him a long time ago.

Lauren gasped. "You're joking. That fucking bitch!"

"Babe, we're running late." Nate, my other next-door neighbor, filled the doorway, eyes impatient. He was a tall well-built guy with an edge. Normally, I envied Lauren her boyfriend. Right then the glory of Nate was lost on me. I was so fucked.

"What's going on?" he asked, looking around. "Hey, Anne."

"Hi, Nate."

"Where's your shit?"

Lauren threw her hands in the air. "Skye took her shit!"

"No," I corrected. "Skye took *her* shit. But she took *my* money."

"How much money?" Nate asked, displeasure dropping his voice by about an octave.

"Enough," I said. "I've been covering for her since she lost her job."

"Damn," muttered Nate.

"Yeah." Seriously, *yeah*.

I picked up my purse and flipped it open. Sixty-five dollars and one lone shiny quarter. How had I let it get this far? My pay check from the bookshop was gone and my credit card maxed. Lizzy had needed help yesterday paying for textbooks and no way would I turn her down. Getting my sister through college came first.

This morning I'd told Skye we needed to talk. All day I'd felt crappy about it, my stomach churning. Because the truth was, the sum total of my talk involved telling her that she needed to ask her parents, or her fancy ass new boyfriend, for a loan to pay me back. I couldn't keep the both of us housed and fed any longer while she searched for a new job. So she also needed to talk to one of them about a place to stay. Yes, I was kicking her to the curb. The guilt had weighed in my stomach like a stone.

Ironic really.

What were the chances of her feeling any remorse for screwing me over? Not likely.

I finished retrieving the contents of my handbag and zipped it up tight. "Ah, yeah, Lauren, the coat's in my closet. At least I hope it is. Help yourself."

Rent was due in eight days. Maybe I could work a miracle. There were sure to be some cash-savvy twenty-three-year-olds with savings in the bank out there. At least one of them must need a place to stay? I'd been doing fine before this. But there'd always been something my sister or I needed more than future financial stability. Books, clothes, a night on the town, all those little treats that made living worthwhile. We'd sacrificed enough already. Yet here I was, broke and on my knees.

Guess I should have prioritized better. Hindsight sucked.

Worst-case scenario, I could probably get away with sleeping on the floor of Lizzy's dorm room if we were super sly. God knows our mom didn't have the cash. Asking her for help was out. If I sold my great-aunt's pearls it might help toward the deposit on another apartment, a smaller one that I could afford on my own.

I'd fix this somehow. Of course, I would. Fixing shit was my specialty.

And if I ever saw Skye again I was going to fucking kill her.

"What'll you do?" asked Nate, lounging against the door frame.

I rose to my feet, dusting off the knees of my black pants. "I'll work something out."

Nate gave me a look and I returned it as calmly as I could.

The next thing to come out of his mouth had better not be pity. My day had been crappy enough. With great determination, I gave him a smile. "So, where are you guys off to?"

"Party at David and Ev's," Lauren answered from inside my room. "You should come with us."

Ev, Nate's sister and Lauren's former roomie, had married David Ferris, premier rock god and lead guitarist for the band Stage Dive, a few months ago. Long story. I was still trying to get my head around it, frankly. One minute, she'd been the nice blond girl next door who went to the same college as Lizzy and made killer coffee at Ruby's Café. The next, our apartment block had been surrounded by paparazzi. Skye had given interviews on the front step—not that she'd known anything. I'd snuck out the back.

Mostly, my relationship with Ev had involved saying hi when we'd passed on the stairs, back when she used to live here, and with me hitting Ruby's Café every morning for a big-ass coffee on my way to work. We'd always been friendly. But I wouldn't say we were friends exactly. Given Lauren's penchant for borrowing my clothes, I knew her much better.

"She should come, right, Nate?"

Nate grunted his affirmation. Either that or his disinterest. With him it was kind of hard to tell.

"That's okay," I demurred. Debris lined the walls where the couch and cabinet had stood; all of the collected crap Skye had left behind. "I had a new book to read, but I should probably get busy cleaning. Guess we hadn't dusted under the furniture for a while. At least I won't have much to move when the time comes."

"Come with us."

"Lauren, I wasn't invited," I said.

"Neither are we half the time," said Nate.

"They love us! Of course they want us there." Lauren re-emerged from my room and gave her boyfriend the stink eye. She looked better in the black vintage jacket than I ever would, a fact that I chose not to secretly hate her for. If that didn't earn me points into heaven then nothing would. Maybe I'd give it to her as a good-bye present before I left.

"Come on, Anne," she said. "Ev won't mind."

"Good to go?" Nate jiggled his car keys impatiently.

Hanging with rock stars didn't seem the appropriate response to learning you'd soon be out on the street. Maybe one day when I was at my sparkling, buffed-up best I could strut on by and say hi. That day was not today. Mostly I felt tired, defeated. Given I'd been feeling that way since I turned sixteen, it wasn't the strongest of excuses. Lauren didn't need to know that, however.

"Thanks, guys," I said. "But I only just got home."

"Um, honey, your home kind of sucks ass right now," said Lauren, taking in my dust bunnies and lack of décor with a sweeping glance. "Besides, it's Friday night. Who sits at home on a Friday night? You wearing your work gear or jumping into jeans? I'd suggest the jeans."

"Lauren . . ."

"Don't."

"But—"

"No." Lauren grasped my shoulders and looked me in the eye. "You have been fucked over by a friend. I have no words to tell you how furious that makes me. You're coming with us. Hide in a corner all night if you want. But you're not sitting here alone dwelling on that thieving ho. You know I never did like her."

Stupidly, I did. Or had. Whatever.

"Didn't I say that, Nate?"

Nate shrugged and jangled his keys some more.

"Go. Get ready." Lauren gave me a push in the general direction of my bedroom.

In my current situation, this might be my only opportunity to meet David Ferris. Ev still showed up here now and then, but I'd never seen him, despite occasionally "hanging out" on the steps just in case. He wasn't my absolute favorite out of the four members of Stage Dive. That honor was reserved for the drummer, Mal Ericson. A few years ago, I'd crushed on him something hard. But still . . . *the* David Ferris. For the chance to meet even just one of them, I had to go. A few years ago, I'd had a bit of a thing for the band. Nothing to do with their being buff rock gods. No, I was a musical purist.

"Alright, give me ten minutes." It was the absolute minimum time frame within which I could mentally, if not physically, prepare myself to face the rich and famous. Fortunately, my care factor was now dangerously close to fuck-it levels. Tonight would probably be the best time to meet Mr. Ferris. I might actually manage to keep my cool and not be an awestruck waste of space.

"Five minutes," said Nate. "The game will be starting."

"Would you relax?" asked Lauren.

"No." The man made a snapping sound and Lauren giggled. I didn't look back. I didn't want to know. The walls here were disgustingly thin so Lauren and Nate's nocturnal mating habits weren't much of a secret. Happily I was usually at work during the day. Those hours were a mystery to me, and not one that I pondered.

Oh, alright. Occasionally I pondered because I hadn't gotten anything non-self-induced in a while. Also, apparently I had some repressed voyeuristic tendencies in need of addressing.

Was I really up to a night of watching couples rubbing against one another?

I could call Reece, though he'd said he had a date tonight. Of course, he always had a date. Reece was perfect in every way apart from his man-whore tendencies. My best guy friend liked to spread his love around, to put it mildly. He seemed to be on a conjugal-related first-name basis with the better part of the straight Portland female population aged eighteen to forty-eight. Everyone except me, basically.

Which was fine.

There was nothing wrong with just being friends. Though someday I truly believed we'd make a great couple. He was just so easy to be around. With everything we had in common, we could go the distance. In the meantime, I was content to wait, do my own thing. Not that lately I'd been doing anything or anyone, but you get what I mean.

Reece would listen to me whine about Skye. He'd probably even cancel his date, come over, and keep me company while I moped. He would, however, definitely say "I told you so." When he'd found out I'd been covering for her, he hadn't been happy. He'd outright accused her of using me. Turned out he'd been 110 percent right on that score.

The wound, however, was too raw to be prodded and poked. So . . . no Reece. In all likelihood, Lizzy would give me the exact same ass kicking Reece had. Neither had been a fan of the save Skye plan. Decision made. I'd go to the party and have fun before my world turned to shit.

Excellent. I could do this.

CHAPTER TWO

I couldn't do this.

David and Ev lived in a luxury condo in the Pearl District. The place was sprawling, taking up half the top floor of a beautiful old brown brick building. It must have been surreal for Ev, going from our poky, drafty, thin-walled building to this sort of splendor. It must have been awesome. The old apartment building sat on the edge of downtown, close to the university, but David and Ev lived smack-dab in the middle of the very cool and expensive Pearl District.

Happily, Ev seemed delighted to see me. One potentially awkward moment negated. Mr. Ev, the rock star, gave me a chin tip in greeting while I did my best not to stare. I itched to ask him to sign something. My forehead would do.

"Help yourself to anything in the kitchen," said Ev. "There are plenty of drinks and pizza should be here soon."

"Thanks."

"You live next to Lauren and Nate?" asked David, speaking for the first time. Good lord, his dark hair and sculpted face were breathtaking. People shouldn't be so greedy; was it not enough that he was insanely talented?

"Yes," I said. "I used to be Ev's neighbor and I'm a regular at Ruby's Café."

"Every morning without fail," said Ev with a wink. "Double shot skinny latte with a hit of caramel coming right up."

David nodded and seemed to relax. He slipped an arm around his wife's waist and she grinned up at him. Love looked good on her. I hoped they lasted.

I'd loved, really loved, four people in my lifetime. They weren't all romantic love, of course. But I'd trusted my heart to all of them. Three had failed me. So I figured there was a twenty-five percent chance for success.

When David and Ev started sucking face, I took it as my cue to go explore.

I grabbed a beer from the kitchen (state of the art and beyond fancy) and faced the big living room with renewed determination. I could totally do this. Socializing and me were about to be best buds. A couple dozen people were scattered around the place. A huge flat screen blared out the game and Nate sat dead center in front of it, enraptured. There were a few faces amongst the crowd that I recognized; most belonged to people I'd never dare approach. I took a sip of beer to wet my parched throat. Being the odd one out at a party is a unique sort of torture. Given today's events, I lacked the courage to start a conversation. With my talent for picking who to trust, I'd probably ask the only axe murderer in the room for his sign.

Lauren gestured to me to join her right when my cell starting buzzing in my back jeans pocket. My butt cheek vibrated, giving me a thrill. I waved to Lauren and pulled out my cell, walking quickly out onto the balcony to escape the noise and chatter. Reece's name flashed on the screen as I shut the balcony doors.

"Hey," I said, smiling.

"Date canceled on me."

"That's a shame."

"What are you up to?"

Wind whipped up my hair, making me shiver. Typical weather for Portland at this time of year—October could definitely get cold, wet, dark, and miserable. I huddled down deeper into my blue woolen jacket. "I'm at a party. You're going to have to entertain yourself. Sorry."

"A party? What party?" he asked, the interest in his voice moving up a notch.

"One I wasn't exactly invited to, so I can't extend the offer to you."

"Damn." He yawned. "Never mind. Might get an early night for a change."

"Good idea." I wandered over to the railing. Cars rushed by on the street below. The Pearl District was a mecca of bars, cafés, and general coolness. Plenty of people were out and about braving the weather. All around me, the city lights broke up the darkness and the wind howled. It was lovely in a moody, existential-crisis sort of way. No matter the weather, I loved Portland. It was so different from back home in southern California, something I appreciated immensely. Here the houses were built for snow and ice instead of sunshine. The culture was weirder, more lenient in ways. Or maybe I just had a hard time remembering any of the good regarding my hometown. I'd escaped. That was all that mattered.

"I should go be social, Reece."

"You sound off. What's up?"

Groan. "Let's talk tomorrow at work."

"Let's talk now."

"Later, Reece. I need to put on my happy face and go make Lauren proud."

"Anne, cut the shit. What's going on?"

I screwed up my face and took another sip of beer before

answering. We'd been working together for almost two years now. Apparently, plenty of time for him to figure out my tells. "Skye's gone."

"Good. About time. She pay you back?"

I let my silence do the talking.

"Fuuuuck. Anne. Seriously."

"I know."

"What did I tell you?" he snarled. "Didn't I say—"

"Reece, don't go there. Please. At the time, I thought it was the right thing to do. She was a friend and she needed help. I couldn't just—"

"Yeah, you could. She was fucking using you!"

I took a deep breath and let it out slowly. "Yes, Skye was fucking using me. You were right, I was wrong."

He mumbled a long string of expletives while I waited mostly patiently. No wonder I hadn't wanted to have this conversation. There'd never be a good way to spin such a shitty tale. Frustration boiled up inside of me, warming me against the cold.

"How much do you need?" he asked, voice resigned.

"What? No. I'm not borrowing money off you, Reece. Getting further into debt is not the answer." Besides, business owner or not, I wasn't sure he had it to spare. Reece wasn't any better at saving than I was. I knew this because of the designer gear he wore to work on a daily basis. Apparently being Portland's resident Mr. Lover-Lover required one hell of a wardrobe. To be fair, he wore it extremely well.

He sighed. "You know, for someone who's always helping others, you're shit at accepting help yourself."

"I'll figure something out."

Another pained sigh. I leaned over the railing and hung my head, letting the cold, wet wind batter my face. It felt nice, off-setting the tension headache threatening to start up behind my forehead. "I'm going to hang up now, Reece. They have beer and pizza here. I'm pretty sure if I try hard enough I can find my happy place."

"You're going to lose the apartment, aren't you?"

"It's likely I'll have to move, yes."

"Stay with me. You can crash on my sofa."

"That's sweet of you." I tried to laugh, but the noise that came out was more of a strangled cough. My situation sucked too much for humor. Me sleeping on Reece's couch while he went hard at it in the next room with some stranger. No. Not happening. As it was, I felt small and stupid for letting Skye play me. Bearing witness to Reece's oh-so-active sex life would be too much.

"Thanks, Reece. But I'm pretty sure you've done unspeakable things to many, many people on that couch. I'm not sure anyone could sleep there."

"You think it's haunted by the ghosts of coitus past?"

"It wouldn't surprise me."

He snorted. "My gross sofa is there if you need it, okay?"

"Thank you. I mean that."

"Call me if you need anything."

"Bye, Reece."

"Oh, hey, Anne?"

"Yeah?"

"Can you work Sunday? Tara's had something come up. I told her you'd cover for her."

"I spend Sundays with Lizzy," I said carefully. "You know that."

Reece's answer was silence.

I could actually feel the guilt slinking up on me. "What if I do a different shift for her? Is it something she can move?"

"Ah, look, never mind. I'll deal with it."

"Sorry."

"No problem. Talk to you later."

And he hung up on me.

I put away my cell, took another mouthful of beer, and stared out at the city. Dark clouds drifted across the crescent moon. The air seemed colder now, making my bones ache like I was an old woman. I needed to drink more. That would solve everything, for tonight at least. My beer, however, was almost finished and I hesitated to head back inside.

Ugh.

Enough of this.

Once the drink was done, my lonely-girl pity party was up. I'd quit lurking in the shadows, pull my head out of my ass, and go back inside. This was an opportunity not to be missed, like I hadn't wished a million times or more to cross paths with someone from the band. I'd already met David Ferris. So there, wishes could come true. I should put in a request for bigger boobs, a smaller ass, and better choice in friends while I was at it.

And money enough to pay for my sister's college education and to keep a roof over my head, of course.

"Want another?" a deep voice asked, startling me. My chin jerked up, eyes wide. I'd thought I was alone but a guy sat slouched in the corner. Wavy, shoulder-length blond hair shone dully but the rest of him remained in shadow.

Whoa.

No. It couldn't be him.

I mean it could be, of course. But it couldn't be, surely.

Whoever he was, he had to have heard my half of the phone conversation, which was more than enough to mark me out as being one of the great idiots of our time. There was the clink and hiss of a beer being opened then he held it out to me. Light from inside reflected off the perspiration on the bottle, making it gleam.

"Thanks." I stepped closer, close enough to make him out even with the low lighting, and reached for the beer.

Holy shit. It was him, Malcolm Ericson.

The pinnacle moment of my life was officially upon me. So I might have had one or two photos of Stage Dive on my bedroom wall when I was a teenager. Fine, maybe there were three. Or twelve. Whatever. The point is there was one poster of the whole band. At least, the photographer probably thought it was of the whole band. Jimmy was out in front, his face contorted as he screamed into the microphone. To his right, half shrouded in shadow and smoke, was David, smoldering over his guitar. And to the left, toward the front of the stage, stood the bulk that was Ben, playing his bass.

But they didn't matter. Not really.

Because behind them all, there he was with the lights shining up through his drum kit. Naked from the waist up and dripping sweat, the picture had caught him mid-strike. His right arm cut across his body, his focus on his target, the cymbal he was about to strike. To smash.

He played with abandon and he looked like a god.

How many times after a day of looking after my mother and sister, working hard and doing the good, responsible thing, had I lay on my bed and looked at that photo. And now here he was.

Our fingers grazed in the way that's pretty much inevitable during such a hand over. No way could he have failed to miss the trembling in mine. Thankfully, he didn't comment. I scurried back to my place by the edge, leaning casually with a beer in hand. Cool people leaned. They looked relaxed.

He chuckled softly, letting me know I wasn't fooling anybody. Then he sat forward, resting his elbows on his knees. His face came fully into the light and I was caught, captivated. My mind blanked.

No question about it. It really was most definitely without a doubt him.

The man had hooker lips, I shit you not. High cheekbones and one of those notches in his chin. I'd never understood the appeal of those things before. Now I got it. But it was him as a whole that blew my mind. The parts meant nothing without the amused gleam in his eye and the hint of a smirk. God, I hated people who smirked. Apparently, I also wanted to lick them all over because my mouth started watering.

"I'm Mal," he said.

"I—I know," I stuttered.

His smirk heightened. "I know you know."

Huh. I kept my mouth shut.

"Sounds like someone had a bad day."

Nope, I still had nothing. A brain-dead stare was the best I could do.

Why was he out here in the dark? From all reports, the man was the life of the party. Yet here he was, drinking alone, hiding like me. Slowly, he stretched, rising out of his seat. Thank you, Lord. He'd go back inside and I'd be off the hook. I wouldn't have to try and make conversation. Fortunate, given my sudden bout of starstruck stupidity.

Only he didn't leave.

Instead, he walked toward me, his lean, muscular frame moving with careless grace. He had maybe five, six inches on me height wise. Enough to intimidate if it was his purpose. Muscular arms put the sleeves of his shirt to the test. Drummer's arms. They were certainly nice as body parts went, covered in ink and bulging in all the right ways. I bet they felt good, too.

And I was so obviously checking him out someone should slap me.

If I kept this up, I would slap me. Hard.

"What's your name?" he asked, joining me at the railing. God, even his voice felt good. The little hairs on the back of my neck stood on end with delight.

"My name?"

He stood close enough that our elbows bumped. His bare elbow, since he wore only jeans, a pair of Chucks, and a fitted "Queens of the Stone Age" T-shirt. Mal Ericson had touched me. I'd never wash again.

"Yeeeah, your name," he drawled. "The point of me telling you my name, even when you already knew it, was so you'd give me yours. That's how these things go."

"You knew I knew?"

"The crazy eyes kinda gave it away."

"Oh."

A moment later, he groaned. "Never mind, this is taking too long. I'll just make one up for you."

"Anne."

"Anne, what?"

"Anne Rollins."

A brilliant grin lit his face. "Anne Rollins. See, that wasn't so tough."

I gritted my teeth and tried to smile. Most likely I resembled a lunatic. One that had spent way too much time imagining him naked. Good god, the shame.

Gently, he tapped his bottle of beer against mine. "Cheers, Anne. Nice to meet you."

I took another sip, hoping it would calm the shaking. The booze wasn't hitting me hard enough fast enough to deal with this. Maybe I should move on to something stronger. One's first intimate conversation with a rock star should probably be conducted over hard liquor. Ev was definitely on to something with her tequila-fueled antics in Vegas. And look how well it had worked out for her.

"What brings you here tonight, Anne?"

"I came with Nate and Lauren. They brought me. They're my neighbors. They live next door."

He nodded. "You're friends with Ev?"

"Yeah, I, well . . . I've always been friendly with her. I wouldn't want to presume . . . I mean, I don't know that I'd say we were close friends, exactly, but—"

"Yes or no, Anne?"

"Yes," I answered, then snapped my mouth shut against another outbreak of verbal diarrhea.

"Yeah, Ev's good people. Davie was lucky to find her." He stared off at the city lights in silence. The amusement fell from his face and a frown creased his brow. He seemed sad, a little lost, maybe. For certain, his much-vaunted party-rocker personality was nowhere in evidence. I should know better. People had painted Ev to be the next Yoko Ono, riding on David's coattails, sucking him dry of fame and fortune. I didn't have to be her BFF to know it couldn't be further from the truth. Chances were, whoever Mal was had little to do with the nonsense flowing freely on the Internet.

But more important, how badly had I embarrassed myself?

"I didn't really get a crazy look in my eyes, did I?" I asked, dreading the answer.

"Yeah, you did."

Crap.

"So you're a friend of Ev's? I mean, you're not in the music business or anything?" he asked, focusing on me once more. His face had cleared, his mood shifting. I couldn't keep up. With the flats of his palms he beat out a swift rhythm on the balcony railing.

"No. I work in a bookshop a few blocks from here."

"Okay." He gazed down at me, apparently pleased with my answer. "So what was that phone call about?"

"Nothing."

"No?" He stepped closer. "What happened to your nose?"

Immediately my hand flew up to block his view of my face. It was only a small bump, but still. "My sister broke it when we were little."

"Don't cover it. I think it's cute."

"Great." I lowered my arm. He'd already seen the flaw, so what was the use?

"Why'd she break it?"

"She got mad one day and threw a toy truck at me."

"Not how. Why?"

I smothered a sigh. "She wanted a kitten and I'm allergic to cats."

"You couldn't get a puppy instead?"

"I wanted to but Mom said no. My sister still blamed me."

He scowled. "So you never had any pets growing up?"

I shook my head.

"That's fucking terrible. Every kid should get to have a pet." He appeared sincerely outraged on my behalf.

"Yeah, well, time's past and I'm kind of over it now." I frowned and swallowed some more beer. Everything told me I was going to need it. This conversation was just plain weird.

He stood, watching me with his faint smile. Just that easily I was riveted once again. My lips curled into some sort of vaguely hopeful idiotic half grin of their own accord.

Mal.

Mal Ericson.

Damn, he was beautiful. My long-dormant hormones broke into a dance of joy. Something was definitely going on in my pants. Something that hadn't happened in a very long time.

"There go the crazy eyes again," he whispered.

"Shit." I shut my eyes tight. Lizzy walking in on me and my boyfriend seven years ago had been pretty damn embarrassing, especially given that she then ran and told mom. Not that mom had been coherent enough to care. This, however, topped it.

"Your cheeks have gone all rosy. Are you thinking rude thoughts about me, Anne?"

"No."

"Liar," he taunted in a soft voice. "You're totally thinking of me with no pants on."

I totally was.

"That's just gross, dude. A massive invasion of my privacy." He leaned in closer, his breath warming my ear. "Whatever you're imagining, it's bigger."

"I'm not imagining anything."

"I'm serious. It's basically a monster. I cannot control it."

"Malcolm—"

"You're pretty much going to need a whip and chair to tame it, Anne."

"Stop it."

"That okay with you?"

I covered my hot face with my hands. Not giggling. Not even a little, because grown women didn't do that shit. What was I, sixteen?

Inside the condo, Nate started shouting. The sound was only slightly muted by the sliding glass doors. My eyelids flew open as he hurled abuse at the TV, arms waving madly. Lauren laughed and my brain came back on line, sending all sorts of emergency signals throughout my body. Like I didn't already realize I needed to get the hell out of there before I humiliated myself further. Good one, frontal lobe. At least I could think if I didn't look at Mal directly.

This was a brilliant and timely discovery.

And it worked right up until he leaned over, getting in my face, making my lungs feel like they were about to explode.

"You have a little gap between your two front teeth," he informed me, eyes narrowed in perusal. "You know that?"

"Yes."

He studied me like I was an alien species, a curiosity that had been dumped on his doorstep. His gaze slid down my body. It wasn't as if he could possibly see anything what with me wearing a coat, jeans, and boots. But that knowledge didn't help at all. His lazy, appreciative grin made my knees knock. It took about forever for his gaze to return to my face.

Damn, he was good. I'd been professionally sullied without a single item of clothing removed.

"Your eyes are a pleasing shade of . . . Is that blue?" he asked. "It's hard to tell in this light."

I cleared my throat. "Yep, blue. Will you please not do that?"

"What?" he asked, sounding vaguely aggrieved. "What am I doing?"

"You're staring at me and making me feel all uptight. I don't like it."

"You stared at me first. Besides, you were wired long before you came out here. If I had to guess, I'd say you're uptight in general. But don't worry, I'm here to help. Go on; tell Uncle Mal all your troubles."

"Wow, that's really kind of you. But I'm good."

He shuffled closer and I shuffled back. Pity there was nowhere for me to go. "What were you talking about on the phone before, Anne?"

"Oh, you know . . . personal stuff. I don't really want to discuss it."

"You were saying your friend ripped you off and you're going to lose your place, right?"

"Right." I slumped, my heart hurting. Fucking Skye. I wasn't a pleaser, but I did look after the people I loved. Stupid me, I thought that's what you did. When mom got sick, I'd stepped up, done what needed doing. There'd been no other choice. The state of my finances right now, however, would suggest it had become a bit of a bad habit. "Yeah. That about sums it up."

His eyes widened in sudden alarm. "Shit. Don't cry. I'm not Davie. I don't know how to deal with that."

"Shut up, I'm not going to cry." I blinked furiously, turning my face away. "I told you I didn't want to talk about it."

"Didn't think you'd burst into tears. Christ."

My beer was empty; time to go. Besides, I needed to escape before my watery eyes betrayed me. And Mal had to have better things to do with his time than talking to me. Teasing me. This had been the most excruciatingly awkward and awesome conversation in my entire life. For a while there, I'd forgotten all about my problems.

He'd made me smile.

"So." I thrust my hand out for shaking, wanting that final contact, needing to touch him properly just once. He'd been on my bedroom wall back home for years. I'd end meeting him on a high if it killed me. "It's been lovely to meet you."

"Are you trying to get rid of me?" he asked, laughing.

"No, I—"

"Stop looking over my shoulder, Anne. Look me in the face," he ordered.

"I am!"

"Are you scared you're going to make crazy eyes at me again?"

"Yes, probably." I clicked my tongue, exasperated. "Do you normally taunt your fans like this?"

"No. I never realized it could be this much fun."

My hand hung in the air between us. I was about to retract it when he grabbed hold. I stared him in the face, determined not to lose it this time. The problem with Mal Ericson was that he was physically flawless. Not a single imperfection marred him, big or small. If he kept riding my ass, though, I'd fix that for him.

"What's that look mean?" he asked, leaning in. "What are you thinking now?"

My stomach swooped and all thoughts of violence were pushed aside. "Nothing."

"Hmm. You're not a very good liar."

I tried to pull my hand from his grasp. Instead, he held it firmly.

"One last quick question. This shit with your friend, that sort of thing happen often?"

"What?"

"'Cause when you were on the phone, talking with your other friend, it sounded like it did." He loomed over me, blocking out the night sky. "It sounded like it was a problem for you, people using you."

"We don't need to talk about this." I twisted my hand, trying to get free. Even with the sweaty palms it was an impossible task.

"Did you notice how your friend asked for a favor even knowing you were all sad faced about this other friend ripping you off? How do you feel about that?"

I yanked on my arm, but he held fast. Seriously, how strong was this bastard?

"Because I think that was kind of a low move. Between you and me, I don't think you have very good friends, Anne."

"Hey. I have great friends."

"Are you fucking kidding me? They rip you off and expect shit from you when you're down. Seriously, dude. Only assholes would do that."

"Mal—"

"But what's worse is that you're letting them. I don't get that."

"I'm not letting them do anything."

"Yes, you are," he said, voice rising in volume. "You so are."

"Good god, do you have a mute switch?"

"It's appalling! I'm officially appalled," he yelled, clueing the whole damn neighborhood in on my life. "This must end! I will stand for it no longer. Do you hear me, Portland?"

"Let me go," I said through gritted teeth.

"You, Miss Rollins, are a doormat."

"I am not a doormat," I growled, everything in me rebelling at the idea. Either that or running in fear of it. I was so worked up it was hard to tell.

He rolled his eyes. "C'mon, you know you are. It's right there on your face."

I shook my head, beyond words.

"So, I've given this absolutely no thought and decided that you need boundaries, Anne. Boundaries. Are. Your. Friends." Each word was punctuated with his finger tapping the tip of my nose. "Do you hear me? Is this getting through?"

Which is about when I snapped and started screaming. "You want boundaries? How about getting the hell out of my face! How's that for a boundary, huh? None of this is any of your damn business, you obnoxious dickhead."

He opened his mouth to reply but I charged on regardless.

"You don't know a damn thing about me. And you think you can get in my face and tear my psyche apart for fun? No. Fuck you, buddy. Fuck you hard."

Everything went quiet, even the music inside. The most horrible silence reigned supreme. People were watching us through the glass with curious faces. Lauren's mouth was a perfect O.

"Shit," I muttered.

"Anne?"

What had I done? Lauren had invited me to this nice party and I'd just gone psycho on one of the guests. It was time to wither and die, I could feel it. "Please let my hand go."

"Anne, look at me."

Never.

"C'mon, gimme your eyes."

Slowly, wearily, I turned back to him. The slowest of smiles curled his perfect lips. "That was fucking awesome. I'm so proud of you right now."

"You're insane."

"Nooo."

"Yes. You really are."

"You're just thinking that now. But give it some time. Think about what I said."

I just shook my head in silence.

"It was great to meet you, Anne. We'll talk again real soon," he said, pressing a kiss to the back of my hand before releasing it. There was a light in his eyes, one I didn't want to decipher. One I certainly didn't trust. "I promise."

CHAPTER THREE

I'd only just wandered back inside when David Ferris appeared at my elbow, probably to throw me out. Yelling at rock stars had to be severely frowned upon at such events.

"Hey." David spoke to me but his gaze stayed on the other side of the room where Lauren and Ev were huddled together. A possible problem, since Lauren talked with her hands. Every few seconds Ev got whacked in the arm. She didn't seem to mind, however.

"Hi."

"Having fun?" he asked.

"Um, sure."

He nodded, his demeanor as cool and detached as earlier.

"Great," I whispered.

The two beers and bizarre confrontation had left me a little light-headed. Maybe drinking wasn't such a good idea after all. Especially if I had to keep talking to important people and actually making sense as opposed to yelling abuse at them. Music was pumping once again, people mingling and chatting their hearts out. No one even really gave me a second glance. I could only hope that picking random strangers' lives apart was Mal's thing and they'd seen it all before. "You talked to him?" he asked.

"Him? Mal?"

"Yeah."

"Ah, yes. I did." I'd thought everyone had heard.

"Hmm." Across the room, Ev burst out laughing. An answering smile tugged at his lips. "You argue about something?"

"No, nothing really," I stumbled. "Just nothing."

David turned to me and his forehead creased, the smile long gone. For a long time he just looked at me.

"Never mind." He slinked away, leaving me boggled.

Was I not supposed to have talked to Mal? He'd talked to me first. I might have started the staring, but he'd definitely kicked off the conversation. And the yelling, for that matter. Not my fault I'd interacted with one of the most famous drummers on the planet. But a memory of Mal looking out over the city came back to me. The frown he'd had on his face before he'd gotten busy poking fun at me once more. The way he'd bounced between moods. And now with David checking up on him . . .

Curiouser and curiouser.

If cash and conquests were everything, then Mal had it covered. I'd seen a picture of his beautiful beach house down in L.A. Photos of him covered in scantily clad women were the norm. Money didn't buy happiness. I knew that. Given my current situation, though, the knowledge wouldn't quite stick. Plus the man had fame, worldwide adoration, and an awesome job involving lots of travel. How dare he not be deliriously, ridiculously happy! What was his problem?

Good question.

"That's a big frown." Lauren hooked her arm with mine, drawing me further into the party. "You okay?"

"Fine."

"I heard you and Mal fighting."

"I'm assuming pretty much everyone did." I winced. "Sorry about that."

She laughed. "Please, Mal lives to get a reaction."

"He certainly got one from me."

"Let me guess, that was your friend, Reecy, calling earlier?" Her voice dripped with disdain. Lauren and I started spending time together when Ev got married and moved out. Often on weekends Nate would wind up needing to work. Lauren had a low boredom threshold for her own company. So we'd grab a coffee or go see a movie. It was good. Especially since Skye had taken to avoiding me the past few months. It had been on the pretext of spending time with her new boyfriend but now I had to wonder.

I hated doubting everything that'd happened. The feeling of losing all trust. It was skin crawling and noxious.

"Reece's date bailed on him," I said. "Did Ev say something about pizza? I'm starving."

"One day, you're going to stop being that boy's back-up plan."

My spine straightened. "We're just friends, Lauren."

She steered me into the kitchen. A vast array of pizza boxes had been spread across the marble benchtop.

"Please," she huffed. "He's a cunt tease. He knows you like him and plays on it."

"No, he doesn't. I repeat, just friends." I'd only recently finished embarrassing myself in front of Malcolm Ericson. Thoughts regarding my possible foolish behavior around Reece Lewis could wait for another time.

Or never. Never would also be fine.

"You could do better if you bothered to," she said.

I made some vague noise. Hopefully it was enough to end this topic of conversation. Then my stomach rumbled loudly. Yum, melted cheese. Earlier, I'd been so worried about the talk with Skye, I'd skipped lunch. With two beers sloshing around inside my belly, food was long overdue. Though the toppings laid out weren't what I expected. "Is that artichoke and spinach?"

"Probably." Lauren shook her head and shoved a piping-hot piece of ham and pineapple at me, taking the time to sit it on a napkin first. "Here, try this one. Evelyn hasn't wrecked it with any of her vegetable nonsense. I love her, I do. But the girl has the strangest taste in pizza toppings of anyone I've ever met. It's unnatural."

I bit into it immediately, scalding my tongue and the roof of my mouth. One day I'd learn to wait until it cooled down. Not today, but one day.

Out in the living room, the music suddenly jumped in volume by about a billion decibels. My ears started ringing. The walls shuddered. Black Rebel Motorcycle Club thundered through the condo. Someone else managed to be louder. "Par-tay!"

Lauren smiled and leaned in closer to be heard. "Mal's decided to join in!" she shouted. "Now the fun begins."

Ben Nicholson, Stage Dive's bull-necked bass player arrived, blowing my mind just a bit more. He and Mal started pouring shots. I stuck to my mostly full beer. Holding it gave my hands something to do. What followed was pretty much everything I'd ever expected from a rock star party. Well, there weren't really drugs or groupies so much. But plenty of pretty people getting drunk and lots of noise. It was a bit like the college parties Lizzy talked me into attending now and then. Only instead of cheap beer in red Solo cups, they passed around bottles of CÎROC and Patrón. Most everyone's clothes were top-of-the-line designer goodies and we were sitting in a million-dollar condo instead of some crappy student apartment.

So, actually, it was nothing like the parties I went to with Lizzy. Forget I said that.

Lauren, Ev, and I had danced and chatted earlier. It'd been fun. For certain, Lauren had done me a favor dragging me out tonight. I'd had a hell of a lot better time than I ever would have sitting at home all by my lonesome. Mal had gone off with David and Ben to another room for a while. Not that I'd been keeping an eye out for him.

For a while I'd hung out in the kitchen, talking to a sound technician by the name of Dean. Apparently he worked with someone called Tyler, who'd been with the band for forever and was basically a family friend. Dean was nice, intelligent, with cool black hair and a piercing through his lip. Yes, he was sort of hot. He asked me back to his hotel room, and it was tempting. But all of my current stresses were running on a loop in the back of my mind. It would basically take a Sex God to make me unwind right now.

I bid Dean good night at the kitchen door.

Then Mal and the guys returned and the music got turned way up again. As inevitably happened, everyone had started pairing up. David and Ev disappeared. No one commented. Lauren sat on Nate's lap in the corner of the couch, their hands all over each other. I stifled a yawn. It'd been a blast, but it was nearing three in the morning. I was running out of steam. We'd probably be leaving soon.

I hoped we'd be leaving soon. In a few hours I had to rise and shine. The shining part might be problematic with the way Mal's words were beating around inside my brain. Overly trusting and broke? Yes. Doormat, my ass.

"Benny boy," hollered Mal. He was dancing on top of the coffee table with a long-legged brunette. The girl seemed hell-bent on wrapping herself around him, strangler-vine style. Somehow he managed to keep her at a polite distance. Well, almost.

"Yo," replied Ben in a very manly manner.

"You met my girl, Anne?" Mal nodded to where I sat perched on the end of a couch. I froze. For hours he'd been otherwise occupied. I'd thought he'd forgotten about me entirely.

"You got a girl?" asked Ben.

"Yeah. Isn't she cute?"

I got a brief looking over from Ben, followed by a chin tip. It seemed eerily similar to the one I'd gotten from David. Maybe this was the equivalent of a rock star's secret handshake.

"We were talking earlier outside. We're moving in together," Mal informed him. The brunette in his arms scowled. He didn't even notice. But more important, what the hell was he talking about? "It's serious, man. Real serious. She's got a few issues with her friends going on. It's a fucking mess. Anyway, she really needs me with her right now for support and shit, you know?"

My hands quietly throttled the poor innocent bottle of beer.

"You doing the Dave and Ev thing?" asked Ben.

"Abso-fucking-lutely. I'm settling down. I'm a changed man. True love and all that."

"Right. This should be interesting," said Ben. "How long you think it'll last?"

"Mine and Anne's lustful passion will be eternal, Benny boy. Just you wait and see."

Ben's eyebrow arched. "You willing to bet on this?"

"Name your price, punk!"

"Five large says you can't make it till we go on tour."

"Fuck that. Make it worth my time. Twenty."

Ben guffawed. "Easiest twenty grand I'll ever make."

"You're moving in with me?" I asked, interrupting all the

male bravado and talk of money. I wasn't even touching upon my supposed friend issues.

"Yes, pumpkin," said Mal, his face deadly serious. "I am moving in with you."

I cringed at the horrid nickname but chose to focus on the real concern for now. "When did we talk about this exactly?"

"Actually, you might have left by then. But it doesn't change the facts." He turned back to Ben. "Perfect timing with Mom coming to town. She's going to love her. Mom always wanted me to find a nice girl and settle down and shit."

"Thought you didn't like Portland," commented Ben.

"I don't like Portland. But I like Anne." He gave me a wink. "Besides, Davie's not moving back to L.A. anytime soon. Even Jimmy's been talking about relocating, maybe buying the place next door."

"Has he?"

"Yeah. You met his new babysitter?"

"Nah, not yet. What happened to the old one, the big black dude?"

"Ha, no. He's long gone. There's been several since him. New girl started a while back." Mal chuckled. The sound was distinctly evil. "If Jimmy doesn't want someone around, he has ways of making their life fucking intolerable."

"Sh-i-i-t. Tell me later."

Mal chuckled some more. "Anyways, things are tight between me and Anne. I may as well stay."

The brunette turned her glare up to high beam. My look was probably more confused. Maybe he meant another Anne. One that had a clue what the hell he was talking about.

"Your girl doesn't mind watching some chick crawling all over you?" Ben gave me a raised brow. "I need a girlfriend like that."

"Ah, fuck. Good point. Honestly, this whole monogamy thing. It takes so much getting used to, man." Mal set the distinctly cranky brunette away from him, the muscles in his arms flexing. He deposited her gently back down onto the floor. "Apologies. I'm sure you're very nice and all but my heart beats only for Anne."

The brunette threw a withering glance my way, flicked her hair, and turned to leave. Ignoring her huffing, Ben caught the girl around the waist, pulling her onto his lap. The girl's transfer of affections took all of a millisecond. To be fair, Ben was a big burly guy. Few would say no.

Mal threw himself at my feet. I scuttled back in my chair in surprise.

"Forgive me, Anne! I didn't mean to stray."

"It's fine." I didn't know exactly how much he'd had to drink. A truckload would probably be a good guess.

"Guess what, pumpkin?" Mal jumped onto the couch beside me, towering over me on his knees. "You don't make crazy eyes at Ben."

I needed to shoot him at least twice. Once for calling me pumpkin and then again for embarrassing me every damn chance he got. Instead, I studied my beer with great intensity.

"She makes crazy eyes at you?" asked Ben.

"Oh, yeah. Anne?" A finger slid beneath my chin and gently lifted, forcing me to face him.

Mal stared at me and I stared back despite my best intentions. His face gentled. None of the drunken amusement remained. He just looked at me and all that stuff about seeing someone's soul began to make sense. It was terrifying. I could almost feel a connection between us. Like there was something I could reach out and grab hold of.

It couldn't be real.

But for one perfect moment, it was just me and him. We were in our own little bubble and nothing or no one else existed. It was strangely peaceful.

"There we go," he said, not taking his eyes off me. "She doesn't do it for you or Davie though. Only I get the crazy eyes. Because I'm special."

Ben said something. I didn't hear what. Then Mal looked away and the moment was gone. The spell was broken. "It's sweet, really. She can't live without me."

"Obviously." Ben laughed.

My jaw clenched. Fuck Mal Ericson and his games very much.

"I haven't met your lead singer, Jimmy, yet," I said, finally finding my fight. It was either words or fists. Given the way he just exposed me to ridicule, I was good with either. "Maybe he's the real favorite and you're just the runner-up. Did you think of that?"

His mouth fell open. "You did not just say that to me."

I didn't answer. Let's see how he enjoyed being teased.

"Anne, are you trying to make me jealous? You wouldn't like me when I'm jealous!" The drunken lunatic roared and started pounding on his chest like King Kong or the Hulk or whatever the hell he was trying to be. "Take it back."

"No."

"Don't toy with me, Anne. Take it back or I'll make you."

I screwed up my face, incredulous. And he said I was crazy. Or crazy eyed. Whatever.

The madman shrugged. "Okay, pumpkin. Don't say I didn't warn you."

Without further ado, he launched himself at me. I screeched in alarm. The noise was awesome. My beer bottle went flying across the floor.

It could be said I'm somewhat ticklish. Sure as shit, I hated being tickled. His fingers were dancing and digging in turn, hitting all my sensitive spots, damn it. It was like someone had given him a map to my body. I was panting and squirming, trying to get away from him.

"Boundaries, you bastard," I hissed.

His answering laugh was no less than wicked.

Then I started to slip off the couch.

To be fair, he did try to break my fall and he used himself to do so. Hands grabbed hold of me, turning as opposed to torturing. We fell in a tangle of limbs, me landing flat on top of him. Mal grunted as the back of his head bounced off the hardwood floor.

Ouch; that had to hurt.

Despite the knock, his arms remained tight, holding me to him. The man felt good, better than I'd ever imagined. And you had to know I'd done some serious imagining, even out there on the balcony. The playful light disappeared from his eyes and every inch of him tensed. He stared up at me, unblinking, his mouth slightly open. I got the distinct feeling he was waiting to see what I'd do next. If I'd take things further. Mostly, I concentrated on breathing. Then he looked at my lips.

Breathing was out.

He couldn't want me to kiss him. Surely this was just another game. Except it wasn't, not entirely. I could feel him hardening against my thigh. Things low inside of me tightened in response. I hadn't been this wound up in ages.

Fuck it, I was going for it. I had to know how his lips felt. In that moment, not kissing him was out of the question.

"Malcolm, no!" Ev stared down at us sprawled on the floor, her face a picture of dismay. "Let her go. Not my friends. You promised."

All trace of sexual tension melted away as embarrassment filled me to overflowing. Everyone was laughing. Well, everyone except for David and Ev. Sadly, they'd chosen that moment to rejoin the party.

"Your friend and I are meant to be together. Suck it up." He gave me a squeeze. "You know, I thought you at least would recognize true love when you saw it. I'm very disappointed in you right now, Evelyn."

"Let her go."

"Davie, control your wife, she's making a scene." Distracted, Mal's hold on me loosened and I managed to scurry off of him. Lucky for him, my knee didn't land in his groin.

"You're the one rolling around on the floor, dude," said David.

"Not. My. Friends." Ev repeated through gritted teeth.

"Your shirt is on inside out, child bride," said Mal, the side of his mouth kicking up. "What have you been doing?"

Ears turning pink, Evelyn crossed her arms over her chest. Her husband did a bad job of hiding a smile. "None of your fucking business what we've been doing," he said in a gruff voice.

"You two disgust me." Mal climbed to his feet then grabbed hold of my hand, hauling me upright. "You okay?" he asked.

"Yeah. You?"

He gave me a goofy grin and rubbed at the back of his skull. "My head would probably hurt if I could feel it."

There was my answer. He was plastered. I was entertainment. Any romantic notions were strictly mine. The story of my life, really.

Finally the laughter quieted down. We were still the focus of every eye in the room, however.

"Malcolm, is that your beer on the floor?" asked Ev, pointing at the mess my fallen bottle had made.

Before I could open my mouth to apologize, Mal was there.

"Yes. Yes, it is. But do not despair. I've got this." He ripped off his T-shirt and knelt, mopping up the spill. There was a whole lot of hard flesh and bronzed skin right there. A truly impressive amount. His back was covered in ink, an intricate scene of a bird taking flight, the opening wings spanning across the breadth of his shoulders. A sigh rippled around the room at the sight of him half naked on his knees. It wasn't just me making the noise, I swear. Though yes, I definitely contributed heartily.

"Christ, Mal," said Lauren. "Put some clothes on before you start a riot."

The man just looked up and grinned.

"And I think that's our cue to leave." Lauren pushed herself off Nate's lap. "It's been fun. But we've got work tomorrow, unlike you musical slackers."

"You're taking my Anne?" Mal asked. His lips turned down at the edges. He climbed to his feet, leaving his sodden shirt on the ground. "You can't take my Anne. I need her for stuff . . . private stuff, in my room."

"Another time." Lauren patted him on the back.

"Stay and play with me, Anne."

"No," repeated Ev.

"Night, Mal," I said. I couldn't tell if he was serious or not. But no way, come morning, would I be scraping myself out of his bed and doing the walk of shame down my friend's hallway.

Nuh-uh.

"Anne, pumpkin, don't leave me," he wailed.

"Run. Go." Ev ushered me toward the door. "He's impossible when he gets like this. You'd swear he didn't get enough hugs as a child."

"Good to see you again, Ev," I said.

She pulled me in for a quick kiss on the cheek. "You too."

"I need sexual healing," Mal continued behind us. He then did a new dance. This one consisted of rhythmic pelvic thrusting while his hand swung through the air, mimicking spanking someone's ass. The "Oh yeah" and "harder baby" only made it better. If ever a vagina was going to sit up and take notice, this would surely do it. The man had all the moves.

"You need some fucking impulse control and coffee. That's what you need." David's forehead crinkled. He pushed Mal back with a hand, bringing his porno dance performance to a halt. "Better yet, when was the last time you actually slept?"

"I'll sleep with Anne."

"No, you won't."

"Yes, I will." He raised a hand high. "For I am, Malcolm, Lord of the Sex!"

With a muttered oath, David went nose to nose with him. Immediately Ben stood, sending the brunette sliding onto the floor. Poor girl, she wasn't having the best night.

"You heard Ev," said David, getting in his face. "Not her friend. That's not cool."

Mal's eyes hardened. "You cock-blocking me, Davie?"

"You bet I am."

"That's not okay, bro."

Ben slung an arm over Mal's shoulders, ruffled his hair. "Come find another toy."

"I am not a child." Mal pouted.

"How about her?" Ben pointed to a sleek blond who smiled and preened in response. "I bet she'd like to meet you."

"Ooh, she's shiny."

"Why don't you go ask her what her name is?" suggested Ben, patting him on the back.

"Do I need to know her name?"

"I've heard it helps."

"Maybe for you," Mal scoffed. "I just call out my own name during sex."

Laughter broke out across the room. Even the corner of David's mouth started twitching.

But when it came to women, Mal was clearly a whore. I'd seen more than enough to confirm it. David and Ev had done me a favor, warning him off. Jealousy didn't hit me in the gut when he leered at the other woman. Something else did. I don't know what it was, but it was definitely something else.

Weirdest night of my life. Hands down, this was the absolute winner.

Wait till I told Skye about it when I got home. She'd laugh her ass off. Shit, no she wouldn't. Mal's antics had momentarily made me forget all about her. Surprisingly enough, as annoying as he'd been, he kept making me smile.

The man himself apparently remembered me again then. I stood ensconced between Evelyn and Lauren as if I needed protecting. Maybe I did. All I know is, when he looked at me my mind went far, far away.

What was it about bad boys? Someone needed to invent a cure.

My lust object gave me a wink. "See you later, crazy eyes."

CHAPTER FOUR

"The skank unfriended me too," said Reece, staring at the shop's computer, sitting on the front sales counter. Facebook sat open on the screen in all its blue brilliance.

"Bitch," I muttered.

Skye had a new name and it wasn't nice. Much deserved, but not nice.

Between Reece and I, we'd called everyone who might have known where she'd gone. Lucky it'd been a quiet morning so far. We'd had no luck with our search. People either didn't know or weren't saying. Everyone sounded sorry. But no one could, or would, help. Some days, humanity sucked.

"I think we should stop," I said.

"What? Why?"

"Think about it. Realistically, what would I even do if I found her?" I crossed my arms and leaned my hip against the counter. The pose was all the better for holding my shit together. "Slapping her silly is illegal. As nice as it would be to rip her a new one, it won't get me my money back. There's no point going to the police because it's just her word against mine. I'm screwed."

"There's the defeatist attitude I've come to know and love."

"Shuddup." I smiled.

Reece smiled back at me, little lines appearing at the corners of his eyes behind his cool-guy thick-rimmed black glasses. A dimple popped in his cheek. He had an awesome smile. No matter how many times I'd seen it, I'd never quite become inured. Though, upon reflection, it didn't make me stupid like Mal's cocky grin.

Huh, interesting.

There was, however, a lot to be said for not being reduced to brain-dead hormonal mush by a man. Reece and I were solid. Though, for some reason, the usual rush I got from being around him was missing. Still, I barely knew Mal. Reece was real. Mal was just a dream on my teenage bedroom wall.

And since when did I compare Reece's smile to anyone's?

"What was the party you went to?" Reece asked, scratching his head in his usual adorable manner. His dark hair flopped over his forehead and I just knew we'd make great babies together one day. Marriage would never be in the cards, not for me. The institution meant so little. But there was a lot to be achieved just by living in sin, by being a life partner.

Reece would make a great life partner.

When Lauren had hinted at my having a thing for Reece last night, she might have known what she was talking about.

Ah, Reece.

I'd worked at Lewis's bookshop since moving to Portland two years ago. Lizzy had asked me to come out for a while, to help her settle in. Obviously, I was still here. I liked being close to my sister and Portland was a cool city. I liked my job and the friends I'd made. Everything was better here.

"Lauren invited me to drinks at Ev's," I said.

Reece's chin retreated in what appeared to be amazement. "The girl that married the dude from Stage Dive?"

"That's the one."

"And you didn't invite me? Damn, A. I like a couple of their songs. That *San Pedro* album wasn't bad. Their new stuff is shit, though, gotta say."

"I love the new album. 'Over Me' is a great song."

He snickered, the corner of his mouth lifting. "It's a song about someone doing your friend."

"I choose to ignore that aspect."

An elderly woman in tie-dye wandered in, heading straight for the self-help/philosophy section. Two teenagers started making out next to the new cookbook display. Sweet, but this was hardly the place for it. When a hand wandered too far south I cleared my throat, loudly. "Keep it above the waist, boys."

The bell above the door jangled crazily as they bolted from the shop at light speed. One turned on the most amazing blush. I almost felt bad for him. Guess he'd wanted that grope something fierce.

Reece chuckled. Well, he might. He picked up regularly within these four walls. A habit he'd hopefully grow out of one day soon. "Calm down. They weren't hurting anyone."

"There's a time and a place."

The little bell above the door dinged again as about the last person I expected strolled on in. Evelyn entered with a cup of coffee in hand and a hesitant smile on her face. Despite only working a couple of blocks away, I don't think she'd ever been in the shop before. For certain, she'd never delivered coffee to me. If that was what was about to happen.

I stared in surprise.

Reece perked up. Then he spotted her humongous wedding engagement ring combo and perked back down again. Coming in from across the river, he didn't go past Ruby's Café like I did. Ev was unknown to him.

"We missed you this morning," she said, sliding the tall

cardboard cup of coffee onto the counter in front of me. "You didn't stop by for your regular. Figured I'd bring it to you."

"You're wonderful. I woke up late for some reason."

"Fancy that." She smiled.

I took a sip of the superhot brew. Perfect. It was fucking perfect. Evelyn was basically the patron saint of the coffee bean. What I'd do in a few weeks when she left to go on tour with the band, I had no idea.

Cry, most likely.

Ev's long blond hair was tied back in a braid. Like me, she wore head-to-toe black. Only she wore a pencil skirt while I'd gone for skinny jeans. "Ruby's Café" was plastered across her bounty of boobs while "Lewis's Independent Book Store" was written over my more sedate mounds. Apart from the chunk of ice on her finger she could have been any other local girl. Why she kept working as a barista when she'd married a millionaire I had no idea and it wasn't my place to ask.

I turned to introduce her to Reece but he'd taken the opportunity to disappear out back, all interest in Ev gone as soon as he saw the ring.

"I also wanted to apologize for last night," she said, resting her arms on the counter.

"What for?"

"The part where Mal tackled you onto the floor, mostly. Unless there's something else I missed I should also be apologizing for?"

"No." I waved her words away, smiling. No need to bring up my shouting abuse at her guest earlier in the evening. "That was fine. He was just playing."

"Yeah. He's kind of like a puppy on steroids. Doesn't know his own strength." She looked around the shop, face open, curious. "This place is great. Why haven't I been in here before?"

"Time, probably. When you weren't working you were studying. Now you're married."

"True." She beamed. "It was good to see you last night, Anne. I'm glad to hear Mal didn't do any permanent damage."

"No, I'm fine. And thank you very much for the coffee. I seriously needed it. I don't know how you handle getting up so early after the late nights."

She lifted a shoulder in a half shrug. "Things wound down pretty much straight after you left. Ben and Mal went out, taking everyone with them. David and I crashed. We don't do the party thing often. If we did I'd be ruined this morning."

"Ah."

"Sooo, David said you were talking to Mal out on the balcony for a while. . . ." Which was about when her coffee-bearing visit started to make sense.

"Yeah, I was," I said. "And then David asked me if he'd said anything. I still don't know what that was about."

Ev's lips pressed tight. "Mm."

"He sent you to ask me about it," I guessed. Correctly, if the flash of guilt in her eyes was any indicator.

"You deserved coffee, anyway. But yes, he did ask if I would mind talking to you."

"Okay." I licked my lips, buying some time to get my thoughts in order. Out of sight my foot fidgeted, doing its best to wear a hole in the carpet. "Honestly, we didn't talk about much, nothing particularly personal or private. Just some nonsense about my ex-roommate."

"Lauren mentioned." Pity filled Ev's eyes.

I shrugged. "Yeah, never mind. I'll figure it out. But really, Mal and I didn't talk much about himself. Mostly, he just teased me."

"He does that." For a moment longer, she looked at me.

Trying to gage the truth, I guess. She was clearly pretty worried about Mal, but the fact was we didn't know one another well enough for this sort of heart-to-heart. It felt awkward, stilted.

"Thanks for letting me know," she said at last. "Mal's been acting strange since he came up a week ago. Manic . . . more so than usual. Then other times he just stares into space. We've tried talking to him, but he says nothing's wrong."

"I'm sorry."

"We don't know if he's depressed or on drugs or what. And after having Jimmy go through rehab so recently . . ." She gave me a small, sad smile. "I'd appreciate you not mentioning this to anyone."

"Of course."

"Anyway, I'm done for the day. I'd better get going. David will be wondering where I am. It was good to see you."

"You too."

"Come over again soon, okay?" She backed toward the door, waving good-bye. The request seemed genuine. It soothed my heart. After the horror of Skye I could do with some real friends.

"I will. Thanks again for the caffeine."

She gave me the rock-star chin tip and then she was gone.

Reece wandered back out, his own cup of coffee in hand. "Your friend go?"

I snapped back to reality, dragging my mind away from the six-foot something conundrum that was Mal. My mind liked lingering on him far too much. He'd apparently become my new go-to thought despite all of the other things happening in my life. "Yeah, she had to get back to work."

"You're frowning. Still worrying about the bitch?"

I nodded the lie. Though it wasn't exactly a lie. I worried about everything. Mal had been wrong. Uptight wasn't my thing, worry was, and right now I was worrying about him. I shook off my frown, drank some more coffee. "Why don't we do some work today, boss?"

"This is why you should be in charge." Reece sighed dramatically. He had an impressive business degree behind him while I'd only barely finished high school, but most days it seemed I was the one with the work ethic. When mom went through her darkest time after Dad left, I couldn't just leave her on her own. The day I came home to find her lining up codeine and sleeping pills on her bedside table convinced me of that. So I was "home-schooled." Child Protection Services came around once and we put on a good enough show.

I made damn sure Lizzy turned up to classes at the local high school Monday to Friday, however.

Reece lifted a box of new stock onto the counter so we could start pricing it out. "Tell me more about last night."

"Ah, I got to meet a couple of the band members. That was cool."

"You got to talk to them?" Reece's expression was rapt. Usually shop talk revolved around his innuendos and escapades due to my life being boring. His language, not mine. I'm pretty sure you don't need to be balling every female in the downtown Portland area to make conversation. Perhaps that was why we'd never gotten together. Our hobbies differed so wildly.

My thoughts were remarkably bitter and twisted today.

Where had I left my happy face? Most likely it still lay on my doorstep, where it had fallen some sixteen hours ago. Malcolm Ericson had briefly resuscitated my joy before he'd started in on my supposed failings. Still, just thinking about him made me feel lighter.

How strange.

Lizzy hadn't texted me back yet. Not a surprise. Her college lifestyle kept her pretty busy. She could also be crap at remembering to charge her cell. I didn't doubt my sister would be there for me, though. Her and her dorm-room floor. I'd left a message for my landlord and received no response from him either. Fat chance he'd give me an extension on the rent. Even if I found a new roommate in record time, I still couldn't come up with my half of the money.

Time to admit defeat whether Reece liked it or not. Time to move on.

Said friend waved his hand in my face. "Anne, fill me in. You get to talk to them or not?"

"Sorry. Yes, I talked to Mal, the drummer."

"About?"

There was the question on everyone's lips.

"Not much, it was only briefly. He was busy. There were lots of people there." For some reason, I was loath to admit to more. Actually, for several reasons. Talking to Reece about another man would be weird. Also, I'd clearly blown the night out of proportion when it came to Mal Ericson. There'd been no connection. No one had looked into anyone else's soul. My fevered imagination had obviously been working overtime last night. So I rushed right on. "David seemed nice. Ben was there too, but I didn't really get to speak to him."

"You're totally dropping names right now." He chuckled.

I gave him a friendly smack in the ribs. "You asked. It's not name dropping if you asked."

"Okay, okay, I believe you. Don't beat me up. So can you get me into the next party there?"

"I doubt I'll be going to another party there, Reece. It was a pure fluke I wound up there last night."

"What use are you?" he joked.

The elderly tie-dyed woman shuffled toward the counter with a copy of *The Alchemist* in hand.

"That's a great book. I think you'll really like it." I rang up her purchase and handed it over for her to put in her reusable bag. Was there anything more wonderful than sending someone home with a book you loved? No, there was not.

I turned to Reece, who was straightening up some credit card receipts. "So you want to hang out tonight?" I asked. "If you're not doing anything. Maybe I'll try to perfect my martini."

"Hmm, I'm kind of leaving my calendar open tonight. There's a girl I'm waiting to hear from."

Of course there was.

"Buuut," he strung out the word. "If she doesn't call me, how about I come over for a martini?"

My heart sank a little bit. Stupid heart. I put on a fake smile. "Sure, Reece, it's not like I have anything better to do than wait around for you all night."

"Exactly," he said, and I couldn't tell if he was joking or not. At that moment, I wondered what exactly I had been chasing and why. Answer: a dream, because I was an idiot. Maybe Mal had a point about my usability. I'd covered for mom for so many years, perhaps the habit had stuck.

He was fiddling with his phone now, a goofy half smile on his face. "She wants to meet up," he said. "So . . . I have a huge favor. Could you close up tonight? Since you're not doing anything?"

"I should really say no. Shit, Reece. I'm not a total loser. I do have some boundaries." No matter what Malcolm Ericson said.

"Please. I'm sorry. You're right, I shouldn't have asked that. And I respect your boundaries, I do. I'm an ass and you're a name-dropping celebrity party animal. Forgive me?" He didn't look sorry, just vaguely desperate. But whatever, this was Reece. The man had offered me his couch last night as an emergency home.

And let's face facts. He was right; I didn't have any grand plans outside of reading.

"Alright," I said, resentment burning deep down in my soul. It soon gave way to sadness. Probably, I should buy chocolate or alcohol on my way home. A truly wise use of the extra money made from the extra hours. Chocolate martini, here I come.

"Thanks. I owe you."

"No worries. Not like I have anything going on."

It wasn't as if I'd be seeing Mal ever again.

CHAPTER FIVE

Something was wrong. Again. This time, I knew it before I walked in the door.

Work had picked up in the afternoon. There'd been no more time for worry, or bitter and twisted thoughts. Definitely a good thing. Now, I was ten types of tired. Two hours of sleep and stressing over money had done me in. The icy cold wind I'd walked in after getting off the MAX had frozen my neck and the tip of my nose. Any chocolate- and booze-fetching plan had flown straight out the window. I wanted a bath and bed. That was my entire plan for the night and it was a beautiful thing.

In a daze, I slid my key into the lock, which was when the door flew in—it wasn't even latched. Balance shot to shit, I fell, face planting in the middle of a hot, hard, sweaty chest.

I oomphed.

He grunted.

Strong hands grabbed me about the waist, holding me steady. A good thing, I really needed a hand right then or my ass might've met the floor. Perhaps I'd entered the wrong apartment. My mind had been elsewhere, worlds away from reality. Another apartment would certainly explain the delicious warm body I was up against.

Since when did sweat smell so good?

It was all I could do not to rub my face in, breathing deep. A sniff or two shouldn't be going too far. Discreetly done, of course.

"Anne. Dude." The chest vibrated beneath my cheek. "Welcome home!"

I knew that voice. I did. But what the hell was it doing in my apartment? Stunned, I blinked up at a familiar beautiful face. "Mal?"

"'Course it's me." He laughed. "You on drugs or something? You shouldn't do drugs. They're not good for you."

"I'm not doing drugs." Though drugs might have gone a ways toward explaining what I was seeing. Because what I was seeing was surreal. "You're here."

No doubt about it. He definitely was. I would know because my hands were still all over his hot, half-naked body. My hormones sidetracked any thoughts about their removal. I couldn't blame them.

"I know," he said. "Isn't it great?"

"Yeah. Wow."

He nodded.

I stared. How the hell did he get in? The door had been locked when I left.

"Work good?" he asked.

"Fine. Thank you."

He smiled down at me. "I was expecting you hours ago."

"Yeah, I had to close up and some people came in at the last minute. Mal, why are you here in my apartment without a shirt on? How did that happen?"

"It got hot moving shit." He rolled his neck, stretching out the muscles. "You're only on the second floor, but the stairs start to add up, you know? Nate and Lauren helped out for a bit, then they had to go. Anyway, not like you care, right? No dress code I need to know about?"

I still stared. Words came out of his mouth but they continued to make no sense. Nothing about this did.

His eyes narrowed on me. "Hang on, I've got my shirt off and everything and you're not giving me crazy eyes. What's with that?"

"Ah, I guess I'm too surprised at seeing you here."

His brows descended, as did the corners of his gorgeous lips. The man looked seriously sad. "Been looking forward to it all day."

"Sorry."

"Never mind. Come on, check it out." He pulled me into the apartment, my apartment, slamming the door shut behind me. Not answering the important question about his presence even a little. But what was truly upsetting was the way he separated my hands from his body. They wept silently. Either that or I was sweating. Most likely the latter. He had the weirdest effect on me.

"Ta-da," he sang, waving a hand about in a grand gesture, presenting my small living room to me.

"Wow."

"Awesome, right?"

"Yeah?"

"Yeah! I knew you'd love this."

I stared some more. Then I rubbed my eyes because they were starting to hurt. It was probably from all the bulging but I couldn't be sure.

What the hell was happening here?

"You moved in with me somehow." There could be no other reason for an entire drum kit appearing in the corner, let alone all the other stuff. The Twilight Zone had officially been entered. "You . . . huh. How about that."

He grimaced and rocked back on the heels of his Chucks. "I

know what you're gonna say, it's sooner than I thought too. But Davie threw me out today so I figured, why wait?"

I just blinked, the rest of me being too frozen to respond.

"Okay. Long story short, I accidentally saw Ev naked." He held up his hands, protesting his innocence. "It was only side boob, I swear. No nipple or anything like that. But you know what he's like with her, the fucking drama queen. He completely lost his shit."

I nodded. I didn't actually have a clue, but it seemed a response was required.

"Exactly. As if it's my fault. It was in the fucking kitchen! I just wanted something to eat and there they are, dry humping against the wall. I didn't even know she'd gotten home from work. As if I want to see that. It's like walking in on your folks. Well, except Ev actually has great tits." His guilty gaze slid to my face. "Alright, there might have been a flash of nipple but I swear it's not like I went out of my way to see it. Not my fault she was topless. Anyway, Davie went ballistic."

"He did?"

"Oh yeah. Huge. Harsh words were said. We may have even wrestled slightly. But I forgive him. Love makes you psycho, right?"

"Right." There was a sentiment I could wholeheartedly get behind. When my first boyfriend broke up with me at sixteen, my tiny little world had been rocked. And look at my mom. She'd lost her shit completely when dad left.

"Mm."

"So you moved in with me?" I said, ever so slowly piecing the story together.

Mal shrugged. "Well, hell yeah!"

"No, I mean, you actually moved in with me. Here. Into my apartment. Um, how did you get in again, just out of interest?"

"Is this going to be an issue?" he asked with a long, winded sigh. "Anne, come on. We talked about this last night. If you were gonna have a problem with me moving in, that was the time to bring it up, not now."

"I thought you were joking."

"Dude, that's offensive. Why would I joke about important stuff like that?"

"Because you were drunk?"

"I get some of my best ideas under the influence."

"I didn't even think you'd remember."

"Again, offended," he said. "I'm not some fifteen-year-old. I know what I can handle."

"Sorry." I don't quite know why I was the one apologizing. But never mind. My legs felt weak. I perched on the edge of the nearest couch. It was incredibly comfortable, though it did little for my sudden light-headedness.

Mal Ericson.

Living with me.

He did indeed look serious as evidenced by the little indent between his brows from frowning back at me. Ever so subtly I kicked myself, to check I was awake and not dreaming. Crap, it hurt. Pain radiated from my anklebone, making me wince. Yep, wide awake. Also, the heel on my Docs packed a punch.

"You're looking at me weird again," he said.

"Am I?"

He rolled his eyes. "Women. Honest, I swear, it was a hint of nipple and no more. I meant no disrespect to Evvie."

I leaned down, surreptitiously rubbing my brand-new bruise. "I believe you."

"Good. Can you please stop bringing it up?"

I opened my mouth to tell him I hadn't. But it seemed safer to keep the thought to myself. Who knew what tangent it would launch him into next? Mal Ericson was a hard man to keep up with.

"Shit, you don't like the couch do you?" he asked. "That's what the look is about."

"The couch?"

"Man." Mal hung his head, hands on his slim hips. "I called Ev to ask what color you'd want but she started asking questions and then she started yelling and it was just a fucking mess. I can't be standing in some furniture shop arguing on the phone with some chick, you know? I've gotta reputation to consider. So I tried calling Lauren 'cause I figured she might have a spare key to your place—which she did."

"Lauren let you in?"

"Yeah. And she said to definitely get that one, said you'd go nuts for it."

"No, it's . . . um, it's really nice." I ran my palm over the velvet fabric. It felt divine, super soft. No way did I want to know what it must have cost.

"Really?" He looked at me from beneath his brows, mouth tight with concern. Still, the green and hazel of his eyes was crystal clear. He seemed almost childlike somehow, vulnerable. "You're sure you like it?"

I couldn't tear my gaze away from him to give the item of furniture a proper perusal. No doubt, however, it looked every bit as good as it felt. "It's beautiful, Mal."

"Phew." His sudden grin lit my world.

I smiled back so hard my face hurt. "Look, I'm not saying no to you moving in. I guess I'm still trying to get my head around the concept. But why do you want to live with me?"

"I like you," he said simply.

"You barely know me."

"You're a friend of Ev's and Lauren's. We talked. I tackled

you. We rolled around on the floor together. It was a real bonding experience."

I blinked.

"More? Seriously?"

"Please."

"You know, I've never lived with a female before. Well, not since my mom and sisters, and they don't count. Gimme a minute, this is way harder than it looks." He threw himself into the black leather wingback chair across from me. Very cool chair. No match for the man sitting in it, but still, nice chair. I waited as he made various pained expressions, finally pinching the bridge of his nose. "You seem like a nice girl, you know?"

I didn't know whether to laugh or cry. Laughter seemed safer. "Thanks."

"Hang on," he groaned. "I'm not used to having to talk women into shit, either. Usually, they're just happy to go along with whatever."

And I did not blame them one bit. But I was reasonably certain there lay the path to ruin. I'd be trailing around behind him like a lovelorn puppy in no time. Not good.

His fingers tapped out a beat on the rolled wooden chair arms. He was a restless soul, was Malcolm Ericson. Never still. You could see how all of his energy made him such a great drummer. "You know, it was fun hanging out with you last night. I enjoyed it. Cool that you weren't being psycho or getting in anyone's face. Despite you being so into me that you get all crazy eyed, I kinda find you strangely soothing to be around right now."

A shadow passed over his face, there and gone in an instant. If not for Ev's visit I might have convinced myself I'd imagined it. But no. Something was definitely up with this man.

"You don't bug me with a lot of questions. Well, you didn't

last night." He reclined in the chair like a king, resting his ankle on his knee. The energy or tension running through him kept his fingers jittering, endlessly tapping. "Let's look at it this way. You need money, right?"

I hesitated, but it was the truth. We both knew it. "Right."

"I need something too."

My eyes narrowed. If he started yelling about sexual healing again I'd throw him out, cool furniture, drum kit, and all. Or I'd lick him all over. With my current confusion and stress levels, chances were fifty/fifty. An opportunity to throw myself at him might just be too good to miss. After all, how many more chances would I get? My luck had to run out eventually.

"And I think you'll suit my needs to perfection," he continued.

"Your needs?"

One side of his mouth hitched higher (forty/sixty). "Every man has needs, young Anne. How old are you, by the way?"

"Twenty-three. I'm aware everyone has needs. But Mal, I'm *not* going to meet yours." My nose went high. Sweet baby Jesus, I so badly wanted to meet his needs, but not when he gave me that smug grin. A girl had to have her pride.

"Sure you are." He laughed softly, evilly, seeing right through me (twenty/eighty). "You're dying to meet my needs. You can't look away from my luscious half-naked body. The minute I opened the door you were pawing at me. It was like you were in heat or something."

Fuck.

I squeezed my eyes shut for a moment, blocking him out in an attempt to regain my wits. If only my heart would stop slipping into cardiac arrest at the sight and sound of him. It would make things so much easier. "No, Mal. I lost my balance when you opened the door on me. Finding you here has actually come

as a bit of a surprise. I'm not used to people just moving themselves in with me without some serious discussion up front."

When I opened my eyes, he was silently watching me. Judging me.

"And I wasn't pawing at you."

The too-calm expression on his face spoke volumes. He
didn't believe me, not even a little. "Hey, now, don't be embarrassed."

I wasn't a clueless virgin. My V-card had been stamped with
my first and last long-term boyfriend at age sixteen. Since coming to Portland, I'd indulged in the odd date. Why wouldn't I?
I was young and free. I enjoyed sex. Thoughts of mounting a
half-naked man on a wingback chair? Not so much.

I was out of control. No way could I let him know this, however.

"It's okay, pumpkin. I don't mind you pawing at me. If that's
how you feel the need to express your affection, that's cool."

"Mal." This was going from bad to worse. I don't even know
why I started laughing. "Please stop talking. I need a minute.
Consider this a boundary."

His eyes lit with delight. "Hey, you've been thinking about
what I said. That's great. I respect your boundary, Anne."

"Then why are you still talking?"

"Right. Sorry."

I tried to find my calm. Why had I never made time for yoga?
Deep breathing exercises would have been so useful.

When I opened my eyes, Mal smiled back at me serenely.
The arrogant jerk. So confident. So hot. And so damn shirtless.
What was with that? It was fall in Portland, cool weather, rain-
ing on and off. Normal people wore clothes this time of year.

"Can you put a shirt on?"

He scratched at his chin. "Mm, no. That's my boundary, sorry. I like your sexy looks too much to get dressed."

Crap, was I making crazy eyes?

"You're perfect," he muttered, smirk firmly in place.

Damn it, I was.

"What do you think my needs are, Anne?"

"I'm aware you're talking about sex, Mal. That's kind of obvious. But why, out of all the women at your disposal, would you choose me? That I don't understand. And why you would move yourself in with me, I don't really get that either. You could have gone to a hotel or rented a place of your own much nicer than here."

"Noooo." He slumped back in the seat, laying his meshed fingers on his flat belly. "I'm not talking about sex. I like to think you and I are above all of that messy, physical stuff, despite your infatuation with me. What I need is a girlfriend . . . well, a pretend girlfriend, and you, Anne Rollins, are perfect."

"Fuck, what?"

He burst out laughing.

"You're joking," I said, relieved. Well, mad and relieved. Were rock stars so bored these days they had to resort to such extremes for entertainment?

"No, I'm not joking. Your reaction was funny, is all." Long fingers brushed back his blond hair, pulling it off his face. "This is serious, a business transaction, and it's gotta be kept on the down low. I've paid your rent. I got you furniture to replace what that asshole friend of yours took. In return, I want you to play my girlfriend for a while."

My jaw gave way to gravity. "You're not serious."

"Why do you never believe anything I say? Anne, I am very serious."

"Why me?"

He sighed and stared at the ceiling long and hard. "I dunno, the way you helped your friend out, even if she didn't do right by you."

"Mal, that doesn't make me a good person. It makes me an idiot." Given how things had gone down it was nothing less than the cold, hard truth. "You basically said as much yourself last night. I let her use me."

Mal bared his teeth. "Hey, I never said you were an idiot and I don't want to hear you talking like that again. There's another boundary, right there."

"O-kay, relax."

"I am perfectly relaxed. Look, we've all got our problems, Anne. I never said you were perfect." He paused, scratched his chin. "Oh, no wait. I did say that. Well, I didn't mean it exactly like . . . not that you're not great and everything but . . . yeah, let's move this on."

"No. Come on, rock star. How did you mean it?" I asked, suppressing a giggle. It was just him. I couldn't help it, the man was hilarious.

He waved away the question. "No, we've moved on. Out of interest, did it even occur to you to hit Ev up for the money you needed last night?"

I reared back in surprise. "What? No."

"She'd have given it to you. Fuck knows her and Davie have got it."

"It's not her problem."

He gave me another smug look.

"That proves nothing. And if you've chosen me for my ethics then am I really the best person to be lying to your friends and family, Mal?"

"Pumpkin . . . we're not going to be hurting anyone. We're just going to be helping each other out, that's all."

"You said I was a hopeless liar."

"You'll be fine." He waved my protests away.

I just sat there and reeled. Was this really something we could pull off?

"Trust me."

"Why do you need a pretend girlfriend?"

"Because I do."

"Mal."

He rolled his eyes, face tensing. "Because it's none of your business why, okay? I've paid up your rent. Your sweet ass will not be evicted. In return, all I ask is that you gaze adoringly at me around other people. You do that anyway; what's the big deal here?"

"So you're not going to tell me?"

"Have you had your hearing tested lately? Let's just say I have a good reason, a personal reason, and leave it at that. Honestly, you're as bad as Davie and Ev. 'What's wrong, Mal?' 'Are you okay, Mal?' Well, I was until everyone asked me a thousand fucking times." He pushed to his feet and started pacing the room. Given the length of his legs, he didn't get very far. Three steps forward, three steps back. After a couple of laps he stopped, stared out the window at the street below.

"Why does everyone insist on being heavy all the fucking time? Life's too short for all this oversharing. You're here. I'm here. We can help each other out and have a good time while we're at it. That's all that matters." He spun on his heel to face me, arms out wide. "Life's a song, Anne. Let's play."

My life hadn't been much of a song . . . at least, not up until this point.

Neither of us spoke for a moment. Expectation and impatience oozed from him. I did indeed have a bad feeling I was being played again. However, not maliciously this time. Mal didn't seem like he'd harm a fly. But he might accidentally trample one.

From the outside, it seemed a good deal. I really did need the money. I also liked being around him. He was about a bazillion times more fun than I'd ever known. Whatever happened, this was bound to be a hell of a ride. And if I knew he would leave, up front, there'd be no risk of getting overly attached. I'd just enjoy the time I had with him and then say good-bye. This could very well be fantastic.

"Alright," I said at last. "You have pulled my ass out of the fire. Thanks for that. But I'm still not completely convinced about this girlfriend plan. I guess we'll see how it goes."

He clapped his hands in glee. "You won't regret this. I won't mess with your life. Much."

"Much?"

"And you know I'm a fucking delight to have around. People don't always get that about me. Plus, I'll open jars and lift heavy shit. I hear those are issues for women." He bounced around the room. Good god, this man had energy to spare like he snorted sugar. "So, what should we do tonight? Wanna order some food? What do you feel like?"

I slumped back in the chair, tired from just watching him. "Mal, I don't have money for that, but you go ahead."

"Would you stop worrying about money? That's why I'm here. Everything's fine. Now what do you feel like?"

"Whatever you want is great."

"That is so the correct answer. We are going to be the best fake couple ever, pumpkin."

"Please don't call me that."

"Puuuumpkin," he drawled, eyebrows waggling. "It's a great nickname. Your hair is kinda that color and we're a couple now. Couples always have dumb-ass names for each other. C'mon, you think up one for me."

"I'll get right to work on that."

"Cool. Then we'll have touching time." He rubbed his hands together. "Actually, never mind, we can do that later in bed."

My mind scrambled for purchase. "Bed? Touching time? Is that a euphemism? I thought we weren't having sex. You said we were just pretending."

"Geez, relax. We're not having sex, we're just sleeping together. The whole plan will totally collapse if we start having sex. What I need is a respectable long-term-looking relationship. We start fucking and you'll be all 'Oh Mal, I never dreamed such ecstasy was possible. I cannot live without you! Fuck me, Mal. Pleeeeease.'" His knees buckled until he fell flat onto the floor. It was an impressive performance. The man knew how to bat his eyelashes.

I giggled like a vapid schoolgirl. A noise that pretty much made me want to shoot myself on principle.

"And then everything will go all psycho Fatal Attraction. Trust me, I've seen it happen and it's not pretty. So let's keep it strictly above the belt. Get your mind out of the gutter, Anne."

"You're that good, huh?"

He leveled me with a look. "Miss Rollins, you have no idea."

"You know, I honestly can't decide if your ego is repulsive or just impressive."

"You want me to lie to you instead?"

"Mal, I can barely tell when you're being serious as it is."

He rolled onto his hands and knees, then crawled over to me, eyes full of mischief. "If I'm talking to you, I'm serious. Now, we'll have to kiss in public, obviously. And what if we're out to dinner and I stick my tongue in your ear and you get all weirded out? People might start to wonder. So we need to practice the touching thing."

"Your tongue? Really? I don't know . . ."

"Lucky for you, I'm here and I do." He stood and picked up a cell phone, his finger flicking over the screen. "We need to make sure we look tight. Lauren's been over fucking constantly. We can't risk separate bedrooms. Do you know she doesn't even knock, just bursts on in like she owns the place? Some people, no manners."

I was too overwhelmed to point out the irony in that statement.

"Yes, but we could lock the door," I suggested, growing slightly palm-sweaty desperate again. Though, to be honest, I'd never really stopped.

Me sleeping with Mal? No. Not a good idea. Him bouncing around my apartment half naked was enough. Touching in the dark would do me in for sure. I'd attack him despite my best intentions. Given we'd be living together for the foreseeable future, pushing for more would be a freaking disaster.

"We can't just lock the door," he said. "Lauren went and got another key made. You need better security, pumpkin."

"Very true."

"Hey, you don't snore do you?"

I gave him my very best withering glare.

"Just asking." He backed away, still playing with his phone. "And I'll make sure I keep any hookups on the down low, okay? I won't embarrass you with any of that."

"Thanks." I shouldn't have been surprised. But I was. Stupid, stupid me. "Were you just setting this up last night? Was that what it was all about?"

"Well, yeah."

I opened my eyes wide. Painfully wide. I took a deep breath in through my nose. It didn't matter really. My pride had taken a hit, but I had a roof over my head for the foreseeable future. Time to suck it up.

This sleeping-together thing wouldn't work. It couldn't. The fact that I was buzzing with tension just from the thought of it confirmed as much. But me playing his girlfriend part? I owed it to him to try. It could even be fun. Serious fun. And god knew I was overdue for some of that in my life.

I sat up straight, took a deep breath. "Okay, I'm agreeing to everything but the touching time."

He opened his mouth to protest but I plowed on before he could get a word out. "And tomorrow we put a sliding lock on the door to keep Lauren out and you start sleeping in the spare room. These are my conditions."

"Look at you, all assertive. I like it. Though really, I'd prefer it if you thought of me as being beyond boundaries."

"I'm serious, Mal. Take it or leave it. I just got out of one clusterfuck of a roommate situation. I won't fall straight into another."

Mal crossed his arms and looked down the length of his nose at me. At first, I thought he would argue. Some evil subversive part of me might have even hoped he would, at least on the sleeping front. But he didn't.

"Very well, I accept your terms. Tell you what," he said slowly. "Why don't I hit the couch tonight?"

My shoulders dropped in what was most likely relief. "That would be great. Thanks."

"No problem." He gave me a vaguely amused look. "Whatever works for you, Anne."

"Great. I'm going to go have a bath."

"Have fun."

"Yeah."

The bathroom door was locked shut behind me in record time. I sat on the edge of the big old battered claw-foot tub, blood rushing loud behind my ears. My mind was a blur. I'd just talked my way out of sleeping with a rock star. What had I done?

Disappointment made my insides ache.

But this was the right move. I needed to remember how into Reece I was. He was a far safer crush option. One day, he and I had a chance of actually working out.

Once all of the noise in my head faded, I looked at myself in the mirror. My hair hung flat around my face. My eyes were wide and wild. Within the space of twenty-four hours I'd been turned upside down. I might not be sleeping with one, but I most certainly now lived with a rock star. Didn't see that one coming.

"What the hell have you gotten yourself into?" I asked the girl in the mirror.

She had nothing but a dazed, surprised smile to offer. Clearly she was a sucker for Mal's particular brand of crazy. Thank goodness I was more mature.

I pulled my work T-shirt off over my head and started in on the laces of my boots. The sudden banging on the door almost made me fall off my perch. I put a hand to the floor and pushed myself upright before I fell face forward.

"Anne?"

"Yeah?" I sat back up and crossed my arms over my black bra, covering things up even though he couldn't possibly see.

"I forgot to say thanks. For letting me live here with you and agreeing to be my girlfriend. I really appreciate it."

"Well, thank you for paying my rent and for the furniture and everything."

"That was nothing. I would've done that anyway. Didn't like seeing you sad last night."

"Really?" My throat tightened and I stared at the door, amazed. That was huge. I really didn't know what to say. He barely knew me and yet he would have come to my rescue? Mal Ericson might be a bad boy, but he was also a good man.

One that I liked very much.

"Yeah. 'Course. It's going to be fun, Anne," he said, his voice close to the door. "You wait and see."

"Okay."

He sounded like he needed me to believe him. Funny thing was, I did.

CHAPTER SIX

I started getting Mal's texts just before lunch.

> Mal: Awake
> Anne: Morning

> Mal: Going for a run with Jim
> Anne: Have fun!

> Mal: Back from run having lunch
> Anne: K

> Mal: Where's cleaning stuff?
> Anne: To clean what?
> Mal: Pizza exploded in microwave
> Anne: Spray bottle under sink

> Mal: When you home?
> Anne: 5:30
> Mal: Bored
> Anne: Sorry
> Mal: What you doing?
> Anne: Working right now. Gotta go. Talk later.

Mal: Your taste in music sucks

Anne: Thanks

Mal: Seriously, we need to talk it's that bad. Everything apart from Stage Dive needs to go.

Anne: Wait. What are you doing?

Mal: Fixing it

Anne: Mal, WTH are you doing?

Mal: Making you new playlists with decent shit. Relax

Anne: K Thanks

Mal: Bored again

Mal: Ben's coming over to play Halo

Anne: Great! But you don't have to tell me everything you do, Mal.

Mal: Davie says communication's important

Mal: When are you on the rag? Davie said to find out if you want cupcakes or ice cream

Anne: I want to not talk about this ever

Mal: Bored. Ben's late

Mal: Let's get a dog

Anne: Apartment has no pets rule

Mal: Nice green lace bra

Anne: Get out of my drawers, Mal.

Mal: Matching panties?

Anne: GET OUT NOW.

Mal: :)

Mal: Sext me

Mal: Come on it'll be funny

Mal: Plz?

Mal: High level of unhealthy codependency traits exhib-
     ited by both parties relationship possibly bordering on
     toxic

Anne: WTF?

Mal: Did magazine quiz. We need help. Especially you

Anne: . . .

Mal: Booking us couples counseling. Tues 4:15 alright?

Anne: We are not going to counseling.

Mal: What's wrong? Don't you love me anymore?

Anne: Turning phone off now.

"Problem?" asked Reece, moseying on up and looking over my shoulder.

"No. Sorry." I shoved my cell into my back pocket. "I'm working, I swear."

"Sure you are." He winked. Being friends with the boss did pay off sometimes. "Do anything interesting last night?"

Had I ever. Mal seemed hell-bent on driving me crazy today, but last night had been fantastic. We'd had a floor picnic with some of the best tapas I'd tasted in a long time, washed down with Spanish beer. He'd told me hilarious stories about big-name musicians. Lots of tawdry sexploits and insane backstage demands, Mal knew about them all. He made for awesome company.

I wasn't ready to explain Mal to Reece, however. Looking at Reece, I might never be ready. Where would I begin? Even if I could keep a straight face, he knew me well enough to know I didn't jump into relationships. Not in this way. Luckily, Reece's attention had already slipped away. I shouldn't have worried.

His gaze rested on a young woman browsing in the True Crime section. You'd have thought he'd have enough sense to turn away when she picked up a book on female serial killers, but no.

"I didn't get up to anything much last night," I lied, feeling zero guilt.

He did a half nod, probably not even listening. "I'll just go see if she needs help."

"Okeydokey." I pulled my cell out, switched it back on. As soon as the screen flashed to life I started one finger typing, a smile already on my face.

Anne: Ben arrive yet?
Mal: He's here. How you doing? Home soon?
Anne: Soon.

Ben was lazed on the love seat, hands busy on the game controls, when I walked in the door. There was lots of blood and guts happening on the TV screen. The novelty of walking in to find famous people hanging in my apartment would probably never fade. I sincerely hoped it wouldn't. Disappointingly, Mal was nowhere in sight. I'd been rushing through tasks, eager to see him all afternoon. Lizzy had called me and it'd almost killed me not telling her about him. But I honestly didn't know how to plausibly explain his sudden appearance in my life. She'd been furious about the shit with Skye. I hadn't been able to muster much anger about it, funnily enough. Good things were happening. That was all in the past.

Now I was finally home, my heart banging around inside my chest, and I felt inexcusably shy. Hesitant almost. Forget it, this was my apartment. My home. And he had chosen to live here, with me, for whatever reason. Back straight and boobs out, what little there was of them.

"Hey, Anne," he said.

"Hi, Ben. Is Mal around?" My ability to play it cool was improving. I hardly stuttered at all.

"In the kitchen."

"Thanks." I dashed past him, trying not to mess with his on-screen killing spree.

Mal was staring out the small kitchen window, his cell to his ear. "What aren't you telling me?"

A pause.

"Yeah, okay. What'd he say?"

Another pause.

"No. Just lay it out for me. C'mon."

The break was longer this time. After a while, he grabbed hold of the edge of the counter, gripping it so hard his knuckles turned white. Obviously, this was a private moment, but I couldn't walk away. The pain in his voice and the lines of his body were acute. He was hurting.

"That can't be right. What about if we—"

He listened in silence. Back out in the living room, the boom of explosions and the rattle of gunfire continued on.

"Okay. Thanks for letting me know." He pressed end on the call and threw his cell aside. Both hands now gripped the edge of the counter, squeezing so hard it creaked.

"Mal?"

The whites of his eyes were huge, rimmed with red. What the hell was going on?

"Anne. Hey. Didn't hear you come in."

"Are you okay?"

He breathed in hard, shook his head. "Yeah! Slept like shit. Then the run with Jimmy wore me out. But all good. Aren't you cute, worrying about me? That's very girlfriendish."

"Ha." I smiled. He didn't smile back.

"Let's, ah . . . You say hi to Ben already?"

"Yes, I did."

His hands grasped my shoulders, turning me and marching me back out into the living room. "You really need to greet your guests properly, pumpkin. You don't want him thinking you're rude."

"Mal, I—"

"Ben. Look, my awesome girlfriend came home."

"Hi, Mal's awesome girlfriend." Ben didn't take his eyes off the screen. "This place is a bit smaller than your L.A. pad, dude. You gonna stay here or buy bigger?"

"Anne's been talking about getting a dog, so I'm thinking we'll trade up eventually."

Ben nodded.

I didn't bother to correct Mal. Really the best way to handle him was to simply roll with it. Plus, this current mood of his concerned me.

"Time to beat drums," Mal announced, rubbing his hands together, then shaking his arms. He still wasn't smiling. The manic energy was clearly back despite his claim of being tired.

This time, Ben did take his eyes off the screen. "Thought we were getting dinner and hanging out with Miss Awesome here."

"Need to burn off some energy. Anne understands, don't you, pumpkin?"

I pushed my disappointment aside and nodded. A man had to do what a man had to do. I just wish I knew what was going on. Whatever the phone call had been about, it wasn't good news. It also wasn't my business, I know.

"She's very supportive of my career. Always has been. In many ways, she is my inspiration."

"You only met her two days ago." Ben turned off the game, throwing the control aside.

"And I've done some of my best work in that time."

"Whatever. So that's what you wanna do, go play some music?" Eyes narrowed, Ben watched Mal bopping up and down beside me.

"That's what I said. Keep up, Benny boy." He curled his hands into fists. "Let's go."

"'Kay." Ben's sharp gaze turned to me like he expected me to have answers. I shrugged. As he'd pointed out, I'd only known Mal for forty-eight hours.

No, I didn't know what was going on with him, but damned if I wasn't going to find out.

CHAPTER SEVEN

Someone was yelling. A male someone. Then another voice joined in, the noise carrying through my bedroom wall. I bolted upright, bewildered but wide awake. Five-fifteen glowed green on the little alarm clock beside my bed.

Damn, it was early.

Due to Mal's nocturnal habits, I hadn't gotten the best night's sleep. When he'd eventually returned just after eleven, he'd been dripping with sweat. I'd crashed earlier in the evening and had been half asleep, dragging my sorry ass out to check if he needed anything. He'd said he'd be crashing soon, so I'd gone back to bed. But for hours I'd lain there, listening to him moving around the apartment. He'd watched TV, talked on the phone, and hummed for hours. Actually, I didn't mind the humming. It was kind of nice. Though humming death metal was more of an art form than you'd imagine. I'd finally fallen asleep to something by Metallica. Good lord, had my dreams been weird.

But why couldn't Mal sleep?

The shouting escalated. I crawled off my bed and bolted for the door, flannel pajamas, bed hair, and all. Out in the living room, Mal's back was to me, barring the front door. He wore only a pair of black boxer briefs. Not that I was complaining because good god, the man's ass. I almost lost my tongue. To the floor or my throat, I'm not sure which. Both were strong contenders.

"Even if you are a friend of pumpkin's this is not a suitable hour to visit," Mal hissed.

"Who the fuck are you and why are you calling Anne *pumpkin*?" That was Reece and he sounded distinctly enraged. Like, rampaging enraged.

My boss and I weren't an item, though. We were just friends. So a semi-naked man answering my door at odd hours of the morning was actually none of his damn business.

"Morning," I said, standing tall.

Mal gave me a brief cranky look over his shoulder. As nice as the couch was, I'd probably be in a bad mood if I'd slept on it too. Maybe that was why he'd stayed up so late. He'd ordered another bed for the spare room, but for some reason it had yet to arrive. Tonight, I'd ask if he wanted to share with me. Just as friends.

His shoulders were distractingly large with his hands on his hips. I was no lightweight, but if he was willing to stand with his arms out, I'd give climbing him a try. Years back, before all the shit with mom, I'd been different, braver. Something about Mal reminded me of the adrenaline-junkie tomboy I'd been. I missed that girl. She'd been fun.

"You woke her, asswipe." For once, Mal didn't sound the least bit light and easy as he gave Reece hell. "Do you have any idea how stressful shit's been for her lately? Plus she had to work late last night."

And as relaxed as Reece was about work, that comment was not good. "Mal, it's okay. This is my friend and *my boss*, Reece."

"Reece?" He sneered. "This is who you were talking to on your phone at the party?"

"Yes."

"Huh. Figured it was a chick."

"Guess again." Reece pushed his way past the mostly naked drummer to shove a box of donuts into my arms. Voodoo Donuts. My saliva glands kicked into overdrive despite the early hour and manly standoff.

To be fair, partly also because of it, yes.

"What the fuck is going on, A? Who is this asshole?"

"Reece, not cool."

His bloodshot eyes blazed angrily, his dark hair sticking out. The scent of stale perfume lingered around him like a miasma. I'd also question his sobriety because his movements seemed a bit off. Here was a man who had not yet been to bed.

At least, not his own bed.

"A?" asked Mal, crossing his arms over his chest. He turned and winked at me. "You call her 'A'? What, saying her whole name's too much of a commitment for you?"

I barked out a laugh. Then attempted to turn it into a cough. Reece didn't look convinced, but I didn't care. Relief made me weak in the knees. My Mal was back, cracking jokes and smiling. A real smile this time, not the harsh manic parody from the night before.

It was amazing. I could actually see Reece's hackles rising. Mal might have had a good half a head on him, but violence was not out of the question. Meanwhile, Mal just looked amused. The depth to which he didn't give a fuck was actually a large part of his charm. I'd never met anyone like him.

Not to say he wouldn't throw down with Reece. I had no doubt the man could handle himself.

"Why don't I make coffee?" I took a hesitant step toward the tiny kitchen, hoping someone would follow. Either one of them would do. Neither made a move so I stayed put.

Reece's brows drew tight together. "Even for a hookup you can do a hell of a lot better."

"What?" Not only was it an extraordinarily rude thing to say, it wasn't even remotely true.

"You heard me."

"Shit, Reece, how can you even . . ." I stared at Mal, frowned, and cocked my head. So much skin. I looked and looked until I hit the dusting of dark blond hair leading down from his belly button, heading straight for No-Anne Land. He had a treasure trail. A map to hidden delights. The donut box trembled in my hands.

I could and should avert my eyes. But I didn't.

"Anne?" Reece demanded angrily, dragging me out of my porny daydreams.

"Um . . ." Yes, such was my genius statement.

"There's the crazy eyes," said Mal in a low, rough voice. "Looks like my pumpkin is ready for round six of the sexin'."

Oh. Crap. He didn't.

Reece's forehead furrowed, his fingers curling into fists.

Alright, so he did.

I crushed the box of donuts against my chest. "That's a really sweet offer, Mal."

"Pumpkin, if you're still walking straight, my work here is clearly not done. Hell, we haven't even gotten around to breaking in the new couch yet." He turned to Reece, enjoying himself way too much if the light in his eyes was any indicator. "She's worried we'd stain the material. Like I wouldn't just buy her another, right? Women."

No answer from Reece apart from the white lines around his mouth.

Mal exhaled hard. "Next time let's stick to leather. Wipe

clean is so much easier and it won't chafe your soft skin nearly as much as you think, Anne. Not if we—"

"Enough," I barked, feeling the cardboard box cave in.

"Too much sex talk in front of friends?"

I nodded.

"Sorry," said Mal. "Real sorry. My bad."

So much hostility in such a confined space. And there was no question, Reece was genuinely jealous. He was all puffed up and radiating fury. His gaze shifted between Mal and me, mouth fierce.

You have to understand, before now, I hadn't been entirely certain Reece even realized I was female. Yet here he was, edging toward me as if I was territory to be protected. Something Mal didn't intend to allow if his side-stepping maneuver meant anything. It was like some strange animalistic caveman dance, the two of them slowly hemming me in. Amusing in a way.

The first male to pee on me, however, would pay with his balls.

"Thinks I'm a hook-up," scoffed Mal with a side look. "Set him straight, pumpkin."

At those words, Reece's nostrils flared. I stood, pinned to the spot. My heart beat so hard, I'm certain ribs were bruised in the process. Wild bed hair or not, this moment was glorious. I wanted it up on YouTube for all time. (Okay, maybe I didn't want it on YouTube. But you get what I mean.)

I cleared my throat and steeled my spine. Today, I stood about ten times taller. "Reece, Mal and I are seeing each other."

"We're living together," Mal corrected.

"Right. That too. I've been meaning to tell you. Mal and I are living very happily together since the day before yesterday."

"Mal?" My boss froze. "Mal Ericson, the drummer?"

"Yep."

Reece's reddened eyes blazed even brighter. Nothing more was said.

"Now that we've got that straightened out, I'm gonna hit the shower," Mal announced. "Give you two kids a chance to talk."

"Thanks," I said.

"No problem." His hand smacked into my ass, making me jump. Then, fingers lazily scratching at stubble, he sauntered into the bathroom. My butt cheek stung. I made a mental note to kill him later, once we were alone. Kill him or screw him, whatevs. My hormones were so confused.

The second the door clicked shut Reece grabbed my arm and hustled me into the tiny kitchen. Dawn had yet to make an appearance. Light from the living room shone weakly on his surly face. His black-rimmed glasses were askew, adding to his whole thoroughly ruffled appearance. I probably should've been jealous. But for once I actually wasn't.

"What the hell is this, Anne? You said you met him, that's all. Fuck, I thought he looked familiar . . ."

"It came as something of a surprise to me as well. But it's great, right?" The boy had bed head and it wasn't from sleeping. No way was he coming into my home and giving me shit over finding me similarly (allegedly) occupied.

"Great," he replied flatly.

"He's a really nice guy when you get to know him."

"Sure."

"He makes me smile, you know? Doesn't take me for granted," I said, going in for the kill. So I had some early morning bloodlust going on. It wasn't like he didn't deserve it for being rude to Mal. I might not like most of the women he had hanging around at various times, but I sure as hell never insulted them. "And I'd appreciate it if you didn't talk to him like that again."

Reece's mouth fell open. "Anne, the way he spoke to me—"

"You're going to go with he started it? Seriously? You don't knock on my door at this hour and call the person that answers it an asshole, Reece. That's not cool."

"Sorry." He gave my battered old fridge a foul look.

"What's happening here? You've never cared about me dating before. Not that I've done much of it recently."

"Nothing. I just wasn't expecting . . ."

I waited, but he didn't finish the sentence. Maybe the subject was best left alone. "Would you like some coffee?"

"No, I'm heading home."

"Okay. Well, thanks for the donuts." I sat the broken box on the counter.

"No problem." He just stared at me, his eyes a mixture of mad and sad. I didn't really know what to do with that. Anger still gripped me.

"Reece . . ."

"It's fine."

"I don't want this affecting our friendship."

His shoulders pushed back. "No. Of course it won't."

"Good." I don't know what came over me, but I had to hug him. He was feeling down, I wanted to fix it. Mom had never been into the touchy-feely stuff and I'd inherited the talent, or lack of one. Accordingly, my arms were stiff, awkward. I patted him once on the back and then got the hell out of there before he could react. A surprise attack, if you will.

"How did your date go last night?" I asked.

"It was nothing special. What were you up to?"

"Mal ordered dinner. Just a quiet night in." As soon as I mentioned Mal's name, Reece's face turned grumpy. It'd have been easier to empathize with him if he hadn't reeked of sex and behaved like an entitled jerk.

"I'm going to go," he said. "I'll see you later."

"Later."

I was still standing there staring after him long after the front door slammed shut. Deep down inside, I was neither angry nor sad. Just a little shocked perhaps to find Reece cared about me in that way after all. How it would affect things, I had no idea.

When Mal reemerged it was with his long hair slicked back. The blond was much darker when wet and the angles of his face were displayed to perfection. He'd put on a pair of jeans and a soft-looking, worn old AC/DC T-shirt. But his feet were bare. His long toes were lightly dusted with hairs. Neat, square nails.

"Coffee?" I asked, already pouring him a cup. It gave me a solid excuse to look away from his apparently fascinating toes. What was it about bare feet?

"Yeah, thanks. Your little hipster friend gone already?"

I set his cup on the counter and he started piling in sugar from the canister. One, two, three heaping spoonfuls. All his energy had to come from somewhere, I guess.

"Reece left a while back," I confirmed, picking through the chunks of donut. Delicious.

"Hard not to think less of you there."

"Why?"

Mal took a sip of coffee, eyeing me over the rim. "You like the douche. You like him a lot."

I filled my mouth with food. Such a great excuse for not answering. If I chewed really slowly it could kill the entire conversation.

"Even with you giving me crazy eyes, I could tell," he unfortunately continued. "You're just lucky I'm not the jealous type."

I choked down the mother load of food in my mouth. "Is that why you started up with the sex adventure stories?"

He laughed, low and mocking. But who he was laughing at exactly, I couldn't tell.

"Mal?"

"He shows up here, fresh from a night out drinking and fucking, fully expecting to find you waiting with open arms . . . I didn't like it."

"We're just friends."

He looked away, licked his lips. "Anne."

The disappointment in his voice stung. I wanted to make excuses. Roll out the old standards. I wanted to protect myself. But I didn't even know what I was protecting myself from. Mal hadn't attacked me. His quiet reproof slipped past my guard in a way Lauren's lectures and demands never could.

"Thing is, you're both straight," he said. "Men and women as friends doesn't really work. One person's always into the other. Fact of life."

"Yes, I like him," I admitted. "I have for a while now. He, ah . . . he doesn't see me that way."

"Maybe. Maybe not. He sure as fuck didn't like finding me here." Mal set down his cup and leaned against the corner of the faded gray kitchen counter, arms braced on either side. His damp hair slid forward, shielding his face. "Were you planning on using me to make him jealous?"

"Manipulating him and being an asshat to you? No, I hadn't planned on doing that. But thank you for asking."

"No skin off my nose." He shrugged. "And he's a douche who deserves what he gets. Turning up here, acting like you owe him something."

I wrapped my arms around myself. "I'm sorry he was rude to you. I had a word with him. That won't happen again."

He snorted out a laugh. "You don't have to protect me, Anne. I'm not that delicate."

"Beside the point." I took a sip of coffee.

"You know, I can live with you using me to get at him. Hell, we're already using each other, right?"

Something in the way he said it stopped me. If only he wasn't hiding behind his hair, I could see him better, gauge where this was going.

"No reason why we can't milk this baby for all it's worth," he said.

"You'd do that for me?"

He half smiled. "If that's what you want. Pushing asswipe's buttons is too easy but I'm willing to make the effort. Hell, this body was born to make mortal men jealous."

I smiled back at him, cautiously. Not committing to anything. This situation called for serious thought. The temptation to leap was huge.

"I do think he's right about one thing. You can do better." Green eyes stared me down. There was amusement there, as always. He seemed to be daring me, pushing me to see what happened. I really wanted to push back.

"But whatever," he said, rolling his shoulders back in some sort of overdeveloped shrug. "Your call. After all, you've known this guy for how long?"

"Two years."

"Two years you've been into him and never done a thing about it? You must have your reasons, right?"

"Right," I said, sounding not the least bit believable.

He laughed and right then, I disliked him just a little. I'd never openly admitted my thing for Reece to anyone and here was Mal, ever so sweetly rubbing my face in it. Problem was, the status quo with Reece was infinitely preferable to anything I'd had since I was sixteen. If he settled down with someone else, my heart wouldn't be broken. But who knew, we might get together one day.

Why act when doing so little was serving me so well?

The big blond guy mocked me with his eyes, smirk in place. He knew. I don't know how he knew, but he definitely did. Man, I hated being a foregone conclusion, especially to him. Hated it with the passion of a thousand fiery hells.

"Alright," I said. "Let's do it."

He stopped laughing.

"I'm serious. I want to make Reece jealous. If you're still willing to help me, of course."

"Said I would not a minute ago. Didn't think you'd actually go for it, but . . ." He picked up his cup of coffee and drained it. "This should be interesting. Exactly how much do you know about being a heartbreaker?"

"I need to be a heartbreaker?" Across the other side of the living room, the bathroom door stood wide open. A wet towel sat forgotten in the middle of the floor. Mal's boxer briefs lay abandoned alongside.

I needed to do some cleaning today.

"Problem?" he asked.

"No."

Funny, when Skye had lived here, I'd usually wound up doing the bulk of the tidying for her too. It hadn't occurred to me at the time. A leftover habit from running a household early, most likely.

"What is it, Anne?"

"Your towel and dirty clothes are on the bathroom floor." I pointed to them, just in case he'd forgotten where the bathroom was.

"Random change of topic." Mal sidled up next to me, standing closer than he needed to. "But you're right. They are indeed decorating the floor and doing a lovely job too."

He said no more.

The dirty laundry lay there, taunting me. And I'm pretty sure that Mal in his silence did the same. Either that or I was a neurotic mess. It was a close call.

"Whatcha gonna do about it, pumpkin?" he asked in a quiet voice.

"I really don't like you calling me that."

He made a dismissive noise in his throat.

I sighed. This was one war I'd likely never win. If taking over the care of a thirteen-year-old had taught me anything, it was to pick my battles.

"That's not my problem," I said.

"No?"

"You need to tidy up after yourself," I said firmly.

"That a boundary I'm hearing there?"

I stood taller. "Yes, it is. I'm not your mommy. You need to pick up your shit, Mal."

He grinned. "I'll get right on that."

"Thanks." I smiled back at him, feeling lighter already. "What was that about being a heartbreaker?"

"You're going to smash me in two, after showing the jerkwad what a momentous girlfriend you make, of course."

I'd only ever been on the receiving end of heartbreak. But fuck that too. Bad habits could be broken. "I can do that."

Mal looked away.

"I can."

"Not doubting you, pumpkin. Not doubting you at all."

CHAPTER EIGHT

Lauren barged in a bit before six in the evening. Or she tried to. The door rattled. Next came the swearing and banging.

"Anne! What's wrong with your door?"

I undid the new sliding bolt and she thundered into the room.

"Your door's broken," she said, her brow creased.

"No, Mal had a new lock put on it. He was worried about security."

A bald, muscular man had appeared after Mal disappeared off to band practice. Apparently, rock stars outsourced household chores to the head of their security team. This guy had the new sliding bolt installed in no time. He was eerily efficient and uber-polite. The whole experience had weirded me out a little.

"Hey, wow. You look great." I said, taking in her slick dress and hairdo. A beautiful white orchid sat behind her ear. "What are you all dressed up for? Where are you off to?"

"What, this old thing?" She smoothed a hand over the slinky caramel-colored silk dress. "Thanks. And can I just take a moment to say, awesome job landing Malcolm Ericson. He probably doesn't deserve you, but go you."

"Uh, thanks."

"When he told me the story, I couldn't believe it. Love at

first sight. That's beautiful." Shit, her eyes actually misted up. "I think you'll be wonderful together. And why aren't you dressed, by the way?"

"Huh?"

Right then, Mal strode out of the second bedroom in a black three-piece suit. Since when had wearing a vest looked so fucking hot? My lungs shrunk a size. Either that or the oxygen in the room had been mixed wrong. He was beyond slick with his hair tucked back behind his ears, the angular line of his jaw perfectly smooth. I'd barely gotten used to him half naked and now he was throwing Armani at me. I never stood a chance. Prostrating myself at his feet was the obvious reaction to such a heavenly sight. How I managed to remain upright I have no idea.

Forget Bond and his ilk. I'd take a drummer in a suit any day of the week.

With a low wolf whistle, Lauren looked him over. "Malcolm. Who's a pretty boy?"

"Only pumpkin is allowed to objectify me," he said, straightening his cuffs. French cuffs with cufflinks.

"Fuck me," I muttered, then smacked a hand over my mouth because crap, my mouth. It was an idiot determined to make an ass out of me.

"Anytime." He winked. The liar.

"Your pumpkin needs to get ready," said Lauren, ignoring our carrying on.

He looked me over and frowned. "Anne, Davie wants everyone dressed up. You can't go in jeans and a T-shirt."

"What are you talking about?"

"The party. Pumpkin, c'mon. We don't have time to mess around."

I shook my head, clueless. "Okay, you two. I have no idea what you're talking about. Will someone please clue me in?"

"I told you about this."

"Like you told me about you moving in here?"

"You didn't tell her you were moving in with her?" asked Lauren, voice low and deadly.

"It was a surprise," he said, recovering quickly. "A great big beautiful romantic gesture because I knew how much my Anne wanted me with her. She was just too shy to say so. Look at her! The woman practically worships the ground I walk on. And you heard her, demanding I sexually service her at all hours of the day. I can't do that shit from afar, you know?"

Lauren raised a brow. "You told me she okayed it and had forgotten to give you a key, Mal."

"Which was basically the truth." He threw his hands out wide. "C'mon, ladies, we don't have time for this."

"Anne, I'm so sorry," said Lauren.

"It's fine. I'm happy he's here." And though a tempting idea, throwing something at him right now wouldn't actually help. I took a deep breath and tried to keep calm. "Let's get back to the 'What the hell is going on here' question. We're meant to go to something formal tonight, I take it?"

"I told you." He pulled out his phone, flicked through a few screens then shoved it in front of my face. "I'm a fucking great boyfriend, see?"

The message on screen read: *AMEX ON TABLE. DRESS UP TONIGHT.* My name, however, was nowhere in sight. Sure enough, over on the dining room table a black credit card sat waiting. I'd figured he'd just forgotten the thing. Him leaving it for me to go on a spending spree had never crossed my mind.

"It says you sent this to someone called Angie," I said tightly. "Not me, Mal."

"I did?" He glared at the phone. "Shit. Sorry."

"Who's Angie?" asked Lauren.

"Fucked if I know, but apparently she's still looking for the card." He laughed. "As if I'd give it to just anyone. Right, sorry. Anyway, Anne, can you throw something on? We gotta go."

"Where?"

"Out."

I scowled at him and didn't move an inch. "Try again."

"It's a thing at David and Ev's, a wedding anniversary party. Not that it's even been a year, but whatever. Davie put lots of effort into it and asked us all to dress up. I'm sorry I screwed up telling you." He fell to his knees, hands clasped to his chest. "Please? I'm sorry. I'm really fucking sorry. See, look, I'm on my knees, Anne. I'm groveling just for you."

"Okay. I'll go. Next time, please make sure I get the message."

"I will. Thank you. Thank you so much," he gushed. "You're the best, pumpkin."

There was only one really good dress in my wardrobe. A vintage black lace dress from the fifties. I'd bought it for my twenty-first birthday two years ago. I liked to believe I'd just stepped off the set of *Mad Men* in it. Luckily, my hair wasn't looking too bad hanging loose. Some concealer, mascara, and lip gloss were about as primed as I could get in less than five minutes. One of these days I'd have time to go all out getting ready to meet the members of Stage Dive. Just not today.

Out in the living room, the pair of them bickered.

"I can't believe you accidentally messaged some stray instead of your girlfriend," said Lauren.

"Does my girlfriend seem bothered? No. So remind me again, what business is it of yours, hmm?"

"If you hurt her, Ev and I are going to take turns disemboweling you with a shovel. Be warned."

A gruesome mental image, but I had to smile. It felt good to have friends watching my back.

Mal scoffed. "You can't disembowel someone with a shovel."

"Sure you can. It's just messier."

He grunted.

"Anyway, why are you in the spare bedroom? She sick of you already?"

"Gotta put my shit somewhere, Anne's closet is packed. You girls, no idea about sharing."

I shut the bedroom door and started shrugging out of my jeans, pulling off my shirt. Next came the panties. The neckline on the dress was wide and strapless bras always dug into my sides. There were few torture devices more horrible than a strapless bra. It wasn't like my breasts were big. The girl in the mirror looked good and happily, the dress still fit just fine. No way could I do up the zipper on the back however. I slid my feet into my super-high black heels saved for special occasions and headed on out, trying to hold my dress together.

"Lauren, would you mind—"

"That's my job now." Mal smiled and stepped behind me. "Cool dress. Classy."

"Thanks."

Mal leaned in closer, his breath warming my neck as he slowly did up the back. I immediately broke out into goose bumps.

"I never noticed how long your neck is. It's very nice."

"Mm."

"And you have sweet little ears."

"Um, thanks."

"No bra?" he asked, his voice casual.

"No. With this dress, I can't . . . We don't actually need to discuss this right now."

The tips of his fingers trailed up my spine, ahead of the zipper. I got shivery, the English language leaving my mind.

"That's going to be a hell of a distraction, pumpkin," he

breathed. "Trying to look down the front of your dress all night."

The look he gave me made me quiver in strange places. This was the problem; my inability to tell if he was serious or not. The whole scene was about establishing ourselves as a couple for Lauren's benefit, right? It just didn't feel like it for some reason. It felt personal. With Mal touching me, I kind of forgot Lauren was even in the room. She was, however, most definitely present.

Lauren groaned, loudly. "Oh good god, my ears are bleeding."

He made me feverish without even trying. I needed to guard my reactions and keep it together. It was the only way this would work.

"Thank you," I said, as my dress finished tightening around my chest and settled into place.

"My pleasure."

I expected him to move back. He didn't. If anything, he got closer. The warm male scent of him, the iron-hard feel, all of it got closer and closer. I tried to bend away from him in an effort to preserve what remained of my sanity, but he just followed. Overwhelming didn't cover it.

"Guys." Lauren was tapping her foot. "Whatever you're doing, stop it."

"Ignore her. She's just jealous of our love." Mal's arm came around my middle, holding me to him. The press of his hardening cock against my rear could not be mistaken. I know we were supposed to be playing the couple, but was rubbing his penis against me really necessary? Me liking it was beside the point. Don't even go there.

"Yes, Malcolm, I'm jealous of your love. That's it." Lauren shook her head slowly. "Come on, let's get moving. Nate will be waiting and he doesn't wait well."

"We better go," I said.

"Yeah." His voice was soft and dreamy, and spoke of good, hard times in bed. Then he shook his head, gave me his usual grin. "Pumpkin, stop rubbing your ass against me. We gotta go! I don't have time to do you now. Prioritize, woman."

Sometimes the temptation to hit him was so huge.

Twice the crowd had gathered at David and Ev's condo tonight. They varied in age from young teens to elderly, from conservative to edgy. All of them primped to perfection. Every inch of David and Ev's condo had been decorated, also. White candles of every size sat in clusters around the room. Vases filled with bright bouquets were on every available flat surface. The ring of fine crystal and the popping of champagne corks battled classic rock for supremacy. Tonight's vibe leaned heavily toward the romantic.

There was a buzz in the air, one of expectation. It was exciting.

Mal kept a tight hold on my hand, his big, warm fingers encasing mine. I took my cues from him, staying close to his side. Whenever some sexy siren tried to approach him he basically shoved me at them with a "Meet my girlfriend, Anne." I'd almost tripped the first few times he'd used me as a human shield, but I was getting the hang of it now. With the last one I'd just held up a hand and said "He's with me." She'd taken it with relatively good grace.

"I thought that one was going to hit me," I said, watching the disappointed girl stalk off into the crowd. "Being your girlfriend is dangerous."

"What can I say? I'm a magnificent specimen of manhood. Of course they all want me. But I do appreciate you protecting my honor."

"I should hope so." I smiled.

"Come and meet Jimmy. This'll give you a thrill." He wound his way through the crowd, drawing me along behind him. " 'Scuse us. Move please. Move."

Jimmy Ferris stood beside the mantle like a painter had positioned him there. The man was living art. Dark hair brushed back, blue eyes bright. He was a lot like his brother, David, long and lean, but smoother and harder. More intense if it was possible. Maybe meeting Ev had chilled David out. Jimmy certainly lacked the lost-in-love eyes.

The dark looks he gave the woman at his side were far less than friendly. She kept her nose high in the air and ignored him. I'm not sure I could have maintained her pose of complete indifference so well. Jimmy Ferris had a lot of presence. There'd been all sorts of rumors going around about what he'd been up to since rehab. Given the size of him, I'd say lifting weights featured heavily. Ben was a big guy in general, heading on into lumberjack territory. But Jimmy appeared to have been working at it, hard.

"Jimbo," said Mal, making room for me beside him. "This is my girlfriend, Anne. Anne, this is Jim."

Yep, Jimmy gave me the same chin tip as the others. It was a secret handshake. So I gave him one back. He smiled, but only just. It was a fleeting thing.

Mal leaned down in front of me, getting in my face. "Nope. No crazy eyes. Your theory is bullshit, pumpkin. They're only for me."

"It's lovely to meet you, Jimmy," I said, pushing my pretend partner out of the way.

"She still doing the eyes thing?" asked Jimmy.

Rock stars gossiped. There you go.

"Lust has no expiration date, Jimbo. And hello, Lena. You

look very nice." Mal offered his free hand to the woman at Jimmy's side. The arctic chill of her manner turned equatorial in an instant. How strange.

"Mal. How are you?" The woman gave his fingers a brief squeeze, before offering her hand to me to shake. Brown hair fell past her shoulders and funky red plastic-rimmed glasses sat on her nose. "And this must be Anne. Great to meet you. Mal's told me so much about you."

"He has?" I shook her hand, returning her smile.

"At band practice today, you were all he could talk about," she said.

"She's the love of my life," sighed Mal, throwing an arm around my shoulders.

"See? You're the love of his life." Lena gave me a charmed smile. Apparently it was only Jimmy she detested.

"This week," said Jimmy.

With a small sigh, Lena half turned her head toward him. That was all it took.

Jimmy gave me a strained smile. "Sorry. That was a shitty thing to say."

"Pumpkin, Lena is what we in the industry call 'a babysitter'," said Mal. "If you're an unmitigated fucking asshole who doesn't know how to behave, you get a gorgeous girl like Lena to follow you around, making sure you're not a PR disaster for the record company."

"I said I was sorry." Jimmy stared out across the room, doing the same crinkly forehead thing his brother did. It kind of reminded me of James Dean.

"Hey." Ben appeared on my free side, staring down at me from his lofty height. There was more chin tipping. All of the band members wore matching black suits, but Jimmy had lost the vest and added a thin black tie. Ben wore the tie but had ditched the vest and jacket and the sleeves of his white shirt were rolled up his strong arms. Both limbs were liberally inked. Tattoos and suits made for a damn good combination.

The quality of the eye candy tonight was off the scale. Mal still had them all beat, of course.

"Pumpkin, guess what?"

"What?"

Before I knew what was happening I'd been dipped back over his arm. The entire room had turned upside down. Fuck, was the front of my dress gaping? I slapped my hand down over my collarbone, just in case.

"Shit, Mal! Up."

He immediately righted me. Blood rushed about inside my head and the room spun. Beside us, Ben and Lena laughed. I think Jimmy was busy doing his bored-stare thing. It was hard to see with my head still spinning. I'm pretty sure people were watching. If I heard an upside-down girl shouting obscenities, I'd probably take a look.

"No one saw anything," Mal said, reading my mind. "You okay?"

I nodded. "Fine."

His thumbs rubbed circles into my hip bones through the fabric of my dress. He held his face close to mine. "Sorry, pumpkin. I didn't think."

"It's okay."

He squinted down at me. "Is it really okay or are you just saying it's okay and you're going to bust my balls about it later?"

I thought about it for a moment to be sure. "No. But don't do it again or I'll hurt you."

"Got it. No more throwing you around."

"Thank you."

"I won't embarrass you again, Anne. Promise."

"I'd appreciate that."

"See," he said, his smile huge. "Our communication skills as a couple are fucking excellent. We're working out great!"

"Yeah, we are," I said, my heart elated. It was strange, we'd only known each other a few days but I trusted him. I liked him and I was really grateful to spend this time with him. After the disaster with Skye, I needed Malcolm Ericson in my life right now. Hell, after the last seven years I needed him. He brought out the sun.

"Yeah," he whispered.

And then he kissed me and ruined everything.

CHAPTER NINE

It wasn't a soft kiss. No passing brush of the lips or token peck of affection would do for Mal. Hell no, of course not. It was an amnesia-inducing drug of a kiss. No memory of another remained. Chemical bliss. I'd obviously never been really and truly kissed before because this . . . he covered my mouth with his and owned me. His tongue slipped over my teeth and his hands slid into my hair. In response, I grabbed two fistfuls of his vest. It might have started out being in surprise or anger. But it turned into a safety measure fast. My knees went weak.

The man kissed me stupid.

His tongue rubbed at mine, encouraging me to play. It might not have been the smart thing to do, but I couldn't hold back. I moaned into his mouth and kissed him hard. Every bit as hard as he was kissing me. My thighs tensed and my toes curled. Every hair on my body stood on end. His hold on me tightened, as if he couldn't let go. I, on the other hand, was basically clawing my way through his three-piece suit. The need to get closer was huge. Nothing else mattered.

All around us applause broke out, which was fair enough. A kiss this awesome deserved a standing ovation. Fireworks wouldn't be overkill. The string quartet seemed a little odd, however. Surely a crazed drum solo would be more in keeping, something primal to match the demented beat of my heart.

"Guys," Ben hissed, nudging us with an elbow. "Knock it off. Guys!"

I tore away from Mal, trying desperately to catch my breath. He was panting too, his green eyes dilated. Stunned was probably a good word. Sordid wasn't too far behind. After all, we were mauling each other's mouths in public.

I stood there staring at him, shaking. Holy shit. What the hell had just happened?

"That was fun!" He grinned, looking at me like he'd just discovered a new game. One that he really, really liked.

No.

Fuck no.

My heart was trying to burst out of my chest, *Aliens* style. I couldn't blame it for wanting to run for cover. This was insane. I had to keep this shit locked down. What if he'd been able to tell what it did to me? He'd call off our arrangement in a heartbeat.

Time for some damage control.

"It was nice." I gave him a pat on the cheek.

His arrogant grin slipped.

People all around us continued clapping. They were also all facing the other way, though many gave us sideways glances. I turned and went up on tippy toes, to see what was going on. In the open front doorway stood Ev in a simple ivory gown. I saw the whites of her big surprised eyes from across the room. Beside her stood David in a suit similar to what the rest of the guys wore. Slowly, he got down on one knee. I was too far away to hear what he said, the room too noisy. But then Ev was nodding and crying and mouthing the word "yes."

"Davie wanted to do a surprise second ceremony," Mal said, joining in with the clapping. "She doesn't remember last time—it was a quickie drunken Vegas wedding—so he's doing it over for her."

"Th-that's sweet." I licked my lips, ignoring the lingering taste of him. So good.

His arm slipped around my waist and it was all I could do to keep still, to not try and move away. Some breathing room would be great. Just until I got my body back under control.

"I think everyone saw us, yeah?" he said.

"Mm." Without a doubt, we'd established ourselves as a couple. We'd probably managed to momentarily upstage the bride and groom. Excellent. They'd be inviting us back here for sure.

A man dressed in a bling-covered Elvis jumpsuit burst out of the hallway, sporting a big black wig and all. He began to sing "Love Me Tender" as played by the string quartet. Everyone laughed and smiled. Ev started laughing and crying. They repeated their vows and even my eyes misted up after I got myself back under control. It was so wildly romantic. Jimmy moved quietly through the crowd and slipped his brother a ring. The gentle smile on his face surprised me just a little.

Ever so damn slowly my heart rate returned to something nearing normal. I glanced over my shoulder at Mal. At first I couldn't work out what he was looking at. His attention was fixed on an older couple on the other side of the room, Ev or David's parents, perhaps? He looked unhappy. The distance was back in his eyes, the line between his brows. Then he caught me watching. He frowned and returned his gaze to the front.

"Can you believe Davie got her another ring?" Mal whispered in my ear. "He is so fucking wrapped around her finger. It's ridiculous."

"They're in love. I think it's sweet."

"At the rate he's giving her diamonds, she's going to have a tiara by Christmas."

It was one thing for me to be caustic within the sanctity of my own skull. But I hated hearing Mal be so against the idea of love or coupledom or whatever it was that had set him off.

"What?" he asked, seeing my down face.

"I can't decide if you sound jealous, bitter, or what."

"I was making a joke," he said, eyes wounded. "Tiaras are funny. Everyone knows that."

"Right."

Mal just blinked. His mouth, those gorgeous wicked lips of his, did not move.

Another round of applause thundered through the room as the remarkably swift service wound up. Though they were already married, no point dragging it out. Or maybe it only seemed fast to me. They kissed and flashbulbs lit the room. People crowded in to congratulate them.

Happy, happy times. What a joyous occasion.

"Back in a minute," I said, squeezing out of Mal's embrace. I needed air, space, shit like that. I needed to get my head on straight. My overreaction to his kiss had unnerved me big-time. Things were cooler and calmer out on the balcony. I knew having Mal cozy up to me at events would be weird. I'd expected feelings, sensations. Nerves, awkwardness, even mild titillation I could understand, but blow my mind, swamp me with lust, and make the world disappear? Not so much. He'd been right, there was every chance Fatal Attraction loomed large around the corner.

"What's wrong?" he asked, coming up behind me.

"Nothing. Everything's fine."

"Bullshit."

"If I say its fine, its fine," I gritted out.

"You're acting weird." He walked toward me, hypnotic eyes messing with my mind. "That was an awesome kiss," he said.

"It was okay," I lied, giving him a serene smile.

"It was okay?" One of his brows arched skyward. "That's it?"

I shrugged.

"Anne, you nearly tore off my clothing. I think it was better than okay."

"Oh, sorry. Was that overkill? I figured with the way you were going at me we were aiming for over the top."

He stopped. "Going at you?"

"Well, it was pretty full on."

"Was it, now?"

Another shrug. "You have to admit, there was a lot of tongue."

He stepped closer, getting into my personal space. My heels needed to be taller. This wasn't the sort of situation where I wanted to be looked down upon. I clenched and unclenched my fingers behind my back, flustered as fuck but trying not to let it show. This was not me. I didn't allow my life to get messed up by men. Been there, done that, had bought the T-shirt and worn it until it had ratty little holes in it.

"I warned you there'd be tongue when we were making our agreement," he said.

God help me, had there been tongue. Lots and lots of it. I could still feel his, sliding against my own, turning me on. Phantom tongue. There was every possibility Malcolm Ericson was driving me insane. He needed to be stopped. But the best I could do right then was to steer this conversation the hell away from all things oral, stat.

"Yeah, about our agreement . . . why did you say you needed a fake girlfriend?"

"We already talked about that."

"You didn't tell me anything."

"Told you as much as I'm going to." He paused, glowering down at me. "Why are you trying to turn this back onto me? What's wrong, Anne, not feeling defensive over one little kiss, are you?"

"No. Of course not." I crossed my arms. "But we agreed to keep sex out of this. Generally, people not having sex don't need to talk about tongues."

"I disagree."

"You really want to keep talking about this? Really?"

"You have no idea how much, pumpkin."

"Great. Let's discuss it." Maybe I should just throw myself over the balcony. It couldn't be that far down. The laws of physics aside, I might bounce. You never know. "You said you'd put your tongue in my ear, Malcolm, not halfway down my throat."

"I didn't put it halfway down your throat." His eyes narrowed. "I've never had any complaints about the way I kiss before."

I said nothing.

"This is bullshit. You liked it. I know you did."

"It was nice enough."

"Nice enough?" he asked, tendons tightening in his neck like he intended to Hulk out on me. "Did you just call my kiss 'nice enough'?"

"We're just pretending, Mal. Remember? Why don't you calm down?" I stepped back, giving him a calm smile.

He stepped forward, his green eyes blazing bright. "That kiss was not just fucking 'nice enough.'"

"Don't you think you're overreacting just a little?" I tried to laugh it off.

He was not appeased. "No."

"I guess we just don't click that way. Which I think is pretty lucky given the situation, right? It keeps things uncomplicated, just the way you wanted them, right?"

"Wrong."

"Careful there. I think your ego's showing. Not every girl needs to fall at your feet."

"You do."

"Ha. No, Mal, I don't."

"Do."

"Don't."

"Do."

"Stop it." I glared at him. Good god, rock stars were so childish. Spoiled brats.

The silence between us was deafening, the depths of space couldn't compete. We had the bubble thing going on again. Inside the condo didn't exist, there was no party, no music, light, and chatter. But I could control this situation. No way would my head be getting messed up by some rock star who'd be gone in no time.

"I want a do-over. Now," he demanded.

"No way." I put a hand to his chest, trying to hold him back. It didn't help. His heart beat hard against the palm of my hand even through the layers of clothing.

He loomed ever more threateningly closer, licking his gorgeous lips. "Right now, Anne. You and me."

"I don't think so."

"I can do better." And closer.

"You don't have to prove anything to me, Mal."

"You'll like it this time, promise."

If I liked his kiss any more I'd have heart failure. "Truly not necessary."

"Just once more," he said, his voice intoxicatingly low and

smooth, lulling me into compliance. Damn him. "No big deal. Just give me one more chance."

His mouth hovered above mine, the anticipation tying me in knots. Damn it, I wasn't going to stop him. Not even a little. I was the worst.

"Trouble in paradise?" Jimmy Ferris stepped out onto the balcony, his trademark sneery smile in place. I could have kissed him for his timely intervention. Except kissing was what had gotten me into this mess.

"Hiding from Lena?" asked Mal calmly.

Jimmy flicked his dark hair back. His gaze slid to me before moving onto the city lights below. There was a non-answer if I'd ever seen one.

"Yeah, that's what I thought." Mal snorted. All of his intensity had evaporated into thin air, thank god. "We're all good thanks, bro. Just picking out names for our future children. Anne wants Malcolm Junior for a boy but I said no, absolutely not. Kid should at least have a chance at a life out from underneath the shadow of his old man."

"That's real big of you," said Jimmy.

"I know, right? Being a parent is all about the sacrifices."

Mal slid his hand behind my neck, rubbing at the tight muscles. "Relax," he ordered. "It isn't good for the baby."

"I am not pregnant."

"Ah, shit, that's right. We were s'posed to be keeping it quiet. Sorry, pumpkin." He smacked himself in the forehead. I would've been happy to do it for him.

"Don't worry," said Jimmy. "We've been friends since we were kids. I know when he's talking shit."

I wish I did.

"Who's pregnant?" asked David Ferris, wandering out onto

the balcony with his wife in one hand and a beer in the other. Ben sauntered out after them.

With a look of great pride, Mal rubbed my belly. Any roundness was far more likely due to a weakness for cake than any acts of procreation.

"I'm not—"

"We were keeping it on the down low," said Mal. "We didn't want to upstage you two lovebirds."

"Fast work," said David with a hint of a smile.

"My boys can swim." Mal winked.

"I don't think you can actually tell that soon, dickhead." Jimmy crossed his arms, leaning against the wall of windows. "Science and stuff, right?"

"A real man *knows* when his woman is knocked up, Jimbo. I don't expect you to understand."

"A real man, huh?" Jimmy pushed off the window, walking slowly toward Mal. His smile would've given a shark second thoughts. Hell, they were both smiling. What was it about males that they felt this primal need to beat the shit out of each other for the fun of it? Why?

"Guys," said Ev. "No punching at my do-over wedding, playful or otherwise."

"What about bitch-slapping?" asked Mal, swinging his arm in Jimmy's direction.

"Let's not." I grabbed his hand and dragged it down by my side before he could do anyone any damage. "And Jimmy is right. Forty-eight hours is a bit too soon to tell. Not that we're trying," I hastened to add.

Mal's brows drew in as he gave me a wounded look. "I can't believe you'd side with him against me. That really hurts, Anne. You, of all people, should know my sperm is of superior quality."

"You wouldn't believe how long I could go never hearing you talk about your spunk, man." Ben shook his head.

"Don't be down, dude. It's only natural my alpha sperm would make you feel pitifully inadequate."

With a long groan, Jimmy covered his face. "You should have just let me hit him. If anyone ever needed some fucking sense knocked into them . . ."

"I'll hold him down," Ben offered.

"Knock it off," said David.

Mal opened his lips, eyes alight with glee. So I slapped my hand over his mouth, quick smart.

"Mal, why don't we discuss your sperm later?" I suggested. He kissed my palm and slowly I lowered my hand. "Thank you. And we are not having a baby."

"Okay, Anne. Whatever you say, Anne."

Ben laughed. "What, you pussy whipped now?"

Without comment, David reached out and smacked the bigger man over the back of the head.

"Hey!"

"Thanks, Davie." Mal drew me back into his arms.

"That was for Anne," said David. "Enough embarrassing shit while the girls are around. Act your fucking age, guys."

"A shovel, Malcolm. A rusty old shovel. That's your fate if you upset my friend. Keep it in mind." Ev stepped forward to give me a kiss on the cheek. "I wish you all the luck in the world with him. You're a brave woman."

"Yes, I'm beginning to think so."

"I like the way he looks at you," she said quietly. "That's new."

"Your second wedding was beautiful." I gave her my biggest, brightest smile, sidestepping the subject of my new fake boyfriend entirely.

Ev threw an arm around her husband's neck, smacking a kiss on his cheek. "Yes it was. It was amazing."

"Love you, baby." David kissed her back.

"Love you too."

He whispered something in her ear. Something that made her giggle. "We can't—my parents are here. Later."

David's mouth turned downward.

"Does this mean you're coming on tour, Anne?" asked Ev. "Please say yes."

"Absolutely!" Mal hugged me to him, squeezing me tight enough to make me wheeze. My feet even briefly left the ground.

"I don't know about that. I haven't had a chance to ask for any time off yet." I wiggled around until Mal gave me breathing room. He didn't allow me much beyond it, however. No biggie, I could ignore him and the crazy feelings he inspired, both. It would've been cool to experience life on the road, but I wasn't actually invited. Plus work, Lizzy, real life, and all that. "When does the tour start, by the way?"

"First show's in Portland in five days' time."

"Five days?" I hadn't been able to afford tickets when they went on sale a few months back. And of course they'd sold out in a matter of minutes. Denied attendance, I'd deliberately ignored what the bulk of the city was buzzing about. Call it petty jealousy, if you will.

My time with Mal was so short. My stomach dropped and my heart ached. The knowledge hurt. No matter how scarily stupid his kisses made me, I didn't want him to go. He made life better, brighter. How idiotic of me to have gotten attached. I hadn't meant to, but the evidence was clear.

"Don't look so sad, pumpkin." He gently cupped my chin, eyes serious. "We'll work something out."

"Guys, they're ready to do photos." Lauren stood in the door-way, a full champagne flute in hand. After some grumbling, Jimmy headed inside. Ev and David, arm in arm, followed behind him.

"Great acting," whispered Mal, laying a soft kiss upon my neck. "I honestly thought you were about to burst into tears."

Funny, I'd thought I might too. I huffed out a laugh and gave him my best fake smile. "I played one of the wicked witches in my middle school's production of *The Wizard of Oz*."

"That explains it."

"It was basically just lying down dead at the start, pretend-ing to be squished while wearing cool red shoes."

"Bet you were the best squished girl ever."

"Thanks. And pregnant? Really?"

He rolled his eyes and pressed a kiss to my cheek. "I'm sorry, I'm sorry. Just got carried away. Do you forgive me?"

I held out for all of two seconds. "Yes."

"Thank you. That's very kind of you. I really didn't mean to stress you out in your delicate condition."

I growled.

He laughed.

"Coming?" asked David, looking back over his shoulder.

"I'll just wait out here," I said, stepping back from Mal while I still could. Immediately the cold evening air rushed in, chilling me.

David shook his head. "No, Anne. You too. If you're with him, you're family. Let's get it done with so we can kick back and relax."

"You heard the groom." Mal grabbed my hand, drawing me in again. "Just one thing first."

"What?"

With the gleam in his eye, I should've known. His lips de-scended, pressing against mine. His arms wound around me, hauling me up against him. My gasp of surprise was just the entry into my mouth he needed. Turned out he knew how to evil laugh and kiss me senseless at the same time. I shouldn't have been surprised about that either. Despite that, the kiss was soul-shatteringly gentle. He kissed me sugar sweet until my head spun and my heart pounded. My knees knocked and my girl parts cried mercy.

And still he kissed me.

"How was that?" he asked eventually, staring into my undoubtedly dazed eyes. "Better?"

"Um, sure?"

He breathed out through his nose, his brows drawn tight. "Shit, I'm still not getting it right. I'm going to figure this kissing thing out. I am. We just gotta keep trying. Never say die!"

I was done for.

CHAPTER TEN

I studied my reflection in the hallway mirror as the party continued out in the living room. One side of my bottom lip was slightly bigger than the other. Honestly, it was. I looked ridiculous. The drummer was nuts. He'd always been riding the edge of needing immediate admission to a nice, soft, padded white room. And for a while, it had even been kind of charming in an offbeat fashion. But now he'd officially lost all semblance of control.

Did I like biting? No. No I did not. Same went for nibbling and most especially hickeys. The mark on my neck did not impress and I'm pretty certain there was a bruise just above my ass from him grinding me into the kitchen counter.

Needless to say, his rough lovin' experiment hadn't been a success.

"God damn maniac."

"Sorry?" asked the woman waiting beside me for the main bathroom.

"Nothing. Just cursing out loud." I gave her a bland, social smile. "Don't mind me."

She nodded and reapplied her lip gloss with the precision of an artist before proceeding to positioning her breasts. What were the chances of me having an early-twenties growth spurt and developing breasts like those? I wished.

"You're with Malcolm Ericson, right?" she asked.

"Right." I wouldn't say that I preened exactly, but I did run my fingers through my hair.

The smile she gave me seemed less than sincere despite being blindingly bright. "I think that's really brave of you."

"How so?"

"Dating out of your weight range like that." Her eyes met mine in the bathroom mirror. They were a dark, evil, pretty hazel kind of color. "I mean, you're clearly not at his level. But why not enjoy him while you can, right?"

I checked in the mirror. But amazingly enough, there was no steam coming out of my ears. My mouth opened, but it took a moment for me to find the words. "Did you really just say that?"

"What?" She did a nervous giggle, hair-flicking thing.

"I'm a complete stranger to you."

"Hey, I think it's great. Go sister and all that."

What petty jealousy bullshit. No way was I giving this bitch the power to make me feel little. "I'm not your sister. I have a sister and she would never say something like that to me."

The woman's perfectly glossy lips popped open.

"Seriously, honey," I said. "Your manners are appalling. Go fuck yourself."

The bathroom door opened and I took my turn, closing the door with a little more zest than needed. My shoulders were up around my ears when I strode back out to the party, the slight throbbing in my lip almost forgotten. I did not look back at the bitch.

People. God damn it.

Hard rock music thumped through me, keeping my agitation fresh. I wanted to hit something. Not someone, but something.

Just give an innocent wall a smack with my hand to let out some of the pressure building inside me. I slowed down my breathing, tried to quiet my ranting mind.

Everything was fine.

Mal, Jimmy, and Ben stood to the side, sipping their drinks, ignoring the hopeful glances of the girls nearby. Crap, was this what it was like for them all the time? It had to get old. A few paces away, Lena chatted to a woman her own age. Her gaze kept sliding back to Jimmy in a way that didn't exactly express professional interest. Imagine that.

Out of the confined space, I could breathe again. It was all good.

"What's up?" Mal asked when I got closer.

Behind us, the woman strutted out of the bathroom, throwing my fake boyfriend a big fake grin. Not a hint of shame about her.

"Promise me something," I said.

"Sure."

I stopped, smiled. "You didn't even hesitate."

"You're pissed about something." He leaned down, making our conversation private despite the packed room. "What's wrong?"

"Promise me you won't sleep with her." I nodded to the beast in question. She was now busy talking to an elderly man, smiling and nodding. In all likelihood, she was Ev's cousin or something equally harmless, not the Harpy Queen of Darkness. Still didn't make her behavior right.

Also sometime soon, I should try to not insult someone every time I entered this building. A great idea.

"I won't sleep with her," said Mal.

"And you won't have sex with her either."

He rolled his eyes.

"Just to clarify."

"What'd she do to you, Anne?"

"She insulted me. But it's fine." I just needed to know she'd never get near him. Now my soul was at peace. "Carry on with your partying."

Mal's face hardened, his mouth drawing tight. "What the fuck did she say?"

"Doesn't matter. I might get another drink. I have no idea where I left mine and suddenly alcohol sounds like a really good idea. I feel I need the social lubrication." I started toward the kitchen, all well once again with my world. Justice would prevail. Mal's pants were closed to the woman.

A hand hooked my elbow, drawing me back into the bath-room. It was a nice bathroom. Dark gray stone surfaces, shiny chrome features. A great bathroom, really, but I didn't need to spend quite this much time in it.

"Mal?"

He slammed the door shut. Whoa, his eyes. There was not a single hint of happy. "What did she say to you?"

"Hey, really, it's okay." I rested my hip against the counter, setting the right example and trying to play it cool. This level of emotion had not been expected.

"Anne."

"I just needed to know she wasn't going to get what she wanted, namely you. Blame it on my little black vindictive heart," I joked.

He did not laugh.

Face still set in furious lines, he stalked toward me, backing me into the counter. The hard gray stone edge connected smack bam with the bruise on my back from earlier. It hurt.

"Ouch." I rubbed at the sore spot, wincing.

"What?"

"I think I've got a bruise from the kitchen bench. Your fault."

He harrumphed in a strangely sexy manner (it had truly never occurred to me that noise could be a turn-on). "I already said sorry about that."

He picked me up by the waist and set me on top of the counter. His able hands pushed my knees apart as far as my skirt would allow and he stepped between.

"Ah, hey there." I put my hands to his shoulders, pressing against the cool material of his suit jacket. "Ease back a bit."

"Tell me what she said."

"Why? You going to challenge her to a duel? Pistols at dawn?"

"You read too many books."

"No such thing!" I cried, aghast.

"No duel. But I'll sure as hell have her ass thrown out of here."

"Mal, seriously. I dealt with it. It's okay."

He just stared at me.

"I very politely thanked her for her opinion and told her to go fuck herself."

The tension in his face eased a little. "You told her to go fuck herself?"

"Yes, I did. I channeled my inner Scarlet O'Hara and took none of her crap."

"Good. Liking that boundary. And you're okay now?" He set his hands on the counter either side of my hips, meaning we were damn close. Much closer with some clothes missing and we'd almost be together in the biblical sense.

"I'm all good. Though my bottom lip sort of hurts. No more biting."

He huffed out a laugh. "Yeah, yeah. I figured that when you pulled half my hair out to get me off of you. You know you can be kind of vicious, pumpkin. I like that."

I smiled and he smiled and everything was fine and dandy.

"You're definitely not going to sleep with her though," I said, just to be sure. I really didn't like the woman. "Seriously."

"My dick doesn't go near anyone that's rude to my friends. That's not cool."

"Your dick has good taste, then."

His eyes went kind of hazy.

"Mal?"

"Hmm? Sorry. I like the way you say 'dick' and 'taste' in the same sentence."

"Right." So not going there. I squirmed ever so discreetly on the countertop. "Thank you for worrying about me. But we should go back out and join the party. People probably want to use the bathroom."

"There's four more." Soft as a feather, he brushed his lips across mine. Every nerve in my body kick-started at the contact.

"I'll make you feel better, Anne."

"Ah, yeah. I already said I was feeling fine. And you remember that line in the sand you drew about us not getting involved in a sexual manner and stuff? You're messing with it big-time tonight."

"It's not a problem."

"It kind of is. I don't want to be your joke, Mal."

"My joke? What the hell are you talking about?" His hands slid around to my butt and suddenly I was pulled in against him. All of him. And by the feel, there was a lot of him in a good and hard mood.

I squeaked and wrapped my legs around his hips. Honest to

god, I didn't mean to. It was an accident. When he pressed his cock against me it made thinking impossible. My hormones were seizing control. All of this talk of babies had obviously given them ideas. Still, I made a token effort to resist. "Okay, big guy. That's enough."

Gently, he kissed my bottom lip. "Still hurting?"

"Totally cured." Oh I hurt, I ached. A bit more of the pressure from his pelvis, making my mind reel, would do the job, however. I rocked against him, unable to stop myself. My eyelids slid half closed. Damn, he felt good.

"You're not my joke, Anne. You're my friend. One I am very fucking into for lots of reasons."

I couldn't help but smile. "You're my friend too."

"But you know, it's okay for us to relax and have some fun." He demonstrated this point by kneading my ass. "You don't have to be so wound up all the time. I'm not going to let anything bad happen."

Malcolm Ericson might have been a lot of things, but omnipotent wasn't one of them. Bad things happened. It was a fact of life.

"What are you thinking about?" he asked, grinding himself against me once more, derailing my sadness.

"Nothing." Sex. Stress. A bit of both, really.

"I really like your dress."

"Thanks. The suit's nice; you look incredible."

"I been thinking about this kissing problem we got."

"There's no kissing problem. Everyone believes we're together so . . . job well done Team Mal and Anne." I raised a fist high. "Yay."

He chuckled softly. "See? You can be funny."

I gave him what had to be a dazed smile. Man, he was beautiful, especially up close like this. He angled his head and nudged my cheek with his nose, kissing the corner of my mouth. Fingers toyed with the zipper on the back of my dress. Not moving it, just casually threatening me with its imminent descent. Good god, did I enjoy being threatened in this way by him. My nipples hardened, more than ready to be on display. They so had no sense.

"Been thinking," he said. "Maybe you need to be kissed in other places."

The man was a fucking genius.

Ever so slowly, he tugged the zipper down an inch or two. His smile dared me to stop him. Pity I'd lost all power over my limbs. The zipper went lower, loosening the bodice of my dress, making the front gape. Mal slipped a finger in the neckline, drawing the black lace out a ways.

"You not going to stop me?" he asked in a soft voice.

"Any minute now." Not a chance.

Then he looked down. Hopefully, he appreciated breasts of all types. If he was a size-based guy, this would not end well.

"Anne. Fuck." He swallowed hard. A very good sign. Softly, his fingers traced over the hollow at the base of my throat.

"Yes?"

"You are so damn—"

Somebody hammered on the door, knocking me out of my lust fog.

"Mal, it's time," a voice hollered.

No. NO!

"Wha—?" Mal turned, scowling, while I got busy frantically holding my dress in place.

The door opened and Ben stuck his head in.

"Fuck's sake, man," said Mal, voice tight and furious. "Anne could've been naked."

Ben scoffed. "You never cared who saw what before. And if it's an issue, there's a lock on the door, dickhead."

"Rules have changed."

"Shit, man," said Ben, flashing his teeth in a big smile. "You're actually serious."

"Of course I'm fucking serious. This is my fucking girlfriend, you moron."

Ben's gaze flitted over my body. "Yeah well, your *fucking* girlfriend's pretty cute. You know what? I think I like her."

Every part of Mal tensed. There was fire in his eyes. "You—"

"No." I grabbed hold of the lapels of his jacket. "No fighting."

He looked at me, nostrils flaring. What was it about weddings that invited so much drama?

"I mean it," I said. "This is Ev and David's special night."

But Ben was apparently having far too much fun to stop now. "Remember that time we shared a girl in Berlin? That was good . . . real good. Always thought I'd like to try that again. What do you say, Anne? Up for a bit of fun? Promise we'll take good care of you."

Mal snarled and I lunged, getting him in a strangle hold. I was basically hanging off him. Damn, the man was strong. Ben might be huge, but given Mal's current mood, I wouldn't bet against him in a fair fight. The muscles in his neck were bulging.

"Mal?" I said his name in my super calm and in control voice. Under different circumstances I'd have probably made an awesome therapist. "Are you listening to me?"

"Yeah." His hands gripped my ass, taking some of my weight. A good thing. Dangling from someone's neck was harder than it looked.

"Everything's fine. Ignore him," I said. "Ben, get out."

The jerk waggled his eyebrows at me.

"Now."

"Sure, Anne. No worries." He winked at me, closing the door.

"Be calm, Mal. The bad man is gone."

"I'm calm," he growled, holding me to him.

"He didn't mean it. He was just messing with you."

"Didn't you see the way he looked at you? Idiot meant it."
Mal hugged me tight. "Piece of shit's bad as Jimmy sometimes.
Should have kicked his ass."

"Hey now, harness that inner caveman. You're very aggressive tonight."

"I don't like people saying stuff about you. You shouldn't have
to put up with that."

"Well, that's sweet. But I don't need you beating up anybody
for me."

"Four of us have been beating each other up since we were
kids. It happens." One handed, Mal tugged my zipper back up
into place. Then he pierced me with a hard look. "You didn't
want to, did you?"

"Generally, I do prefer one penis at a time. It's a failing of mine,
I guess . . ."

"Good."

I gave him a kiss on the cheek because a jealous Mal was an
awesome sight. "What was he talking about 'it's time'?"

"Davie wants to play a few songs for Ev. We gotta go back
out." He sighed and sat me back on the counter. His hands rubbed
over my sides. "You okay?"

"Yes."

Still he frowned.

"You know, you can be kind of intense, Malcolm Ericson."

His watched me in silence.

"You come across as this happy-go-lucky-type dude most of

the time, but you are in fact a man of many layers. You're kind
of complicated."

"Surprised?"

"Yes. And no."

"And you call me complicated. You gonna dance with me
later?" he asked, shaking off the bad mood.

"I'd love to."

"You wanted another drink, didn't you? C'mon, let's go get
that before I set up." He lifted me down, his hands on my hips,
treating me with the utmost care.

"You're the best boyfriend ever. Fake or not."

"How many you had?"

"Boyfriends? Two." I held up a couple of fingers, just in case
he wanted a visual aid. It was good to be helpful.

"So I'm number three?"

"No, you're number two. Relationships aren't my specialty."

"No?" He lifted his chin, looked down at me. "You're doing
real good, Anne."

"Thanks, Mal."

CHAPTER ELEVEN

I had a nice buzz by the time we stumbled home. We shared a cab with Nate and Lauren at around three in the morning after an amazing party.

I'd finally heard Stage Dive play live. They were awesome playing acoustic. Jimmy's and David's voices melding together beautifully. Each one of those men was so damn talented it made my teeth hurt. Ben, with his bass, and even Mal, deprived of his full drum kit, made his presence felt in amazing ways. They were all in perfect balance, integral to the music.

It might have been way past my bedtime, but I didn't want the night to end. Not just yet. I lay on my back, staring at my bedroom ceiling. It'd stopped spinning a short while ago. The gap in my curtains provided just enough light from the street to see by. A few years ago on nights like this when sleep wouldn't come, I'd often talk to Mal—I mean, the poster version of him. Sad and psychotic, but true. Now the man himself slept next door.

Life could be a strange and beautiful thing sometimes.

Other times it was just a disaster. But sometimes beauty won out.

I ran my fingers over my poor, sore lips. They'd almost been kissed into extinction. Once Mal got an idea into his head, he was unstoppable. And apparently dancing with him meant indulging in a mini make-out session. It had gotten more and more difficult to feign dissatisfaction every time he tried something new. So many ways to kiss, I'd truly had no idea. Soft and hard, with or without teeth, the varying depths of penetration by tongue had featured largely. And hand placement. Whoa, the hand placement. He'd done everything from gently stroking my neck to kneading my ass. A man who knew what to do with his hands was truly a force to be reckoned with. I'd only just stopped him from slipping it up my skirt at midnight.

Such a great night.

He'd stripped down to boxer briefs again once we got home. I'd gone into the bathroom to grab a hairbrush and there he'd been, brushing his teeth. A man brushing his teeth had never been such a turn-on, even with the white bubbly drool slipping out of the corner of his mouth. My guess would be he didn't own pajamas. Nope, a guy like him must sleep in the nude. A brilliant scientific deduction based on the hot and hard man currently occupying my couch. All too readily I could imagine his warm, tanned skin exposed. Did he sleep on his back, stomach, or side? Aesthetically, on his back would be most pleasing . . . for various reasons.

But if he did lie on his stomach the long line of his spine would be on show with the bonus addition of his ass. I'd sell something important to see his bare ass. My books, my e-reader, my soul, whatever was necessary.

And I could think about something else anytime I wanted to. But why would I?

No, masturbating was a much more sensible course of action. I was all wired and awake, my nipples hard and breasts aching. The time had come to take matters into my own hands.

"Mm, Nate."

More moaning.

Some groaning.

A thump.

"Baby, yes."

"Lick it, Lauren."

No. Fucking. Way.

I covered my face with my pillow and silently screamed. If I put on music to drown them out (my usual course of action for dealing with Nate and Lauren's nocturnal passions) I'd probably wake Mal.

Two more thumps. The bed next door started creaking. It was so loud I almost didn't hear my bedroom door being opened.

"Pumpkin, am I in hell?" Mal walked in, sat on the edge of my bed.

"Yes. Yes, you are. I'm sorry. This is the first and worst level of all, the one where you can hear your neighbors fucking through paper-thin walls."

Lauren made some screechy noise she was particularly prone to during such encounters. I cringed.

"Make it stop," Mal whispered, mouth opened wide in horror. "Oh, fuck no. This is horrible."

We both started quietly laughing. It was the only sensible response.

"Let's go to a hotel," he said, moving farther onto my bed.

"It's four in the morning."

"How long do they normally take?"

"They've been drinking, so this could go on for a while." I drew up my knees, hugged them tight to my chest. He didn't need to know about my nipple situation. The sad truth was that listening to people having good, noisy sex wasn't helping. Lucky I was wearing my best comfy cotton jammie pants and an old

T-shirt. They were so baggy they hid everything. Otherwise, having Mal sitting on my bed so close might have been a touch embarrassing.

"Isn't there something wrong with this picture?" said Mal, scowling at the wall as if it had personally offended him. "I'm the drummer from Stage Dive. I don't get kept awake by other people having wild sex. I keep them awake. I keep entire fucking neighborhoods awake."

"Damn, baby. You're so good at this," Nate snarled through the wall.

"Did you hear that?" asked Mal.

"Yep."

"Right. That's it." Mal climbed up onto his feet, standing tall on my bed. There was only a foot between him and the ceiling at most. "He's taunting me. He's challenging me."

"He is?"

"The bastard."

"And I always thought Nate was such a nice guy."

He reached out his hand to me. "C'mon, Anne. We must defend our fake sex life."

"Shit." I took his hand, letting him pull me up too. "Don't let me bounce off the side. And don't hit your head."

"I'm not gonna hit my head. Would you stop being such a grown-up for a minute? Relax, have some fun."

"Harder, Nate!" Came from next door.

Mal's cleared his throat, loudly. "Anne!"

"Mal."

"Louder," he hissed, as we started to bounce. The wooden frame of my bed made startling creaking noises. The kind it hadn't made in a very long time, if ever. If only it were due to us being horizontal and naked. That would be so great.

"Mal!"

"You're such a nice girl, Anne," Mal projected for the sake of our neighbors. "I really like you a lot."

"Seriously? That's your version of sex talk?"

"Let's hear you talk dirty, then. C'mon."

I shut my mouth. It stayed shut.

"Coward." Mal turned his face to the wall we shared with Nate and Lauren. "You taste so fucking good."

"Like what?" I asked breathlessly, thigh muscles tightening. The man was lucky I didn't just attack him with my vagina. "What do I taste like?"

"Well, like honey and cream and . . . I dunno, bread?"

I scrunched up my nose. "Bread?"

"Yes. Sexy bread that I could eat all the time because you are so delicious and full of wholegrain goodness."

The next round of giggling made my stomach muscles seize up, but I kept bouncing. How weird to be laughing and jumping and turned on at the same time. Some friends of Lizzy's and mine had a trampoline when we were growing up. It'd never been as much fun as this, however.

Then Mal jumped particularly high and hit the ceiling with his head.

He dropped onto his much-coveted ass, rubbing the top of his skull. "Fuck. Ouch."

"Are you okay?"

The bed suddenly collapsed, one end of the wooden frame crashing to the floor. The noise was most impressive. As was the sudden silence from next door. I stumbled and slid and wound up landing half on his lap. Fortunately, an arm went around me, stopping me from bouncing further. We sat there, basically chest to chest, with one of my legs thrown over both of his.

"We've broken my bed," I said, stating the obvious.

"In battle, sacrifices must be made, pumpkin."

"Is your head okay? Do you need an ice pack?" I pushed his mess of blond hair out of his face. Maybe he needed sexual healing. I was so up for that. It was right on the tip of my tongue to suggest it. Drunken bravado was the best.

"It's good." His smile came ever so slowly.

Someone knocked on the wall from Nate and Lauren's side. "You two okay?"

"We're fine," I called back. "Thanks. Carry on."

I could hear barely subdued laughter. My face felt hot. Flame-worthy hot. You could probably cook a steak on that sucker. Crap, everybody would hear about this. And I do mean everybody. We were never going to live this down.

"They're mocking us," I said.

"Nonsense. We just fucked so hard we broke your bed. They wish they were us. The natural order of sexual status has been restored."

We both laughed. It was all so ridiculous.

But then the laughter kind of dwindled away to nothing and we were sitting there staring at each other. His face was in shadows. It impossible to read him. But his thickening cock made its presence known against my thigh. What I wouldn't have given to know what he was thinking. All of my awareness went directly to between my legs and oh shit, it felt good. I wished he'd do something because I wasn't sure I could. He reacted to me but what did that mean? Dicks did stuff. Mysterious stuff, like getting hard for no reason. Sex was most definitely not part of our agreement. He'd been specific. And yet, all the kissing and teasing tonight . . .

I'd never been so confused in my entire life. Confused and horny.

Next door, the noises started up once more as they took my advice and did indeed carry on.

"I'm pretty sure they're not thinking about us at all," I said.

"Just out of interest, how drunk are you?"

"The room is kind of spinning. Why?"

"Nothing. We better move," he said, voice guttural. Carefully, he lifted me off of him and then climbed out of the ruin of my old bed. We both stood there, collectively ignoring the bulge in his pants. Not awkward at all. It had to be said though; a damp crotch was far easier to hide.

"Let's go watch a movie," he said. "No one's getting any sleep anytime soon."

"Good idea," I lied and let him haul me out of the wreckage. "Poor bed. But that was fun."

"Yeah, it was. Not as much fun as actually fucking, but still, not bad."

My curiosity got the better of me. Either that or I had no manners and was indeed still drunk. "Speaking of which, what happened to your hook-ups? I thought you might go visiting a lady friend after we got back from the party."

"Meh."

"Meh?" He had a half-on and he was giving me 'meh'?

"Between getting ready for this tour and being in a serious fake relationship, I haven't had the time."

"Fair enough." I didn't believe him at all.

Instead, my alcohol-addled mind made giant leaps of logic. Little to no reason was involved. What if his lack of libido had to do with his need for a fake girlfriend somehow? Maybe he had a mysterious real girlfriend hidden away down in L.A. and I existed solely to put people off the scent. Actually, no. That theory hurt. But maybe this was all about the bet he'd made with Ben. He'd backed himself into this ridiculous corner with his insane jokes and now his pride would be wounded if he tried to back out. And that theory hurt even more. Neither probability covered his being sad sometimes, though. I let him lead me into the living room, my head and my heart a not-so-sober mess.

"What about you? You weren't seriously keeping your legs crossed until douche came to his senses, were you?" He sat in the middle of the velvet couch, pulling me down beside him, keeping me close.

"No, I've dated. Just not recently."

"How not recently?" He picked up a remote and the huge TV came to life. His arm rested on the back of the couch behind me, the flat of his hand beating out a fierce rhythm.

"What do you feel like watching?" I asked.

"Not going to tell me?"

"A few months."

Some old horror film was on. From the eighties, if the big hair and spiral perm were any indicators. A pair of barely concealed breasts bounced their way across the screen. A woman screamed.

"This looks good," Mal said.

"Mmm-hmm."

"You don't scare easily, do you?"

"No. Though it does make me sad when Johnny Depp gets turned into tomato soup."

"Bet it does." He smiled. "You know, I meant what I said."

"About what?"

"About you." He looked straight ahead, never meeting my eyes. The light from the TV lit the angles and planes of his perfect face. "I like you."

"Thank you, Mal."

Then why weren't we having sex? Obviously, he didn't *like-like* me. He just *liked* me, like he'd said.

My mind starting spinning all over again.

"You didn't say you liked me back," he prodded, sounding the tiniest bit insecure if my ears weren't deceiving me.

"Oh, well." I turned to look at him, squinting, ignoring the screaming still coming from on screen. "You are . . ."

"I'm what?"

"So . . ."

"C'mon, pumpkin, you're taking too long. Spit it out."

"Very . . ."

"Fuck it. I'm just gonna compliment myself."

I sighed long and loud, enjoying this immensely.

"You're hopeless at this," he bitched.

"How about stupendous? Does stupendous work for you?"

"Hmm." He gave me a small, satisfied smile. "Yeah. That's not bad. I mean, it definitely starts to cover the glory that is me."

"And egotistical. So very egotistical."

"You lie." His fingers danced over my sides, making me giggle and squirm. "I am humble perfection."

"No. Don't tickle me."

"Admit I'm your reason for being. Admit it!" His arm came around me, pulling me back into him as I tried to escape. "Shit, don't fall off the chair again. I can't take any more hits to the head to save you."

"Stop tickling me, then," I huffed.

"Tickling you. Please. As if I'd be so immature." A hand came up and gently pushed my head onto his shoulder and the arm around me tightened. "Shh, quiet time now."

The warm buzz filling me was ten times better than anything alcohol could ever provide. No, a million times better, because it came with the added bonus of smelling and feeling like Mal Ericson.

"Relax," he said.

"I'm relaxing." Stuff happened on the big screen. None of it mattered. My eyes drifted closed as I concentrated on him. Whatever his reasons for being here, there was little chance I'd ever get what I wanted. It was the human condition to always want more. That being said, what I had for the moment was pretty damn good.

CHAPTER TWELVE

People were arguing again when I woke up. Only this time, there was no yelling. Heated whispers passed straight over my head.

"Why is my sister asleep on top of you?" asked Lizzy.

"Because I'm her boyfriend," Mal answered. "Who are you? Anne didn't say anything about having a sister."

"She didn't?"

"No. And how many people have fucking keys to this apartment, anyway? You forget the sliding bolt for a moment and it's open city."

"With Skye gone, just me and Lauren as far as I know."

"Don't say that name. She gets upset when you mention it. Her eyes go all sad and it totally bums me out."

"What, Skye?"

"Yeah," he growled.

"Fine, fine." A pause. "You're kinda hot, aren't you?"

A disinterested grunt.

"I'm not hitting on you, idiot. She's my sister and this is my suspicious voice. Don't I know you from somewhere? Your face is very familiar."

The fingers connected to the big hand cupping my ass tightened. What it was doing there, I had no idea. But did I like it?

Yes. Yes I did. I was sleeping on a bed of Mal. Talk about heavenly. I couldn't even remember falling asleep. Obviously, it had happened sometime during the gory horror movie because we were still on the velvet couch in the living room. My sister was here so it had to be Sunday morning, our day to do our duty and call mom. We always performed this unpleasant task together.

I did not want to move. Not until Wednesday at the very earliest. I was mildly hung over.

But more than that, I didn't want to get off of Mal.

"What the hell did you do to her? Her lips are all puffy and bruised."

"Are they?" Mal's body moved beneath me as he no doubt lifted his head to check out the damage. "Shit. Ah, yeah. She's a bit of a mess, isn't she? But how was I to know if she was into biting or not if I didn't try it out?"

"She's not," said Lizzy. "Or at least, I don't think she is. Anne's never seemed like the biting type to me. She's more . . . restrained."

"Restrained?" Mal laughed softly. "Yeah. Why don't you go check out her bed, then tell me how restrained she is."

Footsteps followed by a gasp. "Fuck me. It's totaled."

"My pumpkin's an animal when she gets going."

"You call her pumpkin?" My sister's voice was filled with awe. "Does she actually answer?"

"Well, she pretends to hate it. But secretly, I know she loves it. Her face goes all soft and everything."

Oh good god, enough. I'd basically raised this girl; she didn't need to hear this sort of shit. Any authority I'd once had would be dust. I cracked open an eyelid. "Quiet, Mal."

"I am your servant in all things."

"What time is it?" I asked as a yawn almost cracked my jaw in two.

"Mal? Did she call you Mal?" asked Lizzy, coming up close beside us. My sister and I didn't look much alike. Her hair was a pretty caramel color as opposed to my carrot. Her features were more delicate than mine, though we both had mom's strong jawline. "No. Way."

Ha, this would be fun.

"Strangely enough yes, way," I said, my voice ever so slightly smug. "Mal, this is my little sister, Lizzy. Lizzy, this is Malcolm Ericson." My sister hadn't been quite as big a Stage Dive fan as me. Doubtful it would stop her from fangirling out, however.

As suspected, Lizzy squealed like a loon. Both Mal and I winced. "Oh my god, Anne loves you. She had an entire wall of her bedroom dedicated to you."

"No!" Shit, how had I not seen this coming? Fear choked me. Someone had to tackle my sister, now. Take her down and lock her in a cupboard. It was absolutely for her own benefit, but mostly mine. I tried to lunge at her, but strong arms held me trapped. "Lizzy. Shut up. Please shut up. He doesn't need to know that."

"Tell me more, Lizzy," demanded Mal. "A whole wall, did you say? That is fascinating. I definitely need to know more."

"No you don't."

"Hush, Anne. I'm listening."

My arms weren't long enough to cover Lizzy's mouth. I had to settle for Mal's ears. I fought him, but he shook off my hands far too easily, the wily man.

"She used to write your name on her thigh in permanent marker," my traitorous wench of a sister reported. It was official: Lizzy sucked. There was a good chance I'd soon be an only child if she kept talking. Given mom rarely noticed she had children at all, the loss shouldn't be too debilitating long-term.

"That's a lie!" I cried, breaking out into a cold sweat.

"Did she write it on her inner thigh? I bet it she did, the minx." Mal grabbed my wrists, holding them against his chest. An effective means of stopping me from beating him bloody. "Did she draw little hearts with arrows sticking out of 'em too?"

"I don't know." My beloved sister settled into the wingback, crossing her legs. "But she did practice signing her name as Anne Ericson *all* the time."

"I am so touched you'd take my name, pumpkin." Mal attempted to smooch my fists. "No shit, that's awesome of you. Means the world to me. My family is gonna love you."

"La-la-la-la," I sang at the top of my voice, drowning them both out as best I could.

"And she'd watch Stage Dive videos over and over. Except for the one where you kissed that girl." Lizzy clicked her fingers, her face tensed in concentration. " 'Last Days of Love', that was the one. She flat-out refused to watch it, would leave the room if it came on."

Beneath me, Mal's body shuddered because he was laughing his ass off. The man was in hysterics. Even his eyes were bright with unshed tears, the douche canoe. A big hand curled around the back of my head, pressing my face into his neck. "Aw, Anne. Were you jealous?"

"No." Yes. Horribly, horribly jealous. That kiss had ravaged my teenage soul and made me listen to sad songs for almost a year.

"My poor girl."

"Shuddup."

"I didn't mean to kiss her. My mouth slipped," he said, trying for earnest and failing. "I swear I was trying to keep myself pure for you. Tell me you believe me, please."

I called him something foul.

He laughed even harder, making the whole couch shake.

Given he wasn't letting me go any time soon, I hid my hot

face in his neck as invited. Everyone in the room, I hated them. I hated them hard. It was tempting to bite him but he'd probably enjoy it. He'd certainly spent quality time nibbling at my lips and jaw after cornering me yet again at the party last night. His kissing crusade had almost undone me, but it had taken my sister to do the real damage, my own flesh and blood.

Now Mal knew everything. I was doomed.

"Lizzy, be a good girl and fetch me a pen," said Mal. "I need to write your sister's name on my junk, right now."

Honest to god, I tried not to laugh. I tried so hard.

"How about I go make coffee instead?" Lizzy hauled herself to her feet. "You know she usually has breakfast cooked for me by now, every Sunday at ten o'clock on the dot. You're a bad influence on her, Mal."

"Let me get dressed, I'll take you both out." He smoothed his hand over my back. "Can't have my future sister-in-law getting mad at me already."

"Won't you get hassled?" Lizzy hollered from the kitchen.

"People have usually been pretty cool around here when I've visited. But I'll wear a hat and sunglasses. And I can call up some security if needed."

"Why don't I cook us something? It's got to be my turn by now," said Lizzy. The clanging of pots and pans and the running of water accompanied her statement. Maybe my sister wasn't so bad after all.

"Thanks," I said.

"Soooo." Mal smacked a kiss on the top of my head. "You weren't just a little into me. You're my biggest fan. You love me."

"I don't love you."

"You totally love me." He gave me a squeeze. "I'm your everything. You'd be lost without me."

Thankfully, this time when I scrambled off of him, he didn't try to fight me. I pulled down my old T-shirt and smoothed back my bed hair, getting myself together. "It was just a stupid teenage crush. Don't let it go to your already swollen head."

"The big one or the little one?"

I groaned.

Mal just laid there, his fingers sitting steepled atop his bare chest. He watched me without comment. His eyes, they saw far too much. After a moment, he sat up, his feet hitting the floor. He yawned and then stretched, cracking his neck. "You know, that's the first decent sleep I've gotten in ages."

"With me passed out on top of you? It can't have been comfortable."

The shadows beneath his eyes had faded and he seemed more relaxed, stretching out his long limbs. Still, he rubbed at the back of his neck. "No, it wasn't really. Go figure. Guess we should be sleeping on the couch every night from now on."

"My bed is broken."

He pushed back his hair, gave me a smile.

"You've been having trouble sleeping?" I asked.

"A bit, I guess."

"Something on your mind?"

"Dunno. It's nothing." He avoided my eyes.

"It's something." This was the first real in he'd given me. Or first vague in. Either way, I needed to take it. "What's going on with you? What's wrong? Sometimes I look at you and you seem so . . ."

"What? I seem so what?"

"Sad."

His face blanked, his hands settling on his hips. Tension radiated from his body like a force field. "Nothing's going on. I told you that shit wasn't up for discussion."

"Sorry. I just thought maybe you'd like to talk about it."

"Not up for discussion kinda means, I don't want to talk about it. Got it?" His voice was hard and he used it like a weapon. Accordingly, it hurt.

"Okay," I said quietly.

Anger thinned his lips. "You know, Anne, you're the last fucking person who should be pushing me about anything. We had a deal, an understanding."

Oh no, he did not. My chin jutted out. "And you've stuck to it so well."

"What the fuck is that supposed to mean?"

"I went to the party. I played my part."

"Yeah? And?"

"And you spent the night trying to prove you're the world's greatest lover or something. There wasn't anyone around to see some of those kisses, Mal. They were all about you proving you're the shit because that's what you decided to do."

"They were about more than that." A muscle popped in his jaw. It was kind of impressive and a little scary. But screw him.

"Were they?"

" 'Course they fucking were."

I stared at him, taken aback. "Okay. I didn't realize. But don't rip my head off for crossing a few lines because I'm worried about you. I don't like seeing you sad either."

"Fuck," he swore and his face stilled. He linked his hands behind his head, muttering some more expletives. Then he let out a long breath, never taking his gaze off of me. His mood had shifted, the anger gone from the air. Ever so gently he reached out and traced my swollen bottom lip. "Looks sore."

"It's okay." My voice wavered.

"I overdid it. Sorry."

I wilted, the anger seeping straight out of me. His eyes were sad again and this time, it was all about me. I had no defense for that. "If the worst thing to happen to me is that you think it's fun to kiss me and lie to people about me being pregnant with your child, my life will probably be pretty sweet."

His smile lacked commitment, there and gone in an instant.

"Mal, if you ever want to talk, I'm here." I should probably have shut up but I couldn't. "It's okay."

He looked away.

"To be honest, I'm not exactly great at sharing either." My hands flexed and fisted, flexed and fisted, as if to demonstrate the point. Awkward as all hell, I hated feeling helpless. Why couldn't he just spill so I could try and fix whatever was wrong already?

"Can we stop talking about this now?" he asked the wall.

"Sure."

"Thanks." He reached out, tugged on a strand of my hair. Then his hand slid around to the back of my neck and he drew me in against him. Damn, he smelled good. I got giddy. Maybe there was also a little relief over the argument ending, hard to tell which. With my cheek pressed to Mal's chest, my brain malfunctioned. I wrapped my arms around his waist, getting a solid hold on him just in case he changed his mind and tried to peel me off of him.

"That was our first fight," he mumbled.

"Yeah. I won."

"Did not."

"Did too."

"Pfft. Okay." His arms tightened around me. "I'll give you that one. But only because you're being so childish about it."

"Thanks."

He breathed out hard. "I don't want to fight again."

"No," I agreed wholeheartedly.

"Is it safe to come out yet?" Lizzy asked, peeking around the kitchen door. She gave Mal a quick once-over and then realized what she was doing and looked away. I didn't blame her, but I didn't like it. Man, now I was getting jealous of my own sister. Ridiculous, especially given the man had an army of women after him. If I planned to hang out with a rock star I'd need to get used to this.

"Your sister and I have to go have make-up sex now. It's very important for the long-term health of our relationship." Mal started forcibly stepping us toward the spare room. "But you have a good breakfast and a very nice day. Just leave the dishes; I'll take care of 'em later. It was lovely to meet you, Lizzy."

"Mal, you're strangling me." Or that's what I tried to say. With my face pressed up against his hard chest, it came out garbled. Most likely my words were completely unintelligible.

"What was that?" He loosened his octopus hold enough to allow me to take a good deep breath. Phew, oxygen, my dear old friend.

"Why don't you put some clothes on? I'm going to help Lizzy cook breakfast," I said.

Lizzy watched us with eyes popping out of her head. Fair enough, really. We'd apparently entered some alternative universe where Mal Ericson was all over me like a rash. How mind-bendingly breathtakingly amazing. I needed to make the most of this before he went on tour. Soak up all the memories I could.

"You're the worst girlfriend I've ever had." He pouted. It shouldn't have been charming. But of course it was.

"Am I?"

"Yes. The very worst ever."

"I'm the only girlfriend you've ever had." Fake or not, it was the truth.

"Yeah, you are." He held my face in his hands and covered it in kisses. Everywhere but my poor, sore lips. I don't know what I'd done exactly to earn such an outpouring of affection, but I was profoundly grateful for it just the same. My heart up and keeled over; gave up the war. Hopefully my panties were made of sterner stuff. Given last night, I highly doubted it, however.

"We good?" he asked, lips brushing against my cheek.

"We're great."

"Okay."

"Clothes, Mal."

He laughed and wandered into the spare room, kicking the door shut behind him with some faux Fred Astaire dance move. The man was all class in his snug boxer briefs.

"I've never seen you smile like that." Lizzy leaned her shoulder against the kitchen door, watching. "You look kind of stoned."

"Ha. Yes, he has that effect."

She had her careful face on. I rarely liked anything I heard when she had her mouth set like that. What with me being the older sibling, I didn't see it often. But when I did, it was never good. "I um, I didn't mean to hear what you guys were saying. But your apartment is pretty small."

"I need you to not ask me any questions about this, please."

"Just one."

I agreed to nothing.

"Whatever is going on between you two, this deal you have, is it going to end up hurting you, Anne?"

I hung my head, scuffed the sole of my foot against the floor. My sister and I didn't lie to each other. It was a rule. One we stuck to without fail. No matter the crap Mom peddled, Lizzy and I were always straight with one another. "I don't know."

"You think it'll be worth it?"

"That's two questions," I said with a small smile.

"Call it an early Christmas present."

"He's great, Lizzy. He's so great. I've never met anyone like him."

She nodded slowly, dusted off her hands, and then squeezed them tight. More nervous traits we'd inherited from our crackpot of a mother. "It's like he's turned you back on. Getting away from home helped but . . . he's found you again or something."

"Found me? I've always been right here, Lizzy."

"No, you've been gone a long time."

I stared at the floor, lost for words.

"So, I thought you were inviting Reece to join us this morning."

My mouth dropped open in surprise. Talk about a first time for everything. "Shit. I said I'd call him. I totally forgot."

"Poor Reece. You know, I think this is going to be character building for him." Lizzy grinned then stopped and sniffed at the air. "Bacon's burning!"

We rushed into the kitchen in time to see smoke rising out of the pan and blackened strips of bacon that had shriveled away to nothing. What a waste. I turned off the burner, emptying the remains of breakfast into the sink. Normally, the fridge would be full for our Sunday brunch. But this week I'd been too busy. "Never mind, we'll have toast instead."

"Sorry."

"You two are coming to band practice, right? The guys won't mind." Mal walked into the kitchen, still zipping up a gray hoodie. The man belonged in a jeans ad he wore them so well. And I was still hanging out in my elegant sleepwear, unwashed, and with what had to be greasy hair. He peered at the charred mess in the sink. "Lemme guess, I'm taking you out for breakfast after all?"

"No, we're having toast. You have practice today after that party?" I asked. The merriment of last night had lasted into the early hours. "That's dedication."

"Only four more days till the tour kicks off. Time's a-wasting." Mal paused. "And we're going out. You can't expect me to live on bread and water. You gotta feed your man better than that, woman."

I did my best not to get weak at the words "your man" and thereby set the feminist movement back fifty years. Proximity to Mal was a dangerous thing. "Sounds great. Let me grab a quick shower."

"Good idea. I'll wash your back," he said, following me into the living room.

"Why don't you keep Lizzy company?"

"Why don't I keep you company?" His voice dropped in volume. "I could clean that special place for you with my tongue. Promise I'll do a good job."

"Wow. That's really sweet of you." Oh, boy. I clutched at the bathroom door handle for support. "Two words for you, Mal. Fatal. Attraction."

His smile was huge as he waved away my concerns. "Hello, I don't even own a rabbit. And let's face facts, you're not that strong, pumpkin. I could easily disarm you if I needed to. We've been getting along so well. Come on, it'll be fun."

"Gah! Stop," I whisper yelled at him. "I can't tell if you're serious or not. You're hurting my head."

He leaned down, getting in close. "Look at me; I am totally serious. You're not drunky Anne today, you know what you're doing, and I feel like fucking. Let's renegotiate. This agreement is no longer working for me. I wanna talk to my lawyer!"

"Oh, you feel like fucking?"

"Well, yeah. I'm not used to going more than a day or two. It's making me antsy." He did a little jig on the spot to demonstrate. "I don't like it. C'mon, Anne. Help a friend out. It'll be good."

"Hands down, that's the most romantic thing I've ever heard. I can pretty much feel my legs just falling wide open for you right now."

"What do you want, some bullshit about love?"

"No." *But maybe* something terrible whispered deep inside of me. It needed to shut up.

"You want a song? No problem. I'll ask Davie to write you one later." He put a hand to either side of the bathroom doorway. "I know you wanted to go for it last night. But I wanted you sober. Now you are. I want you. You want me. Let's fuck."

My heart went into overdrive, but I forced myself to calm down. "You're right, I did want to last night. I still want to. But this is not the time, Mal. My sister is here."

"I'll come quick." His brows bunched up. "Wait, I didn't mean it like that. It'll be fast but great. Anne, you might diss my kissing but I'm telling you now, my oral sex skills are off the chart. I know all about getting dirty down under. Let me show you, pretty please?"

"Mal . . ." I couldn't even think what to say when he gave me pleading eyes. He had me bouncing between emotions as fast as he changed moods. Angry, horny, and amused all blended into one. "Lizzy is just in the kitchen. She can hear every word we're saying."

"We'll shut the bathroom door, turn on the shower. With the water running she won't hear a thing."

"God, you confuse me. I don't think my head has stopped spinning since you walked in the door."

"You can be confused later. But come on my face now, please?"

Which is about the time I started panting. Horny was definitely winning the race. Fortunately my baggy T-shirt hid the worst of the hard nipple evidence. I pushed him back with a hand while I still had the strength. "We'll talk about this later when we're alone. Go bond with your supposed future sister-in-law. Please."

"Fine." His whole body drooped. "But you're missing out big-time."

"I don't doubt it."

"I might not even be in the mood later, Anne. You could completely miss out and that'd be it, life ruined."

"I consider myself duly warned."

"Last chance." He rolled out his big pink tongue like a dog. Though that was probably being mean to dogs. In all likelihood, canines showed more discretion. "Thee? Iths really long."

"Will you please put that away?" I laughed.

Instead he grabbed the back of my head, dragging the length of his warm, damp tongue up the side of my face. I froze against the onslaught. "You did not just do that."

"It's a sign of affection. You think I salivate on just anyone?"

"You . . . I can't even."

"There are women who would kill to have me licking their face. You do not even begin to appreciate just how lucky you are to have my spit. Now lick me back." He pointed to his jaw, demandingly. "Anne, do it. Do it now, woman, before I get offended."

I giggled, my whole body getting in on the act. Which was getting dangerous. "I need to go to the bathroom. Go away. Stop making me laugh."

"I like making you laugh."

"Yeah, well, me peeing my pants would be less cool. Go on."

"Hold up." He grabbed my wrist, his voice quieting. The way he could switch from clown to calm in an instant was nothing short of amazing. "One, that was too much information. Two, you and Lizzy coming to band practice with me?"

"You're sure that's okay?"

"Yes."

"Then we'd love to." I nodded. This had to be the most insanely perfect moment ever. Me with a full bladder and a full heart both at once. "We just have to make a phone call first, then we can go."

"Good. Three, admit you lied about not liking my kisses last night." His gaze held me fast.

No point denying it any longer; I liked him and I wanted him so much it hurt. The minute I had him all alone, it was on. His fingers were still wound around my wrist as I cupped his jaw. The scratch of his stubble against the palm of my hand and the warmth of his skin was divine. But it wasn't enough. I needed to give something back. Some small part of the crazy, confusing, lusty joy he gave me. He held perfectly still while I reached up and pressed a careful kiss to his cheek. "You're right, I lied."

The tension lines around his mouth eased. "You did."

"Yes. I'm sorry. You just kind of overwhelmed me and . . . anyway, you're the best."

He pumped his fists into the air. "I knew it! I'm the best."

"You are."

A simple statement of fact, but it lit up his eyes just the same. "Thanks, pumpkin."

His smile . . . I had no words.

CHAPTER THIRTEEN

We called Mom from my bedroom, perched on the edge of my downed mattress. Mal was busy watching TV in the living room, a cup of coffee in hand.

I nodded and Lizzy took out her cell, selected the contact, and set the phone to speaker. Then she held it between us. My skin prickled. The air seemed cold and hot all at once. Fuck, I hated this. I hated it with a passion. But in my head, Mom was so closely entwined with anger and frustration I couldn't separate her from the emotions. One day, it wouldn't be this way.

"Hi, Mom," said Lizzy, sounding cheery as sunshine in a bottle. She'd forgiven Mom already. I was still getting there.

"Hi, girls. How are you?" Just the sound of her voice brought it all back. Sitting in the dark with her, begging and pleading with her to eat just another spoonful, to get out of bed and have a shower maybe, act like a human being. To start being an adult and look after her daughters so I could go back to being a kid.

"We're great, Mom," I said, doing my best to sound normal. "How are you?"

"Good. Work's been fine."

I nodded like she could see me, relieved she was holding down a job still, being responsible for her own finances. That was good. For years I'd made do with the remains of the savings account, then whatever Dad saw fit to send.

"School's going well." Lizzy swapped her cell over to her other hand, talking on about college all the while. Then she put her arm around me and started rubbing my back. A sweet gesture, but honestly, being touched right then didn't help.

My sister excelled at these conversations. She could babble on for a good ten minutes. And really, ten minutes was a long enough time frame for a weekly call home, right?

"What about you, Anne?" she asked once Lizzy had exhausted herself.

"I'm fine."

"Anne is seeing someone," Lizzy supplied.

I shot her a glance. "It's not that serious."

"He's really great, Mom. He's so into her, you can just see it in his eyes."

"Oh," said Mom, followed by a moment's silence. "You're being careful, aren't you, Anne?"

It could mean so many things, but I knew exactly what my mother was saying. Had I not forgotten men were the sworn enemy? Why, look how our dad had just up and left us! Funny, men being evil wasn't the lesson I'd taken away from my teenage years, no matter what Mom might have intended.

"Yes, mom." I tucked my newly styled hair behind my ears, sat up straighter. "Everything's fine."

Mom let out a little sigh. "Good. I wouldn't want—"

"He's actually waiting to take us to breakfast, Mom. So we better go."

"Alright, I wanted to ask if you girls would like to come home for Thanksgiving, maybe?" Her voice sounded hopeful, pleading. "It would be lovely to see you both."

"Thanksgiving?" Lizzy asked, like she'd never heard of the occasion. "We'll think about it . . . sure."

Like hell.

"I don't think I can get the time off work, Mom," I said. "Sorry."

Mom made a sad little noise and the heart I'd hardened toward her a long time ago paused. There was a twinge of guilt, but not enough to make me go back. Never even remotely enough for that. I had my own life now.

"But, Anne, you never take time off," she said. "It can't be good for you."

"Reece depends on me, Mom."

"Surely you're entitled to some holidays. Are you certain he's not taking advantage of you?"

I just stared at the phone.

"Oh, crap, Mom," said Lizzy. "My cell's about to die. I'm so sorry."

"You're always forgetting to plug it in."

"I know. Look, we love you. Great to talk to you. We'll talk again next week."

"Alright, girls. Take care."

"Bye," cried Lizzy, carrying the show.

I mouthed the word. It was honestly the most I could manage. Thank fuck, we'd made it through another week.

Lizzy ended the call, her hand rubbing up and down my back somewhat frantically. Like I needed nurturing. I'm the one who sat her down and explained what a period was. Oh, and sex too. I'd looked over her homework, making sure she got assignments done on time. I could keep my shit together. So I hadn't quite moved on yet from this issue I had with Mom. I'd get there.

"We're not going home," she said.

"Not a chance." I crawled back up onto my feet, smoothed down the gray sweater dress and straightened my tights. I opened the bedroom door. Mal sat on the wingback, staring at the TV.

"Hey, you good to go?" he asked.

"Yeah. All done."

He cocked his head. "What's up, pumpkin?"

I forced a smile, walking toward him. He made me want to smile. It wasn't a complete lie. The concern didn't fade from his eyes, however.

But my mother wasn't ruining this for me.

I leaned over him, setting my hands on the back of the chair, getting close. "Hey."

"Hi," he said, gripping my upper arms. Despite the feeling of not wanting to be touched, something in me unwound at the contact. At his nearness.

"I need a kiss."

"Do you, now? Then you're in luck. For you, I have an endless supply."

God, he was so sweet.

I pressed my lips to his, kissing him lightly to start with. His hand slid into my hair, supporting my head. Then his tongue slid into my mouth. Warm, glowy, happiness filled me. This man, he had magic. At the very least, he had a magical tongue. And really, wasn't that what life was all about? No, okay. Don't try to follow that logic.

"Mm." My happy place had been found.

"An okay effort," he said, rubbing his lips together. "You could probably use a little practice though."

"Haha."

"You get bad news?" he asked.

"No. My mom just hurts my head." There, let the record show, I'd officially shared.

"Yeah?"

"Yes. Let's go get breakfast. Don't want you to be late for rehearsal."

He wasn't so easily distracted. "Don't have sad eyes, Anne. I can't fucking stand it when you're sad."

"You make it better."

"Dude, of course I do. Have you seen me lately?" He grinned and I laughed. "That's better. C'mon, let's go. Otherwise, we keep kissing, we ain't going anywhere but to bed."

CHAPTER FOURTEEN

We were ten minutes late to band practice and eggs Benedict could take the blame. Mal had sat at the table with his back to the room, a baseball cap on his head. Only the waitress recognized him and quietly asked for his autograph. He'd tipped her big-time. I'm pretty sure I saw love shining in her eyes when we left. Lizzy couldn't be far behind with the sentiment. Sure as hell, he'd gone out of his way to win her over, asking questions about her degree and her life in general. He'd been sincere in his interest, sitting forward, listening carefully to her answers. She'd also been highly impressed with his big black Jeep featuring every accessory known to mankind.

But fancy SUVs aside, Mal Ericson was a man to be proud of. My heart and my hormones both took him very seriously. Beneath the surface, all caution had fled. He had me and if the hand fixed to my knee during breakfast was any indication, he knew it. Strangely enough, I didn't have it in me to worry.

Screw being stressed about Mom. With Mal smiling at me, none of it mattered.

Stage Dive practiced in an old building by the river. Mal switched into business mode the minute we walked into the massive space. The difference was fascinating. He gave the side of my face a quick kiss and then continued on to where the guys waited. A stage had been erected at one end of the place. Amps and equipment sat thick on the ground. Cables snaked out in every direction. A couple of roadies, or sound technicians, or whatever they were, rushed about.

Mal stretched his fingers and rolled his wrists, warming up his muscles. Then he stripped off his hoodie and sat behind a shining drum kit, twirling a stick in his hand. The man was clearly in his element, his focus complete. David and Ben were messing around with their instruments, plucking and strumming strings. Interestingly enough, Jimmy was doing push-ups. Lots of them. Then he climbed to his feet and motioned the guys to gather around Mal's kit.

Lizzy and I joined Ev and Lena sitting over on some storage boxes near the back of the hall.

"Hello, fellow Stage Dive groupies and hanger-oners. How is your Sunday morning?" Ev said, sitting on her hands, kicking her feet.

"Good." I smiled back at her and Lena in greeting. "How are you feeling, Mrs. Ferris?"

"I am feeling very very married, thank you for asking. How are you and Mal doing?"

"Ah, good. All good." Everything was good. I parked my butt on the edge of a box. "This is my sister, Lizzy. She goes to school at PSU. Lizzy this is Ev, David's wife, and Lena, Jimmy's . . ." I faltered.

"Assistant. Hi." Lena did the chin tip.

"Hi." Lizzy waved.

"Nice to meet you," said Ev. "Anne, quickly before they start playing. Tell me the story of you and Malcolm. I still haven't heard how you got together, exactly. But Lauren mentioned he basically invaded your apartment."

My mind scrambled. In the next life I was definitely going

to stress less and prepare more. "Ah, well, we met at your place the other night and hit it off."

Lizzy gave me a long look that I ignored.

"That's it?" Ev asked, eyes incredulous.

"Yes, that's pretty much it," I said.

She did not appear pleased.

"What is this, Ev, a grilling?" I laughed.

"Yes, this is a grilling," said Ev with a hopeful smile. "Give me information, please?"

"He's really great and yes, he kind of moved himself in with me. But I love having him there. He's wonderful, you know?" God, I hoped that would do. Definitely time for a subject change. "So, why are you still working in a café?"

"Touché," she said. "It's complicated. I owed my parents money, it was important that they saw me earning it as opposed to my hot, rich husband just handing it over. Things have calmed on the family front now and I'm moving on to other things. Always find it funny the way people react to me working. Like I should sit at home and spend David's money, be the trophy wife. Screw that. I'd be bored as hell inside of two minutes."

Ev shook her head. "Not saying it's been all smooth sailing. We've had to get restraining orders against one nut of a fan and one ass of a photographer. For a while, Sam the security man had to come hang out with me at work. I did not like that, but them's the breaks. After I failed to do anything interesting the paparazzi moved on. Anybody that bothered me got banned from the shop. Not saying it was easy, but I'm entitled to my own life."

"Yes," I said. "You are."

"You'll probably find out for yourself someday soon. Dating one of these guys can be a headache, but they're worth it. Now back to you. Mal is suddenly living with you. I've never even

seen him with the same girl twice. Didn't think it was possible."
She paused, eyeballing me to add emphasis to this information.
Inside my chest, my heart just sort of shriveled. What would
happen when the novelty wore off and Mal got tired of playing
house with me?

"Anne? Hello? Please give me more."

"Um." I was tempted to flail, but that would give away too
much. "He's very persuasive. And . . . he's Mal Ericson. So, yeah.
How could I say no?"

She paused. "This is your tale of true love? That's the worst
story ever. To think I spilled my guts to you."

"Their eyes met across a crowded room." Lena supplied, busy
playing with her cell.

"Was it love at first sight?" asked Ev.

"Absolutely. Didn't you feel the ground move?"

"So that's what that was. Got it." Ev huddled down into her
gray jacket. "Alright, I'll mind my own business. I'm just happy
you two are happy."

"Thank you," I said, ignoring the continuing sad state of my
heart. I just had to live for the moment. Enjoy being with him
while I could. Sure. Not a problem.

Meanwhile, Lizzy hadn't sat like me. Instead, she stood staring at the stage, transfixed by something. Or someone. To be
fair, it was an awesome sight. The band finished their talk and
separated, moving to their own areas. Then Mal counted them
in and bang! Music poured out, filling the hall. No wonder Ev
had wanted to talk before the boys started playing. The guitar
screamed and the bass thumped, rattling my rib cage. Drums
pounded and I felt the rhythm of the music beating in time with
my heart. Then Jimmy sang. "I've got this feeling that comes and
goes, ten broken fingers and one broken nose . . ."

It was an old song off the *San Pedro* album, one of my favorites. All thought of what the future may or may not hold for me and Mal slipped from my mind. Mal's playing and the music owned me, the smoothness of his movements and his absolute focus. His energy. My face hurt from smiling by the time they reached the chorus. All four of us jumped to our feet and broke out into applause at the end. Jimmy laughed softly and bowed. A group of people huddled by the side of the stage took turns giving us bad looks. No idea what their problem was.

"That's their manager, Adrian, and some of the record company people," said Ev, her voice far from warm. "Piece of advice, steer clear of them."

"Adrian's an asshole." Lena settled back onto one of the wooden boxes. "But he's a hell of a manager."

The man in question was middle-aged, wearing a business shirt with a thick gold chain around his neck.

"Was he there last night?"

"Nope." Ev flicked her hair over her shoulder angrily. "Adrian and I don't get along. He prefers the band to be focused on their music rather than wasting time on relationships."

"Like your sexing up David didn't inspire the last album," said Lena.

"Exactly. He should be thanking me." Ev huffed out a laugh. "If he gives you any crap, Anne, let Mal know. He'll deal with him."

Four hours later the band finally stopped playing and handed their instruments over to roadies. My throat was raw from yelling, my hands red from clapping. God help me if I ever made it to an actual concert. There had been some stopping and starting as they worked on perfecting various parts of songs. Then they'd held meetings, just the four of them and also with some of the record company people. They also toyed with effects via the sound guys with their panel of buttons and dials. Us ladies had danced and hollered and had a great time all around. Each and every member of the band was so talented.

But Mal . . . we needed to get back to my apartment and ruin the remains of my bed.

His hair was dark with sweat and he'd long since lost his T-shirt by the time he approached. "Have fun?"

"Yes, I did," I croaked.

"You losing your voice? I thought that was you screaming." He pulled on his hoodie.

"Oh my god, is that *the* David Ferris?" Ev stood atop one of the boxes we'd been sitting on. Her husband just shook his head and held out his arms, eyes amused. She launched herself at him and with no difficulty at all, David caught her. Her legs went around him and their mouths fused.

"Get a room," groaned Ben.

Mal handed me his drum sticks. "A memento of your first Stage Dive concert."

Someone laughed, but I didn't care. I held the sticks tight to my chest. "I'll treasure them always."

"She heard us play last night." Jimmy hung back from the group, arms crossed. His good mood was apparently gone.

"That was acoustic," said Mal. "And I'm not going to give my love a set of flimsy fucking brushes, am I? Only long, hard, phallic shaped things will do for a girl of her appetites."

"I heard about you two." Carefully, David set his wife back down, keeping an arm around her.

My head snapped up. "What?"

"Ooh, what happened?" asked Lena, ears practically perking up, puppy style.

"They broke the bed." The look on Ev's face—hell, we were never going to live this down. "Can you believe that?"

"Of course we broke the bed. They're just lucky we didn't break the building," announced Mal proudly, taking a bow.

David shook his head. "You two do anything interesting and I get Lauren calling at the crack of fucking dawn to tell my wife. Move already."

"Anne likes it there," said Mal. "No rush."

"You got shit security. People get to know you're in the area, you'll have no privacy. And how fucking small are those apartments?"

"Relax, Davie. We'll think about it. You guys, all so addicted to your mansions and fancy livin'. Why, Anne and I could live in a cardboard box and we wouldn't even notice, our love is so epic. Isn't that right, pumpkin?"

"Um, yes?"

"See?" Mal crowed. "She's insanely psycho crazy about me. Material things mean nothing in the face of such worshipful adoration."

David just shook his head.

"Whatever." Ben ran a hand over his short hair. "I'm starving. We finding somewhere to eat and drink?"

"YES." That was Lizzy. A very loud and determined-sounding Lizzy.

The bass player's eyes moved over her with sudden interest. A slow, salacious smile curled his lips. "Well, okay then."

Red alert. So not okay. My baby sister was not hooking up with a player who had to have eight or more years on her. If I wanted to be stupid with my heart, that was on me. I'd let Lizzy get hurt over my dead body.

"Don't you have to get back to school, Liz?" I asked.

"No, I'm fine."

"I thought you had an assignment to do?" I communicated much with my eyes.

She ignored it all. "Nope."

"Lizzy." I forced her name out through gritted teeth.

"Ladies, ladies," Mal said, sensing the rising hostilities. "We got a problem here?"

A woman who'd been hanging with the record company executives approached, her high-heeled boots tapping across the floor. Her smile was tentative. The woman was gorgeous, breasts about a billion times the size of mine (granted, not hard to do) and blond hair in a cool pixie cut. "Mal?"

He turned and his entire face lit up at the sight of the girl. My insides knotted. Yes, fine. I might have been a bit jealous.

"Ainslie, when did you arrive? Looking good." He sounded super happy. They hugged. Then they hugged some more. The girl giggled and sighed, pressing herself against him. Holy shit, was that bitch actually feeling up my fake boyfriend in front of me? She was practically humping his leg. Given the dynamic between the two, there could be no doubting what their relationship was about. I'd finally met one of Mal's fuck buddies. It had to happen. Surprise was stupid and I had no real right to hurt feelings. Pity that didn't make the pain disappear.

I could feel the other women's eyes on me, boring holes into my skull. No way was I returning their stares. Mal had obviously found someone to scratch his itch. Meanwhile, my face was heating up. The entire scene was fucking horrible and embarrassing.

"Hey, Mal," said Lizzy, interrupting the lovers' reunion. "Should we invite Anne's friend Reece along to eat? He often does stuff with us on Sundays."

Oh the wonderful loyal little shit stirrer. I appreciated the thought, but her intentions were misplaced. I didn't need protecting.

"I think Reece said he'd be busy," I said.

My sister played the wide-eyed innocent so well. "No, really? Why don't you give him a call and check, Anne?"

I shook my head. "Maybe another—"

"Fuck no, Lizzy. I mean, I don't think there'll be room." Mal's arms remained around the woman. Then he noticed the faces of his friends, the disapproving and the curious both. For a moment he looked confused, blinking, his forehead creased. Then he stepped back from her, shoved his hands into his jeans pockets. Talk about compromised. Our fake relationship had entirely slipped his mind. His Chucks shifted restlessly.

Also, apparently the thought of making Reece jealous no longer appealed to him. But I hadn't wanted to call Reece either. I'd been perfectly happy as things were. Either way, right now, it didn't much matter. This woman had changed everything.

Ainslie put a hand on his arm. "Is something wrong?"

"It's cool," I said, not on the verge of tears. The air was just really dusty in the old building. "Why don't you go for a drink with your friend and catch up?"

"I thought we were gonna do something," he said.

"Yeah, but . . ."

Eyes guarded, Mal looked at me. Then he looked right through me. I wasn't even there. Whatever he was thinking, it didn't show on his face. It couldn't be easy for someone who was used to getting what they wanted when they wanted it to back down from an obvious offer of sex. Let's be honest, his impulse control was limited at best.

"I'm sorry, you are?" Ainslie asked. Perfectly polite, I couldn't fault the woman's manners.

"Ainslie, this is Mal's new girlfriend, Anne. Anne, this is

Ainslie." Fucking great, even Ev knew her. This one was a regular. What had happened to never seeing him with the same woman twice?

"Girlfriend?" Ainslie laughed uncertainly, eyes darting around the group. No one laughed with her. Christ on a crutch, this was awkward.

Mal stepped closer. "I was just saying hi to a friend. What's the big deal?"

"There isn't one. It's fine."

"Yeah, there obviously is or you wouldn't be looking at me like that," he said, his tone fierce and pissed off. Like I was inconveniencing him or something.

"You need to not talk to me in that tone of voice," I said. "Especially not in front of other people. Go out with your friend, have a nice time. We can discuss this later."

"We can, huh?"

"Yes."

Ainslie took a big step back. Poor woman.

But Mal looked around the group, pissed and confused. A vein looked about ready to pop in his neck. "Fuck it."

He turned and strode back toward the stage, barking an order for sticks at one of the roadies. Soon the pounding of drums once again filled the warehouse. Everyone was looking somewhere else. What a clusterfuck.

Davie looked to Jimmy. His brother nodded, wandering off also in the direction of the stage. Ben followed while Ainslie just sort of drifted back toward the record company people.

"Crap, I forgot." Ev grabbed at her head dramatically as if struck by a sudden thought. "We women all have to go meet Lauren. Girl's night out."

"You do?" asked David.

"Yep." She gave him a piercing look. "We're starting early."

He got the drift. "Right. Yeah."

I don't remember much about us leaving. Between Ev and Lizzy, I was hustled out of there damn fast to a big black Escalade waiting outside. The beefy, bald man standing beside it was strangely familiar.

"Hi," I said. "Didn't you put the bolt on my door the other day?"

"Yes, ma'am."

"That's Sam. Sam, this is Anne. She's one of us." Ev slid into the backseat and buckled up, while Lizzy jumped in the front. She bounced her butt up and down on the plush leather. It was good to know someone was enjoying the lap of luxury. I could have given two shits if we were in some smelly old cab.

"Lovely to meet you, ma'am," said Sam. "Good to see you as always, Mrs. Ferris."

I climbed in and buckled up.

"I don't understand," said Lizzy.

"About?" I asked.

Lizzy twisted in her seat so she could see me. "This. He makes you happier than I've ever seen. It's like you're a different person. He looks at you like you invented whipped cream. Now this. I don't understand."

I shrugged trying my best to keep my face calm, neutral. "Whirlwind romance. Easy come, easy go."

"I'm going to need a rusty shovel, Sam," said Ev.

"I'll get right on that, Mrs. Ferris." He pulled out of the parking lot.

"Excellent. We better go pick up Lauren. She'll want to be included in this."

"And what is this?" I asked. "We're not really doing girl's night out are we?"

Her face let me know that hell yes we were.

"You know, I'm not really in the mood right now. But that's very sweet of you."

"Sam?" Ev sang out almost merrily.

"Yes, Mrs. Ferris?"

"If I needed your help kidnapping our Anne here and making her drink with me, would that be a problem?"

"Of course not, Mrs. Ferris. Anything for you."

"You sweet dear man," she cooed. "You know he used to be a Navy SEAL. I wouldn't mess with him, but you do whatever you feel you need to, Anne."

"You're kind of evil when you get going." I stared out the window, letting the scenery slip by.

Ev held her peace. For all of a moment. "I don't know what the hell Mal was thinking back there letting that skank climb all over him."

Lizzy snorted. "I'm not sure he was thinking."

Me, neither. But I didn't say that.

The truth was, Mal and I might have broken up. Our fake relationship could be over. Who knew? What a truly god-awful horrible fucking notion. I blinked profusely. Must have had something in my eye. Honestly, I wasn't the crying type. So my crush had been crushed. Life goes on. Whatever Lizzy knew, or thought she knew, she wouldn't say a word. And me, I had no comment to make on the subject.

Nothing.

Though, this was exactly why getting overly attached to people wasn't smart. If there was a chance their absence would make things heartrending, walk away. No one should have the power to make you want to throw some manic-depressive episode and swallow a truckload of gin (my mom's favorite method for dealing with such disappointments). I guess you needed to learn these lessons over sometimes. Well, I had it now. All good.

Mal didn't come home Sunday night. Not that my apartment was home, but you know what I mean.

Despite the drinks poured into me, I didn't get much sleep.

CHAPTER FIFTEEN

By the time I fired off the fifth text for the day, lunchtime had come and gone.

> Anne: I can drop your stuff at David & Ev's if you want.
> Just let me know.

Like the previous ones, this text garnered no response. Zip. Nada. Nothing. I couldn't help myself. I had to try again.

> Anne: I hope we can still be friends.

The minute I sent it regret swamped me. It was such a dumb-ass standard boring thing to say. Why didn't smartphones come with an "undo" button? Now that would be an app worth having. I should've tried to be more original. Maybe if I'd been funny about it, thrown in something witty about his drum kit or something, he'd respond. But again I got nothing.

"Still texting him?" asked Reece from where he was busy reshuffling books in the action/adventure section.

"Mm-hmm."

"No response yet?"

"No."

Worst Monday ever. I'd managed to talk Reece into letting me tidy up out back all morning, thus eliminating any need for conversation. With only two, maybe three, hours of sleep under my belt, I wasn't human. Not really. I was a nasty, bitchy, ball of heartache. Had Ainslie soothed Mal's man pain? Images of them entangled filled my head. I'd seen almost all of his body, so the details were vivid.

Yes, my delicate little feelings had been well and truly hurt. Thank god Mal left when he did. Any more time together and I'd have become completely devastated when he went on tour.

Still nothing from my cell. I checked it twice just to be sure.

He was right on with the Fatal Attraction. So far I'd only stalked him via text, though. Lucky he'd kept his dick in his pants. His mere presence had inspired me enough. The thought that I might lose him entirely made me want to both burst into tears and break shit (preferably over his head). Anger and sadness owned me.

How many days had it been since I met him? Not many.

"Fucking ridiculous."

"What did you say?" asked Reece, casting a nervous eye toward the hipster couple browsing in home renovation.

Crap. "Nothing. Nothing. Sorry."

Reece approached the counter. I kept pounding on the computer keyboard regardless, pretending to process invoices. Maybe if I ignored him he'd go away. A couple of days, and I'd be fine again. Today, however, I kind of needed some space. I didn't want to hear the details about whoever my boss banged over the weekend. Please understand, I wasn't jealous, for once. Or was it twice, now? My crush on Reece had mysteriously (or not so mysteriously) disappeared. Mal Ericson fever was a potent thing.

"You're really upset about this guy, aren't you?" he asked, sounding like the concept defied logic.

"I don't really want to talk about it, Reece."

"Listen." He sighed, bracing his hands on the counter. "How about I take you out tonight for a few drinks? There's a new bar down in Chinatown. We can check it out."

"That's really great of you. But how about another night?"

"You got plans?"

"Sort of." Because sitting alone brooding while wearing one of Mal's T-shirts constituted plans.

Reece rubbed his chin with the palm of his hand, his brows drawing downward. "Anne, realistically, you had to know this was coming. He's Malcolm Ericson. The guy's a living legend."

"Yeah, I know." My shoulders caved in on me. In standard measurement, I stood about two-feet tall. I couldn't have felt any smaller.

"Guys like that don't have a reputation for stable relationships."

"I, ah . . . I get that. I do."

"Hey, you're great. It's his loss."

"Thanks."

Ugh. The pity in Reece's eyes . . . kill me now. A bottle of tequila was now included in tonight's plans. Rock on. This was why I never much bothered with dating, this whole moment right here. Penises were out and self-love was back in. Not that it had ever really left.

I needed to put my life back into context. Mal was the one being a jerk. I'd done nothing wrong. Except for having no idea how to handle a difficult situation, of course.

"Guess we should get back to work." I wasn't really achieving much, but still, a token effort should be made what with him paying me and all.

Reece crossed and uncrossed his arms, watching me. "Listen, why don't you take the rest of the day off? I'll close up."

"Really?"

"Yeah." He smiled, dimples popping. "God knows I owe you some hours. You've never even taken a sick day."

"Thanks, Reece."

My big old claw foot tub was the best place in whole wide world. Nothing could compare. Life seemed so much better from within its warm, soapy watery confines. If I ever had to move, it's what I'd miss the most. I'd been in there, soaking, for a good solid half hour. Frankly, I had no plans to ever get out. I was perfectly content to laze around, staring at the tiles on the wall and thinking of nothing.

Raging, great open seas full of nothing.

Right up until the front door crashed open. I bolted upright, adrenaline pumping through me.

"What the fuck?"

"Anne?" Mal yelled.

Then the bathroom door crashed open too. I grabbed the white towel hanging off the rail overhead, holding it against my chest. Straightaway, the material started soaking up water.

"Anne." Mal stomped in, electric with rage. It spiked out his hair and darkened his eyes. The bathroom door slammed shut behind him.

"Mal?"

"What is this?" he growled, shoving his cell in my face.

"Um, your phone? What the hell are you doing in here?"

"The fucking texts you've been sending me, I mean."

"What?" I stared at him, flabbergasted. "Get out."

"No."

"You want to discuss my texts, you can wait till I'm out of the tub and have some clothes on."

"We'll discuss them now."

For this conversation, I needed armor. The damn towel wasn't working at all. I crossed my arms over my chest, huddling in on myself. "Those messages are me trying to be friendly after yesterday. You barging in here like this, though? I'm not feeling so friendly anymore. Get the fuck out, Mal."

"You're breaking up with me by text." Not a question, a statement. One that made me just a small part livid, though the crashing of doors and yelling might have played a part in it too.

Was he insane? No, seriously, was he?

"That little asswipe Reece push you into this?"

"No," I snapped. "Reece has nothing to do with this. And I can't really be breaking up with you because remember the part where we were never really together? Where it was all fake?"

"It was, huh?" He squatted beside the tub, hands gripping the edge so hard his knuckles whitened.

"Get out."

"I'm not going anywhere till we talk this out."

The vestiges of self-pity disappeared, replaced by flat-out rage. How dare he?

"If you want to talk this out, then you might want to stop acting like a dick. Busting in here and yelling at me, accusing me of crap . . . not smart."

"That right? Why don't you tell me what I'm supposed to do since I'm not so smart and all." He loomed over the side of the tub, eyes bordering on manic. "Tell me how I'm supposed to handle this, Anne. And use small words, okay?"

I tried to sit up, the water sloshing. Could he have picked a more awkward time and place for this? And how had *he* turned into the victim here?

170 | KYLIE SCOTT

"I didn't mean . . ." I started, but gah, fuck him. If he wanted to get all insulted, he could, with my compliments. I cleared my throat, tried again. "Big picture. You didn't come home . . . back here, to the apartment last night. I assume you were with Ainslie. Your friends are probably going to know that, right? So our cover is blown."

"I wasn't with Ainslie," he ground out.

Everything stopped. "You weren't?"

"No; I played drums till I calmed down, then I did some drinking with the guys. Davie said to give you some time to cool off. I crashed in Ben's hotel suite."

"Word to the wise, next time when it comes to us, try talking to me instead of Davie."

He let out a slow breath. "Okay."

"You just crashed in Ben's suite?" This version of reality differed so wildly from the hateful version I'd been playing in my head. It wouldn't sink in at first.

"Yeah, I did." His dark green gaze roamed my face. "I didn't think when Ainslie came up to me after practice. How it would look and everything. Didn't think at all and then I didn't handle it right."

He paused, but I had nothing. It was all I could do not to burst into tears of relief. Not that I was a crier. I'd blame it on PMS but it was nowhere near my time of the month.

"I fucked up and I hurt you," he said, deflating. "I'm sorry."

"Oh, no, you didn't hurt me." I held my eyes wide open, trying to keep my shit together. "I mean, it might have been nice if you'd answered one of my texts but . . . yeah, no, I wasn't *hurt* exactly."

His brows rose and for a moment, he said nothing. "You looked hurt."

"Well, I wasn't. I was fine."

He just watched me.

"Really."

The smudges were back beneath his eyes. It seemed Mal hadn't gotten any more sleep last night than I had.

"Everything's good," I said, not believing it but hoping he did. Meanwhile, I was still bare-ass naked in the bath, horribly exposed. "Now can you please leave?"

Mal's brows rose. "You're alright?"

"Yep. There's the door."

"I didn't hurt you?"

"Noooo."

"Okay," he said eventually, thumb rapping out a beat on the edge of the tub. "So the deal is still on and everything's cool?"

"Sure, I guess so. Why not?" I gave him my very best big, brave smile, clutching the wet towel to my breasts, my knees drawn up to help cover downstairs.

He breathed out hard through his nose, sat back on his heels. This was good. He was accepting it and we were moving on, thank god.

"We're fine. No worries."

Then he slowly shook his head. "Christ, Anne. You're so full of shit I don't even know what the fuck to say to you right now."

"What?" My screech bounced off the tiled walls, echoing around us.

"You heard me."

"But—"

His hand held firm to the back of my neck and he slammed his mouth down on mine. My words were forgotten. His tongue slid into my mouth, teasing me. His hand cradled my head, holding me out of the water. I gave myself up to it, the demanding press of his lips and the scratch of his stubble. I angled my head, getting closer, going deeper and pulling him into me. If I drowned, it'd be worth it.

There was no finesse. Raw hunger took over.

I didn't realize he'd started climbing into the tub with me until half the water sloshed over the sides. No more of this splashing nonsense, we made a god damn waterfall. He got in, jeans, T-shirt, Chucks and all, his legs tangling with mine. One strong arm wrapped around my waist, holding me to him, the other he braced on the top of the tub. Someone had to keep us afloat because I was too busy getting my hands beneath his T-shirt. I could've kissed him for days, but getting him naked was important.

"Off," I demanded, dragging the material up.

"Hang on." He pulled back onto his knees. With one of his hands and two of mine, we got rid of that sucker.

The feel of his hot skin and hard flesh was so fine. My fingers couldn't travel far enough fast enough. I wanted to learn every inch of him. My mouth found his again and *yes*. I groaned and he clutched me harder. We were pressed together, skin on skin for the most part. My pebbled nipples rubbed against his chest.

Fuck yeah, friction.

Friction was beautiful, but wet denim sucked. I wiggled a hand under the back of his waistband, grabbing onto his tight ass. His hips flexed, pushing against me, grinding into me. There was every chance the bath wasn't big enough for this. We'd make do. My elbow clocked the side, vibrating my funny bone. It hurt like a bitch. He must've noticed, because the next thing I knew we were rolling. More water cascaded out onto the floor.

"On top," he grunted.

" 'Kay."

His hands slid over my skin, trying to keep hold. "Fuck, you're slippery."

The man knew how to use his body. All I could do was hold on, my hands tangled in his long hair. His mouth traveled over my collarbone, up my neck, finishing with his teeth at my jaw. Every inch of my skin broke out in goose bumps. My tummy tensed. A large hand palmed my ass, squeezing. Wet denim wasn't so bad after all. Grinding my pussy against the ridge his hard-on made felt rather nice. Not as nice as he'd feel bare, but still.

"You hear that?" he asked.

"What? No." The only thing I could hear was my heart pounding. And anyway, who cared? Now wasn't the time for listening. It was the time to feel and I felt fucking fantastic sitting astride him. Luckily I knew how to prioritize. I fit my lips to his, kissing him deep and wet.

He broke away, turning his head aside. "Wait," he said, followed shortly by, "shit."

Distantly, from ever so far away (like the next room), there it was.

"Malcolm? Honey?" It was a woman's voice, accompanied by several sets of feet. We had company.

What on earth?

"Mom?" he answered, his face skewed with disbelief.

Oh shit, he'd left the front door open.

"We got an earlier flight," his mom called. And for the record, she sounded like a very nice woman. But shit, I didn't want to meet her like this. What a wonderful first impression.

"You did?" asked Mal.

"That's not a problem, is it?"

"Your parents are visiting?" I queried in a furious whisper. "Right now?"

He squeezed his eyes shut and whispered back, "Did I forget to mention that?"

"Mal? Honey?" his Mom called. "Everything okay?"

"No, no. Not a problem at all, Mom. Everything's good."

"We were just so excited when you told us about Anne."

"She is pretty damn exciting." He gave my breasts a long look. "Got to agree with you there."

"We really wanted to just get here and meet her. I guess we should have warned you."

His grin was pure evil. Hell itself would have been jealous. "Oh, you want to meet Anne? Because she's right—"

I slapped my hand over his mouth. "Don't you fucking dare," I hissed.

Crap, the things he thought were amusing might just get one of us killed. In this situation, it was most definitely his life on the line. Despite the laughter in his eyes, he nodded, pressing a kiss to the palm of my hand. Slowly, I removed it, my eyes narrowed on him.

"What was that?" asked his mom.

"I was just saying she'll be home from work soon, Mom."

"Wonderful."

"Sorry," he mouthed to me, laughing silently.

"Asshole," I mouthed back.

He grabbed the back of my head, bringing my lips to his. If only I didn't love kissing him so much.

"Son," a deep voice said from the other room.

"Hi, Dad." Mal rested his forehead on my shoulder. "Don't come in."

"No, no. We won't do that."

"There's a lot of water on the floor," his mom said, matter-of-factly. "Aren't you a bit old to be splashing around like this? What on earth were you doing? Where does Anne keep her mop?"

"Kitchen cabinet," I whispered.

"Ah, kitchen cabinet, Mom. Thanks. Guess I got carried away." Mal rested his head against the back of the tub. He rolled his eyes to the side, checking out the floor. "Look what you did, young lady."

"You're the one that climbed into my tub," I replied quietly. Sure enough, the bathroom was pretty much flooded. Water had spread across the floor, a stream of it leading out beneath the door and into the living room. "What a mess. We better clean this up."

"Sorry, pumpkin. I don't mind picking up my shit and all, but I'm a rock star. Rock stars don't mop. It's just not done."

"You help make the mess, you help clean it up. Boundaries, Mal."

"You don't understand." He shut his eyes, face tight with fake despair. "These are the hands of an artist. Would you expect Bonham to mop?"

"Who?" I asked in confusion.

"John Bonham."

"Right. Well . . . if John Bonham got water on the floor, yes, I would expect him to mop."

"Well, he can't. He's dead."

I cocked my head. "What . . . who are we even talking about?"

"You don't know who John Bonham is?" Mal asked, his voice rising.

"Shh. Your parents are going to hear us."

"Sorry. But c'mon, pumpkin, you have to know who Bonham is. You're fucking with me, right?"

"Sorry."

"Ah, man," he sighed, shaking his head slowly, mournfully. "I'm not sure I can stick my dick in a woman who doesn't even know who John Bonham is."

" 'Stick your dick in'?" I asked, my brows probably touching. "Did you actually just say that?"

"Make love. I meant make love . . . of course. I would never just stick my dick in you. I would make mad, passionate love to this sweet, sweet body of yours for days, no, weeks. It would be beautiful, pumpkin. There'd be little angels, and birdies, and you know . . . all just hanging around, watching. Perverts."

"Right. You are so full of shit." I smiled, cautiously, climbing to my feet.

"What about Kerslake, you know him? How about Wilk, never heard of Wilk?"

"I know Grohl. He's great."

"Oh, no. Fuck, honey. Not Dave Grohl. I mean, he's a good guy and there were flashes of definite genius back in the Nirvana days, sure." His hands slid from my waist down the sides of my thighs, holding me steady. "Whoa, where'd they go?"

"Hmm? Mal, stop."

He stared straight at my sex, studying it. A little line sat between his brows. Deep down inside, I could live without him doing that right now. The man's parents were on the other side of the door. The woman who'd given birth to him was busy cleaning up the mess we'd made. So not the time to be getting familiar with me. Quizzing me on famous drummers could probably also wait.

"Can you not, please? And where'd what go?" I threw a leg over the side of the bath, stepping down carefully onto the slippery floor. Getting the hell away from his overly intrusive eyes. My robe hung on the back of the bathroom door, fortunately. I hadn't thought to bring in a change of clothes and my work wear sat in a soggy heap in the corner.

"Your pubes," he said, angst filling his voice. "Where are they?"

"I wax."

His nose wrinkled up in obvious disgust. "Well, stop it. I want cute carrot-colored pubic hair like on the top of your head. I deserve it."

I bit back a smile. "You've given this a lot of thought, haven't you?"

"It's been almost a week. I had to have something to beat off to."

"You've been masturbating to the thought of me?" I asked, thrilled. Clapping would probably be uncool, plus his parents might hear.

"Do I have a dick, Anne?" Mal climbed out, water running out of his soaked jeans, flowing out of his Chucks. What a beautiful wet disheveled mess.

"Given the size of the bulge in the front of your jeans, I'm going to answer yes to that question, Malcolm."

"Then, yeah, of course I've given this a lot of thought. I've been thinking about your pussy constantly, what it looks like, what it tastes like, how it'll feel." He towered over me, half naked and dripping wet. The dripping-wet part was definitely going around. "Why do you think I was on Ben's couch last night? No one else I wanna fuck. It's gotta be you."

"Wow," I whispered.

"You gonna give me shit about not being romantic like you did last time?"

"Nope."

"Nope?" His fingers toyed with the collar of my robe. Not undoing it, just hanging on.

I gripped the waist of his jeans and lifted my face, pressing my lips to his. "All I heard was blah blah I've been thinking about you constantly. Blah blah it's got to be you. It was perfect, pure romance."

He grinned. "You're crazy."

"We might have that in common, yes."

"I definitely need you to know I have a dick." He rubbed his lips over my jawline, making me shiver.

"Show it to me later?"

"Since you asked so nicely." He drew back slightly. "Shit, we're not going to start acting all nauseating like Davie and Ev are we?"

"Isn't that how we're supposed to be behaving?"

"Yeah, but it was funny while we were faking it. If we're doing it for real . . ." He left the thought hanging.

My lust cooled significantly, chilling me. Because *for real* meant people getting hurt. And *people getting hurt* most likely meant me. It might also mean him, yes. But the odds were not in my favor. I already knew how much it would sting when our fake relationship ended. But a real relationship? That would be so much worse.

"I, um . . . why don't we just take it easy? See how it goes," I said.

"Can't stop now." He rested his forehead against mine. "We really fucking need to have sex, Anne."

"Yes. But things don't have to change if we start sleeping together."

"They don't?"

"No. It'll be fine." God didn't smite me. Who knew, it could even be the truth.

"Cool," he said, cocky grin back in full force. He held one big hand aloft, waiting for me to high-five him. "Damn, we're good."

I slapped our palms together, before slipping my fingers between his and holding on tight. "We so are."

CHAPTER SIXTEEN

When it came to his parents' visit, Mal went all out.

He threw on dry clothes and mopped out the bathroom while I hid in the tub behind the curtain. All in all, he got his parents out of the apartment quite quickly. I heard his mom asking about my decimated bed (because the bedroom doors were wide open too). Our on-and-off, real-and-fake relationship was slowly destroying my apartment and its contents. Though hopefully the water spillage hadn't done too much damage.

Mal mumbled an explanation about the bed and his father changed the topic of conversation. What the hell had he told them? Now they probably thought I was some sort of sex fiend, knowing him. Though the real reason, that we'd been jumping on the bed like a pair of idiots, wasn't something I wanted his parents knowing either.

I got dried and finished up the mopping. Fifteen minutes later Mal texted me.

Mal: Car will b there in 15
Anne: Where are we going?
Mal: Surprise
Anne: I don't like surprises. Where are we going?

Anne: Answer me or I will hurt you while you sleep. I need
      to know what to wear etc
Mal: Wear nothing
Anne: . . . Try again
Mal: Restaurant in town. Wear a skirt
Mal: Plz?
Anne: Your wish is my command
Mal: HAHA I fucking wish

I stood on the curb, freezing my knees off in the bitter cold wind. Also panicking ever so slightly about what his parents would think of me, barely educated and broke. Then a sleek stretch limousine pulled up.

Oh, wow.

My eyes had to be as wide as the wheels. This was a first for me. I'd missed out on prom. I'd missed out on a lot of things. My first boyfriend had moved on to someone who had time to go to games and after-parties.

A young man in a snazzy gray suit and hat stepped out.

"Miss Rollins?" he asked.

"Yes." I pulled open the door, eager to check out the inside. Then paused. "Crap. I was supposed to let you do that, wasn't I?"

"That's alright, miss." He took up his position by the door, waiting for me to get in. Luckily my skirt went to my knees. Given the size of the vehicle, there wasn't really any dainty way to make an entrance.

Glossy leather and a shining crystal decanter and glasses set greeted me. Talk about luxury. The limo dropped me at an upmarket steak place in the Pearl District. We always seemed to end up in that part of town. I'd never been to the restaurant before, but I'd heard all about it. Once upon a time, Reece had taken a woman there in hopes of impressing her. It did the job.

This place reeked of style, with its red booths and low lighting. Honestly, the lighting fixtures looked more like art installations. There were these giant, sparkly orb-type things. I really needed one for home just as soon as I made my first million.

I mentioned Mal's name and the cool guy acting as the host gave me several once-overs. Though I guess after the first time, the look ceased to be a once-over and turned plain rude.

"Whenever you're ready," I said, not bothering with friendly.

Mal was sitting with his back to the room, his hair in a short ponytail. Asking him if his mom had made him tidy it up was tempting but in any teasing war of words, I usually wound up the loser. My nerves were frayed enough from meeting his parents so I kept my mouth shut and admired the cut of his cheekbones.

"Here she is." The pride in Mal's voice both startled and warmed me in turn. He slid out of the booth and put an arm around my waist. "Mom, Dad, this is Anne."

Mal's mom was petite and her smile lit up her entire face. Neil, Mal's dad, stood at my approach. Tall with golden blond hair, he appeared to have Viking blood in him. It made sense once you'd seen the son.

"Lovely to meet you," I said, trying my best to project bright, bubbly, trustworthy . . . shit like that. I'd never been introduced to a man's parents before. Mal and I were forging new ground. Fingers crossed, I didn't let him down.

His mom held her delicate hand out to me. The bones in her fingers felt fragile, obvious to the touch. "Hi, Anne. I'm Lori. And this is Neil. We're so happy to meet you."

"Hi, Lori. Nice to meet you too."

Pleasantries done with, I slid into the booth, Mal following close behind me. His jeans-clad thigh pressed against the length of mine and a hand covered my bare knee. After dithering around in my wardrobe, I'd gone with a navy long-sleeved top, black skirt and ankle boots. A touch of conservative mixed in with a dash of ass kicking for good measure. Maybe it'd been a poor choice. What did I know about the families of rock stars? Neil wore a dress shirt and tie, Lori a white linen top and pants. I hadn't exactly expected piercings and leather, but white linen? I'd have spilled something on myself within the first two minutes given the way my hands were shaking.

"Hey," Mal said, leaning closer.

I definitely didn't want to fuck this up, but a heavy lump of dread sat in my stomach. Things weren't great with my own mother, so what were the chances I'd manage to charm his? My hands were clammy, sticky with sweat. Honestly, put me in a stressful situation and I could rival a rhino for perspiration issues. Assuming rhino's had perspiration issues.

Mal laid a gentle kiss beneath my ear. "Breathe, pumpkin. All good."

"Yep." I gave him two thumbs up.

"Yeah, okay. Not good." He looked around, held out a hand. A waiter rushed over. "Hi. Can you get her a . . . look, whatever you've got that's potent, okay?"

"How about Rocket Fuel, sir?"

Mal clapped his hands together. "Why, that sounds delightful! Excellent, Rocket Fuel it is. Make it a double."

The waiter's eyes went wide. "Uh, yes, sir."

Photos had been spread across the table, a veritable sea of blond-haired babies. Chubby faces and starfish hands were abundant. Lori gave me another warm smile. "These are all our grandchildren."

"I didn't realize Mal was an uncle."

"Eight times over, sweetie." His mother started pointing out faces, naming names. Given his three sisters were such prolific breeders I made a mental note to stock up on condoms. Wherever he and I were at, we definitely weren't ready for Mal Junior, despite his joking. I didn't even know if I wanted to have children. They fell firmly under the "maybe someday" label.

Lori's anecdotes about her grandchildren saw us right through ordering and dinner. She talked while we all ate. Sips of Rocket Fuel loosened me up considerably. So far as I could taste, it consisted of every kind of white liquor with a dash of lemonade. The drink should probably be either illegal or set on fire to burn off some of the alcohol. I laid off it after an inch or two, leaving it for Mal. He stole from my plate and sipped from my drink and I loved it, the intimacy and sense of togetherness. It probably was just plain old thievery but the way he did it, fake distracting me with a smile or wink, made the game worthwhile.

I was so easy for him.

"So you have three older sisters," I said. "You know, I can definitely see you as the youngest child."

His mother guffawed. She might have been little but she laughed big. It spoke well of Mal's childhood. The adoration in her eyes when she looked at her son just backed it up. I couldn't even remember what my mom sounded like laughing. It'd been too long.

"Why?" Mal asked, glaring at me down the length of his nose. "Are you saying I'm loud and immature? Because it's just plain rude to point that shit out, pumpkin."

His mother cleared her throat in an obvious language warning.

Mal sat with his arm stretched across the back of our bench. He'd put on a black Henley to cover his tats, and a dry pair of Chucks. I tried not to look at him too long, terrified of going crazy eyed in front of his parents. Memories of what we'd gotten up to in the bath simmered too near the surface.

"Explain yourself," he ordered.

"All I'm saying is that you're a natural performer. It just makes sense you'd be the youngest."

"Right." He cocked a brow, his gaze shifting to his folks. His hand, however, shifted higher on my leg, sliding up beneath my skirt. I grabbed hold of his fingers, squeezing them hard in warning, before he could make a move for anything important. Only a quirk of his smile betrayed him. "Anne's the oldest. You should see how she is with her sister, Mom. Protective doesn't cover it. I'm surprised the girl isn't bubble wrapped."

His mother smothered a smile.

"I am not overly protective," I said. "She's twenty. She's an adult now. I respect that."

"Do you?" Damn, I liked him teasing me. I liked the familiarity in his gaze. "Ben said he was afraid for his life when you caught him checking her out. He was wondering if he needed to protect the family jewels."

Lori made another admonishing noise at the mention of testicles but Mal just charged on. "He said you looked ready to annihilate him."

This information I liked much less.

"He talked about Lizzy?" My eyes narrowed, all good humor long gone. I didn't even want Ben Nicholson to know she existed. "She's too young for him. She needs to be concentrating on school."

"Relax, momma bear. So happens, I agree." Mal smiled broadly, rubbing the back of my neck, soothing me instantly. Christ, his hands. As much as I liked his parents, hopefully this wouldn't be a long, drawn-out dinner. Short and sweet was the way to go. Mal and I had things to do.

"We'll keep Benny boy away from your baby sister," he promised quietly. "Don't worry."

"What about your mother, Anne?" asked Lori. "Where is she?"

I flinched and Mal's fingers paused against my neck. I didn't need to see what look he was giving me. What I needed was to move the conversation onward and upward. "She's, um . . . she's back in So Cal. She's fine."

"And your father?"

"He left. Many years ago." It was better than saying "Fuck knows." And why sugarcoat it, right? Facts were facts. I picked up my remaining half slice of sourdough bread, nibbled at the crust. It was nice but I was full. We needed something neutral to talk about but the now-empty dinner plate offered no inspiration. My brain wouldn't cough up a damn thing.

"You two staying for the first few tour dates?" asked Mal. I could have kissed his feet for the save.

"We'll see," said his dad.

"Of course we will. At least the first," Lori corrected. "We love seeing you and the boys play. How are they all? Jimmy feeling better?"

"He's good, Mom. They're all doing good. Davie wants to introduce you to Ev as soon as possible."

His mom happy sighed. "I would love to meet her. I always knew David would settle down first. He's such a sensitive soul, more so than the rest of you."

"I'm sensitive. I'm nothing but a big ball of mushy sensitive stuff inside. Tell her, pumpkin."

"Your son is very sensitive," I dutifully recited.

"That didn't sound believable." He gently tugged on a strand of my hair, moving in closer. "My feelings are hurt. You've wounded me. Kiss it better."

"Apologies." I gave him a brief but sweet kiss on the lips.

"That the best you got?" He rubbed his lips against mine, trying to lure me in deeper. "You should be ashamed of yourself. I think you can do much, much better than that. Why, you missed my mouth entirely."

"Later," I whispered, doing my best to keep things below an R rating in front of his parents. But damn, it was hard.

"Promise?"

"Yes."

"Such a pity you weren't home when we dropped by your place earlier, Anne," said Lori. "But you have a lovely little apartment."

"Thank you."

"Malcolm just needs to stop breaking your furniture and causing floods."

Mal groaned. "A man needs to be free to bounce on beds and bathe as he sees fit, Mother."

"You're twenty-seven years old, honey."

"And?"

"Isn't it time to start acting like a grown-up?"

"I pay my bills, see to my responsibilities. Beyond that, does it really matter?" Mal sat up straighter, staring his mom down with a smile. You couldn't help but get the feeling they'd had this conversation many times before.

"Funny," said Neil, talking for the first time in forever. "Could've sworn I heard two voices in that bathroom."

"Thin walls," Mal and I both said at once. Yeah, my smile . . . I highly doubt it was even the tiniest bit believable. Excellent.

His dad grunted.

Lori tried to cover her smile by dabbing her lips with the napkin.

Shit. We were so busted.

"Eat more, hon." Neil pushed Lori's plate closer to her. The rest of us had wolfed the excellent food down, but Lori had barely touched hers.

"I'm not all that hungry." She patted his hand.

The fingers rubbing my neck froze.

"But . . ." Neil leaned in, whispering in her ear.

After a moment Lori shut him down with a quick kiss. She put on a bright smile, a fake one. It was an expression I knew well. Hers wasn't bad, but it still jarred. I guess I hadn't expected it from her. What was going on here? Of course, there could be a hundred and one explanations. Couples fight.

A rousing rendition of "Happy Birthday" broke out on the opposite side of the room. A large group of people around Lizzy's age were starting to get seriously loud. The host on the front desk watched them with wary eyes.

"Malcolm, you have to bring Anne home for the party so she can meet your sisters," she said. "We're having a big family get-together next week in Coeur d'Alene and you both have to be there. It's between the Seattle and Chicago shows, so the boys all have time to come."

"That's where you're from?" I asked Mal without thinking. A real girlfriend would know these things. But Mal and I hadn't gotten around to discussing normal everyday stuff yet. Though the past wasn't a topic I tended to encourage. Fortunately, Lori didn't appear to be concerned.

"Yeah." He nodded, eyes fixed on his dad.

"What's it like?" I asked.

His gaze stayed on his parents and he wasn't smiling. "Trees, lake, a couple of good bars. It's nice enough."

"It's lovely, especially in fall," said Lori enthusiastically. "You have to come, Anne."

"I'll see what I can do." I moved restlessly in my seat. Something had changed. Both Mal and his father seemed subdued, preoccupied. Neither would meet my eyes. The atmosphere in the booth had cooled and I didn't understand why.

"You'll make sure she comes, won't you, sweetie?" Lori reached over and squeezed Mal's hand, ignoring whatever weirdness had come over the table. If anything her smile was larger than before, like she was making up for the lack. "We'll have a wonderful time showing you around."

"Sure," Mal said, his voice hollow. Someone had flicked a switch and turned him off. He simply wasn't there anymore. I recognized that too.

"We better get back to the hotel," announced Neil. "Don't want to get tired out."

Lori smiled glumly. "I suppose so. Say, do you think it's really haunted, Anne? I saw something about a ghost tour. Wouldn't that be a blast?"

"It sure would."

From his pocket, Mal pulled out his mobile and fired off a text. "They're bringing the car around."

His arm disappeared from around my shoulders and he slid out of the booth. Suddenly, a pair of girls, maybe eighteen years old, appeared out of thin air. Mal took a step back as if startled.

"Oh my god, we thought it was you," gushed the first, giggling.

"We're your biggest fans."

"Ah, hey. Thanks." Mal took the pen they held out and signed their napkins, notebooks, and whatever else. His hand was a blur. Clearly, he'd done this a million times or more. I climbed out after him as Neil helped Lori, his hand to her elbow.

Heads turned and soon more people from the rowdy table joined the two girls circling Mal. The crowd gathered incredibly fast. Flashes went off, blinding me, and I raised a hand to guard my eyes from the glare. There were two, three people between me and him now. Hands pushed me aside and I stumbled into the end of a table, hitting it hard with my hip. A glass smashed on the floor at my feet and suddenly Mal was there.

"You okay?" he asked, steadying me.

"Yes. It just caught me by surprise." If anything, I was embarrassed.

"Let's go." He tucked me in against his side as people around us started to complain and press in once more. One guy tried to shove his phone number at Mal. Mal ignored him, moving us through the crowd mostly by force. When someone yelled right in my face, my heart went boom and I broke out in a cold sweat. These people were fucking insane, well off or not. What would have happened if he'd been recognized at a fast-food joint?

We rushed out of the restaurant, shouts coming from behind us. Neil ushered Lori into the limousine, and we followed fast behind. Hands hammered on the windows as the driver struggled to close the door without maiming anyone. A minute later the limo pulled out into traffic and I could breathe again. We were on our way.

No one said anything and the silence was killing me. Even Lori could only raise a thin smile, apparently running out of steam as Neil had predicted. In the rush to get in, Mal hadn't wound up sitting beside me. A pity; I could have done with some hand holding.

"That was exciting," I said.

"Mostly they're content to just look. But now and then they get carried away," said Lori. "Don't let it scare you, Anne."

No one spoke again.

She kissed me on the cheek before climbing out of the limo once we reached the hotel. The mood from dinner hadn't shifted. I stared at Mal, willing him to look at me. He hadn't had time to shave, and the hint of a beard framed his jaw, his mouth. The need to kiss him, to cover the distance between us, made my heart race.

"Are you alright?" I asked.

"Yeah. You?" he asked, sitting across from me on the seat stretching along the back. He was the picture of cool, calm, and disconnected. "Sorry about the scene at the restaurant."

"I'm fine. Not a big deal."

He scrubbed his face with his hands. "It happens."

"The food was wonderful. Thanks for inviting me."

"Mm."

"Your parents were lovely. I really like your mom."

"Great."

"Your dad was nice too."

He nodded, staring off at nothing.

"No, seriously, Mal. What's wrong?" I blurted out. We needed to go home and get back in the bath. Things had been better there.

"Nothing."

This conversation sucked. Somewhere along the line, things had turned to shit and I had no idea how to salvage them. I lacked the skills.

I so badly wanted to go sit beside him, but something held me back. For some reason, I wasn't sure of my welcome. Tonight was meant to be the night, skin on skin, sweaty sex, the whole shebang. Now I wasn't so sure. Not about whether I wanted him or not, because I did, the need I had for him made me a fool-hardy mess. I just didn't want to be there alone.

Outside, it started to rain.

"I'm going to go play the drums for a while," he asked. "I'll drop you back at the apartment first."

"There's a practice session tonight?"

His smile didn't even get close to his eyes. "No. I just feel like hitting the drums."

"You didn't want to come home with me?" I asked, and he knew to what I was referring; he had to know.

Mal shrugged.

Oh, no. No way. He did not just shrug off us finally having sex. This was not a situation where ambivalence could be considered cool in any way, shape, or form. The limo pulled into the nighttime traffic, awaiting notification of our destination, no doubt.

Mal pulled out his cell and started flipping through the screens. I crossed my arms over my chest. Fine, if that was the way he wanted to play it. Outside, downtown Portland passed us by in all its beauty. The trees in one of the little parks were lit up. Everything glistened in the wet weather. Tiny streams ran down the car windows, obscuring the view.

Fuck it; if he really wanted to go and drum he could just go. Obviously, he wasn't in the mood for company. I opened my mouth to agree to the plan but nothing came out. This wasn't working. Truth was, I could be a stubborn bitch and horny didn't really sit well with me. Might be best if I had some space.

"Can you ask him to pull over?" I pushed a strand of carrot-colored hair out of my face. "There's no need for you to go out of your way. I'll find my own way home. Catch up with you later."

His eyes narrowed. "I'm not dropping you on a street corner in the rain, Anne. I'll take you home."

"Alright. Thanks."

He opened his mouth and then shut it again.

"What?"

He said nothing.

Ugh, avoidance. I knew it so well. I couldn't keep demanding that he share with me when I had no intention of spilling my whole sorry history to him. No one needed to hear that.

Still, we were better than this. Or we should be.

"Fuck this," I muttered.

"What did you say?"

"Fuck. This."

He cocked his head.

"Safety in moving vehicles is highly overrated."

"Wha—"

I crossed to the seat beside him. Then went one better, climbing onto his lap, straddling him. He blinked, his hands hovering over my hips as if unsure where to set down. His cell fell to the side, forgotten apparently. Thank god I'd worn a skirt. It was shortish and made of a stretchy material, useful for so many occasions but particularly this one.

"Anne."

"Mal."

"What's going on?"

"The night isn't ending this way," I told him, perfectly calm. "I won't let it."

He looked at me like I'd started speaking in tongues. Which was actually an excellent idea, given I had no real idea what the problem was here.

I slipped my hands around the back of his neck. Now I got why he always did this, the skin was so soft and warm there. In all honesty, I had no idea what to say; kissing him made much more sense than blurting out the wrong thing again. I brushed my lips against his, plump and perfect. His swift intake of breath was music to my ears. Given half a chance, I could have paid homage to his lips all night. Hooker lips. No other man was this kissable.

"I hate seeing you sad."

We stared at each other, our faces close. Whatever was going on with him, hurting him, it needed to stay away from the here and now. Mal and I had earned this moment. He'd just forgotten it somewhere along the way, gotten sidetracked. Lucky for him, I hadn't.

"Whatever it is, let me fix it. Just for a little while . . ."

I angled my head and kissed him, tracing my tongue over his lips. He tasted wonderful. Already my hips shifted restlessly in his lap, seeking more. I was in heat and it was all his fault, so he'd just have to deal with it. With a groan he gave up and opened his mouth. Fuck, I loved the feel of his tongue, the sweet taste of him. It went straight to my head, making me giddy.

He didn't hesitate. His hands slid up my legs, under my skirt, going straight for the kill, god love him.

"Need something?" he asked, fingers stroking over my thighs.

"You."

"Fuck. Anne." His mouth chased mine, pushing for more, deeper. And holy hell, was I happy to give. The tips of his clever fingers stroked the crotch of my panties, making every corner of me light up in response. If anything stopped us this time, I couldn't be held responsible for my actions.

"Keep doing that," I panted, tugging the tie from his pony-tail to loosen his hair.

"You don't want this instead?" The pad of his thumb pressed against my clit, moving in small circles.

"Oh, god." My head fall back, sensation rushing through me. I was so turned on it was embarrassing. The damp fabric of my panties told the tale. But we'd had days and days of foreplay, really. Long before I'd met him I'd wanted him, though reality far exceeded my expectations. Mal Ericson was my dream come true. The kissathon at David and Ev's, lying awake missing him last night, these things had already pushed me to the edge. Safety and sensible be damned. I'd get as much of him as I could for as long as I could.

"That's it," he murmured.

I pushed forward against his hand, seeking more. He cradled the back of my skull, holding up my head so he could see. "You are so fucking pretty. Have I told you that?"

No idea. And if he expected me to answer, he'd be waiting a while.

"I should've told you that," he said.

I just stared at him, dazed. He was, without a doubt, the most beautiful man I'd ever seen. The elegant lines of his face made me want to write bad poetry. And the sound of his voice, his words, they were all so perfect and good. But then my insides tightened, and there was nothing there to hold on to. I was so horribly empty I ached.

"I need . . ." Forget talking. I started tearing at his belt buckle instead, ripping into the button and zip of his jeans. My thigh muscles burned from gripping him and if the car stopped suddenly I'd be in serious trouble.

"You can have whatever you want, Anne. Just ask for it."

"I want you."

Fingers traced the seam of my sex, making my head swim.

"How do you want me?" he asked, his hand coaxing a moan from me. I rested my cheek against his, lungs struggling for air. "Hmm?"

"Inside me." Words were a hassle and so was his zipper. "Mal, please . . . stop playing with me."

"But you love me playing with you."

I held his face in my hands, my mouth rigid. "Enough."

Just as well I was sitting down, otherwise his smile would have floored me. Arrogant, gorgeous bastard.

"Okay." Mal pulled his hand out from under my skirt. I could have wept for the loss of the lovely pressure. Much more important, however, to get him into me as soon as humanly possible.

"Hop off a sec," he said.

He lifted me aside and pushed down his jeans and underwear, dug a condom out of his pocket. I stopped dead at the sight of his cock, jutting out large and loud. I needed more time to look. How mad would he get if I tried to take a picture? It would be purely for my own personal use, of course.

"Anne," he said, breaking my concentration. "Panties off. Now."

"Right." My skirt had already bunched up around my waist. I hooked my thumbs in either side and shimmied them down, kicking off my ankle boots at the same time. Coordinated and cool I was not, but only getting myself bare from the waist down mattered.

He opened the condom wrapper with his teeth and rolled it on.

"C'mon." Big hands gripped my hips, pulling me back over his lap. I grabbed hold of his shoulders for balance and stared at his face, memorizing him. This moment needed to go down in history with every last detail imprinted for all time. From the curve of his cheekbones and line of his jaw to the small dip in his top lip that I was dying to kiss and lick, I didn't want to forget a thing.

He slipped a finger into me and my muscles spasmed in shock at the intrusion.

"Okay?" he asked, holding still.

I nodded. "Just caught me by surprise."

Slowly, he eased in deeper, making me squirm. Ever so skillfully he worked me higher and higher. His thumb rubbed around my clit while he stroked over some sweet spot inside of me. Someone somewhere had given up the secrets of my pussy; the man knew everything. I couldn't remember anyone ever turning me on so effortlessly.

"Fuck, you feel good, my finger's in heaven."

"Mal, please . . ." I wasn't even sure what I was asking for. I wanted his fingers, his cock, his mouth, his everything. The man made me greedy.

His finger slid out of me, teasing over my lips, spreading me gently open. My pelvis moved of its own accord, grinding against his hand. My moans were so loud the driver had to have heard them despite the divider. Did I care? Nope.

"We're ready," Mal announced.

We so were.

One hand held my hip while the other moved his cock into position. The press of him sliding against my labia had me seeing stars. I didn't know how I'd survive more. Slowly, steadily, I sunk down on him. His nostrils flared as I took him deep. I didn't stop until I sat atop his bare thighs, the hair on his legs tickling me.

"There we go." His focus on me was complete, his gaze searching my face, taking in everything. It left me no room to hide. A problem, given I had the stupidest impulse to burst into tears or something.

Since when did sex mean so much?

"I want to move," I said. But the hands on my waist held me down. The feel of him filling me couldn't be described. It bordered on being too much.

"Wait." He reached up, kissing me soft and slow. "Just gimme a minute. Fucking perfect. Been waiting to feel you for forever."

I rocked against him, getting past desperate.

We were still dressed up top, but oh man, the things we were doing down below.

"Mal," I breathed. "Now."

Fingers dug into my ass, drawing me up his hard length before easing me slowly back down, letting me get used to the feel of his thick cock. That same motion, over and over, again and again, was heaven. The slide of him into me made my blood run red hot. Slow was too good. It melted my mind.

Gradually, I started picking up the pace, his hands helping me along. Faster and harder, I rode him. Nothing could compare to the solid heat of him dragging over sweet places inside of me, turning me liquid. I slammed down onto his hard length, working us both into a frenzy. Sweat slicked our skin. My spine tingled; my whole body was shaking with need. This was life and death and a billion other things I never even knew existed. The tension inside me grew to exquisite gigantic proportions. His thumb slid back and forth over my clit and the whole wide world burst open. My hips bucked and I hid my face against his shoulder as I came hard, biting down through his Henley. A mouthful of cotton tried to muffle the noise escaping my throat.

It went on and on until I fell limp against him, lost and found and everything in between.

Mal groaned, holding me down on his cock. He was growling something. It might have been my name, in which case I appreciated the sentiment. The minute I could, I'd be sure to tell him thanks.

I never wanted to move. Never ever. Or at least, not until the next round.

We sat slumped on the limousine's backseat in silence. Sweat and body fluids glued our thighs and groins together. Every muscle in me trembled. Holy fucking hell. That had been epic.

"You alive?" he asked after a while, brushing my hair back behind my ear.

I gazed up at him, slack jawed and fuck drunk. Best feeling ever. "It was okay, I guess."

Crap, my words were slurred. My tongue had turned thick and dumb.

"Yeah?" He didn't bother to hold back the smile.

"I'm sure you tried your hardest."

"I appreciate the vote of confidence."

I kind of grunted at him in a completely ladylike manner, out of energy.

"Sweetie pie? Pumpkin? You screamed so loud my ears are still ringing. I can't actually hear whatever bullshit you're peddling right now. Tell me later after I get a couple of stitches put in my shoulder, okay?" He chuckled, the sound rumbling through his chest in the nicest way. "A biter and a screamer. And you seem like such a nice, quiet girl. I'm shocked."

I pushed the neck of his shirt aside, inspecting his shoulder. "You're not bleeding. There'll be a bruise at the most."

"I'll wear it with pride."

Damn, he smelled good. The limo should just keep circling the city until it ran out of gas so I could keep breathing him in. Sex and sweat and man.

"Did you still want to go to practice?" I asked, mostly being polite. The desire to keep him all to myself kept my arms around his neck in something close to a strangle hold. But if he wanted to go, I'd go. Orgasms tended to leave me in a pretty benevolent mood. "I could hang out, listen to you play again."

"Fuck, no," he said.

"Fuck, no?"

He snorted, his lips twisted like I was lacking in the mental department. "Home. Bed. Now."

"You got it." I grinned.

CHAPTER SEVENTEEN

We fell out of the limousine, still tugging our clothes into place. Things between my legs were sticky and swollen. Upon reflection, I don't think I'd make a very cowgirl because my thigh muscles still hadn't quite recovered from the ride. I really did need to get back into going to Pilates. A mild bit of muscle strain wasn't wiping the stupid smile off my face, however. More practice was required and odds were, the way Mal kept putting his hands on me, he wouldn't mind.

"There's so many stars. Look how clear it is." I let my head fall back, inspecting the heavens. Fresh from a great orgasm with Mal Ericson at my side, the world was a pretty fucking awesome place.

Mal kissed my chin. He tucked a finger in the waistband of my skirt and towed me toward our apartment building's front door. "C'mon, your shirt looks uncomfortable. You need to get it off."

"But nature, it's beautiful and stuff."

"Your tits are beautiful and stuff. I'm more than willing to spend serious time looking at them. Will that do?"

"Yes."

He laughed.

I fumbled the key in the door, clumsy in my haste. The lock

turned, the door swinging open, slamming into the wall. Crap, what a noise. It echoed through the hall, up the stairs. We really would break the building before we were through. Mrs. Lucia was going to give us hell for being so loud. She lived on the first floor and considered herself the sheriff in these here parts. No one had the nerve to tell her otherwise. But if I had to, I'd pull up my big-girl panties and deal with Mrs. Lucia.

What I didn't know was how to deal with the sight of Reece sitting on the stairs with a bunch of flowers in hand. They were every color of the rainbow. I stumbled to a halt, Mal beside me.

Reece bought me donuts now and then. A bottle of wine when we went out for my birthday or his. He didn't bring me flowers. And he sure as hell didn't sit on my stairs looking forlorn, a lock of hair hanging over his forehead.

"Reece . . ." I climbed the stairs toward him.

Mal stayed put, his hand slipping from my grasp.

The color had fallen out of Reece's face. He looked as white as a blank piece of paper. My and Mal's disheveled state couldn't be interpreted too many different ways. Reece looked like a child who'd lost his favorite toy. I don't think I'd fully appreciated the differences between Mal and him before now. But for all of his joking, Mal was in his head and heart a man. Reece was a boy. I'm not even sure I could explain the distinctions. They simply played in different ways.

"Anne." Reece gave the flowers a perplexed look, like he wasn't quite sure how they'd come to be in his possession. "Didn't realize you'd have company. Sorry."

I silently held my keys out to Mal. His mouth flatlined. He gave me a harsh little shake of the head and I shoved the keys at him. What the hell did he expect me to do? I couldn't just leave Reece sitting on the fucking stairs. Mal stared at me and I stared back, silently willing him to understand. God, this was basically my best friend.

After a moment he snatched the keys out of my hand and went ahead, stepping around Reece. Mal went inside, closing the door (not slamming it, thank god).

Reece offered me a stiff smile. "This is awkward."

What an understatement. I sat down beside him, resting my elbows on my knees. "Nice flowers."

"They're for you." He handed them over, the scent sweet and heady. He didn't meet my eyes.

"Thank you. They're beautiful."

"I was worried about you."

The statement sat there like an accusation. I didn't know what to say. Emotion had never been my strong point. I was woefully unprepared for this mix of sadness and guilt and whatever the fuck else he'd bought in on his boot heels. Mom had taught me a long time ago to play it safe and keep your mouth shut.

"You two worked things out," he said.

"Yes." On the other hand, my mom was a beyond-shitty role model. Reece deserved better. "What's going on here?"

"I got to thinking about things. About us." He shoved a hand through his hair, pushing back the floppy fringe. I'd always adored the way he did that, the accompanying toss of his head. But my heart didn't roll over and give it up to him. Not like it did for Mal. Reece had waited too long.

"Us?" I prompted, both angry and bewildered.

His smile was far from happy. He nodded toward the upper floor. "Thought he was gone."

"So did I. Apparently, I misunderstood."

"Guess that's good for you. Think it'll last?" His voice wasn't unkind exactly. But the question garnered an immediate reaction.

I sucked in a breath, an honest answer eluding me. My happy-sex high hadn't dissipated enough for brutal honesty, not with Mal waiting upstairs. My mind didn't want to know. Mom had always said love made you stupid. Guess I hadn't learned that lesson yet after all. "I don't know. But I hope so."

It was still relatively early but the building sat in silence. Our voices barely made a dint.

Reece rose to his feet, moving slowly like he'd been hit. "I'm going to go. See you tomorrow."

"Reece," I said, my voice tight and high. Something was breaking right there beside me and like so much lately, I didn't think I could fix it. I couldn't give Reece what he'd finally decided he just might want. "I'm sorry."

He hung his head. "It's my fault, Anne. I was an asshole. I was too stupid to see what was right in front of my eyes until it was too late."

I had nothing. Absolutely nothing.

He waited a moment, lips skewed with disappointment perhaps. Then he started moving.

"Night." He jogged down the stairs, taking them two at a time, obviously eager to get gone.

"Bye."

I sat there, holding my flowers, staring into space. I just needed a moment to get my head together. The world was so strange. Nothing made sense. A minute later Mal came out and sat down beside me. He leaned over, sniffed at the bouquet. His hands bashed out a beat against his thighs, but he said nothing. Finger tapping seemed to mean restless or busy thinking things out. This savage piece of percussion was something altogether different.

"Reece left," I said, breaking the silence.

"Mm."

"This has been a strange day," I said, quite possibly making the understatement of the century.

"Strange good or strange bad?"

"Both."

"Mm." He grabbed the back of his neck, sucked in a deep breath. "You breaking up with me here or what?"

My head shot around. "You want to break up?"

He didn't respond. For a minute or more, I said nothing and neither did he. We had apparently entered into some messed-up contest of wills. When I gave him a questioning look, he simply raised a brow, waiting me out.

"I couldn't just leave him sitting here. He's my friend."

Mal jerked his chin.

"Was I supposed to let you two arm wrestle over me or something? Because that was never going to happen."

"We screwed and then you sent me on my way with a pat on the head." The low, cold way he said it didn't help at all.

"No," I answered, matching his tone of voice. "Come on, Mal. You know that's not what happened. I sent Reece on his way. You I asked to wait in my home. To give me a chance to speak to him."

He stared at me and I stared straight back.

"Don't do this," I said.

"God!" He scrubbed at his face with his hands, growling in frustration. "I fucking hate being jealous. Hate it."

"Tell me about it." I threw up my hands in equal frustration. "You are aware that a healthy portion of the vagina-owning population wants to do you? Don't even get me started about the penis-wielding people, because there's quite a few of them into you as well."

"The shit you say . . ." He sputtered out a laugh. "Fuck."

The storm seemed to be over, thank god. I leaned my head on his shoulder, needing to get closer. Happily, he let me.

"I don't usually fight with other people," he said, rubbing his cheek against the top of my head. "In the band, I usually keep the guys from ripping into each other over stupid shit. Tell a joke, get 'em smiling again."

"You're the peacekeeper. But you were ready to rip into Ben the other night."

"About you. You're turning out to be kind of a mind fuck for me, pumpkin."

I frowned.

"Not saying you mean to be."

"Yeah, that doesn't make me feel any better."

We sat in silence. Eventually, he lifted the flowers out of my arms, stood, and headed down the stairs. The only noise the entire time was the soft thud of his shoes on the worn wooden steps. Carefully, he placed the flowers on Mrs. Lucia's doorstep, before returning to sit beside me. A statement had been made by confiscating those flowers, but what exactly did it mean? That was the question. Mal Ericson was quite the mind fuck himself. And he went on tour in a couple of days. It'd be foolish of me to ignore this oh-so-salient fact. I tugged at the buckles on my boots, all agitated. Too many emotions were stirred up inside of me.

He did that.

"When I was sitting up there, waiting for you, a couple of things occurred to me," he said.

"Yes?"

"Well, you're my girlfriend for real now."

I stopped breathing for a moment, thrown. "I think I needed to hear you say that."

"You have been for a while. Didn't mean for you to be, but you are. I just have to get used to it."

Of course, when he put it like that I sort of wanted to physically hurt him. Instead, I sat and waited to see where he was going with this.

"Don't get mad," he said. "Just stating a fact."

"I'm not mad."

"Liar. See, now this is why we should have gone to counseling when I suggested it right at the start."

"What?" I scrunched up my nose. "When did that happen?"

"Day after I moved in, when we were sexting."

"We weren't sexting, we were just texting. You said you wanted to get a dog too, if I recall correctly. So I really didn't think you were serious about counseling."

The slow curl of his lips made something hot and delicious unfurl deep in my stomach. "Pumpkin, I'm always serious when it comes to you. Even when I'm messing around, I'm still serious as shit. Whatever you need, whatever I have to do. It's been that way since we met. Haven't you noticed yet? We're fucking destined or something. I can't help myself. It's pathetic, really."

"Huh." I stuffed my hands beneath my thighs, giving his words a moment to sink in. "That's what you figured out waiting upstairs?"

"Yep." He shuffled closer, pressing his hip to mine. "Think about it. Things were shit and then I met you at the party and you amused me. I wanted more time with you and then I saw Ev's side boob and Davie threw me out so I had to move in with you. I wanted to sleep with you and we accidentally broke your bed jumping around on it so you had to crash on the couch with me. I wanted to have sex with you and you got bored on the ride home and jumped my bones. See? Destiny."

I burst out laughing. "That's beautiful. But I'm not sure it completely makes sense."

"It's fate, Anne. Written in the stars. Leave it the fuck alone."

"You're crazy." I hung my head and sighed. What else could I do?

"That's better. Can't stand it when you're sad either." His arm slipped around my shoulders, drawing me in against him. I grabbed hold of his fingers, just hanging on.

That was better. Everything would be okay. But there was still an issue I was curious about. "Why did you ask me to be your fake girlfriend?"

He shrugged, looked away. "I wanted to spend time with you. You make me happy."

I scrunched up my forehead. "That's all it was?"

"That's pretty fucking important. Guess with Davie pairing up I was feeling a bit lonely or something. I thought we could be friends."

I just stared at him.

"Needed a chance to get to know you a little better, just you and me alone. Moving in seemed a good way to do that. And you needed the help. Okay?"

"Okay."

We sat in silence for a moment.

"Whatever shit you're telling yourself, stop it," he said.

"What? What are you talking about now?"

"Reece." He rested his head atop of mine. "You're worrying about him. Stop it."

"Mal . . ." How could I explain this to him? The words were weighted in lead, impossible to get out. I hadn't been thinking about Reece, but now that he mentioned it . . .

"You didn't do anything wrong."

I wiggled out from underneath him, needing to see his face. Since when could he read me and why couldn't I do the same?

He appeared calm and sure, beautiful as sin. His lips sat slightly apart, his eyes serene. Suddenly, the words weren't so impossible to find after all.

"I hurt him."

"Maybe. But he's the one that left you hanging on. He hurt you too."

"But I fix things," I said. "It's what I do."

"You can't fix this." He toyed with my hair, wrapping the short strands around a finger.

"Why not?"

"You going to dump my ass? Send me packing?"

"No. Absolutely not."

He smiled and shrugged. "There you go."

"You make it sound so simple."

"It is. I'm your boyfriend now, which means there's no room for your hipster admirer. He'll just have to lick his wounds while we lick other things." He raised a devilish eyebrow.

My head filled with so many needy questions. A hundred and one ways to beg him for reassurance. No god damn way any of it was getting past my lips. He was so insanely perfect and I'd had him inside of me. My body buzzed with the memories, sliding straight toward overload. I wanted him again. Maybe I should just shackle myself to his ankle and be done with it. This could be the answer.

"I didn't want to upset you," I said. "But I needed to talk to him alone."

"Yeah, I know. I was being a dick." He moaned, looked to the heavens. "That enough of an apology?"

"You're sorry?"

"Yeah. I get Reece is part of your life. I'll try to be nice to him."

"Thank you."

His hair was in his face again. Carefully, I tucked some behind his ear and then cupped his cheek.

"Hey, crazy eyes. Operation Fake Girlfriend is off," he murmured. "In case you were wondering."

"It is, huh?"

"Way I figure it, we're together until we decide we're not together anymore. Let's not put too much thought into it. Let it sort itself out, yeah?"

It was a sound plan, considering we'd only started sleeping together less than an hour ago. "I approve."

"Glad to have you on board, Miss Rollins." He covered my hand with his own, pressing it against his face. "I don't wanna be unduly crass or any shit like that, but I'm worried about something."

"What might that be?"

"Your shirt."

I opened my mouth, shut it. "My shirt?"

"I think it's chafing you. Subconsciously like." His eyes were intense, his expression grave.

"My shirt is chafing my subconscious?"

"No, I believe it's chafing the delicate skin of your nipples and the area around . . . what's it called?"

"The areola?"

"Yeah, that bit. 'Cause it's all pink and sensitive, you know? It's delicate, so I believe my concern with regards to the harsh and unyielding nature of your shirt is real important even though you have yet to acknowledge the discomfort it's causing you."

"You know you could have been one hell of a salesman." He was so convincing, I almost felt bad for the soft cotton of my long-sleeved top. "I'm wearing a bra. But my nipples really appreciate your concern."

"Yeah, your bra's in on it too. They're both against you."

"No way!" I said. He made it damn hard not to smile.

"I know, right? Thank fuck I'm here to deal with these things."

"How about we go upstairs and I take my shirt and bra off, would that ease your mind?"

"I'd definitely feel a lot better if you did that, yes."

"Well, alrighty then. Race you." I jumped to my feet, barreling up the stairs, giggling. Mal's arm came around me from behind, lifting me off my feet, pulling me back up against his chest.

"I win," he said, and carried me into the apartment where we both won, big-time.

CHAPTER EIGHTEEN

Fingers were playing with me. Clever fingers.

My alarm hadn't gone off for work yet. It was just before dawn. Sleep, however, wasn't an option with him stirring me up the way he was. Since when was Mal a morning person? Answer, since he wanted sex.

God bless him for his base desires.

I lay on my stomach with him beside me, the hardness and heat of his body a wonderful thing to wake up to. Ever so gently, he stroked me between my legs. He trailed his knuckles softly back and forth along the seam of my sex. Everything low in me tensed in approval. I arched my pelvis, giving him better access to my pussy. We'd dragged my mattress out into the living room, away from the destruction of my wooden bed frame, and gone at it again last night.

"You awake?" he asked, voice husky from sleep.

"No."

He trailed kisses down my spine, making me get all quivery. The graze of his stubble made for a delicious tactile sensory whatever. Yeah, I was still half asleep.

"Okay, don't mind me. I just need something. Shouldn't take too long . . . I'll try not to disturb you."

"Mm, thanks."

His hard-on prodded my thigh. Then a strong hand slid beneath my hips, lifting. "Up," he said, sliding the soft bulk of a pillow under me. "This is sweet. Anne, really, your ass looks great raised up like this."

Wet fingers slid around my clit, turning me on like nobody's business. He circled and stroked and tickled in turn, touching me just right. My thigh muscles tensed, knees digging into the bed. Damn, the man knew what he was doing. I clutched at the sheets, already breathing hard. It would be futile to try and express exactly how much I enjoyed having him touch me. Especially when my brain had shut down for the duration. I moaned in disappointment when he took to kneading my butt cheeks instead, trailing his fingers up and down my thighs.

"Wider," he murmured, pushing my legs farther apart. The mattress shifted beneath me as he moved into place. From behind wasn't my favorite position, but I had no doubt Mal could make it work. The man had skills.

There was the crinkle of a condom wrapper as he changed over to teasing me one-handed. Even just one of his hands was pretty damn good. Then the broad head of his cock nudged my sex. I squeezed my eyes shut, pushed back against him, groaning as he slid into me. With his cock filling me, there was no room for thought. I could only feel.

So damn good.

The way he gripped my ass, his fingers digging into my flesh, gave this tiny thrill of pain. He was truly a whole-body experience, quite possibly involving the astral plane. There were all the usual five senses and then something more I couldn't begin to describe. Something addictive only he could give me. If my brain had been working, I would have been worried about this.

Big hands stroked over my back. Then the heat of his body

covered me. Teeth nipped the lobe of my ear, stinging. My shoulders hitched and my muscles clenched.

"Ah, yeah. Fuck, that's hot." Mal pushed himself hard into me. Like he could get any deeper . . . as if. "You're a lazy lay in the morning, Anne."

"Hmm. I did all the work last night in the limousine."

He chuckled, his chest moving against my back. Then he flexed his hips, pushing in, then drawing out, making every inch of me tremble. With his arms set on either side of me, he proceeded to fuck me leisurely into the mattress. My butt jiggled and it didn't matter one iota. Not with Mal buried inside me. It seemed to take forever for him to pick up the pace. And he called *me* lazy. I needed more. Pushing my hips back against him, I urged him on. He got the message, moving faster, going harder. Sweat dripped off of him, onto me.

Gray noise filled my ears and white light filled my head. So damn close I could taste it. The sublime knot of tension drew tighter, but it wasn't quite enough.

Yes.

YES.

But no. Shit. Damn it.

Mal ground himself against me, groaning. His cock jerked deep inside me.

I hadn't even realized I'd been holding myself tense until I collapsed facedown on the mattress. Made it kind of hard to breathe. I turned my head to the side, concentrated on catching my breath, on letting go of the ache. I'd almost gotten there, a first for the position.

Never mind, I just needed to think happy thoughts. Good thoughts. You couldn't win every time.

Mal pulled out of me and fell onto the bed at my side. Outside, birds were singing. The faint hum of traffic came from not too far away. Nate was clumping around in the apartment next door.

"Anne?"

"Yes?" I rolled onto my back.

Mal was busy pulling off the used condom and tying a knot in it. Then he rolled off the mattress and walked into the bathroom.

"What, Mal?"

The toilet flushed. He walked back out, face carefully blank. We'd only been sleeping together for approximately five minutes and this felt weird. Like all relationships didn't have their average sex moments. But did he know? I couldn't tell. Maybe he was about to ask about breakfast or comment on the weather.

I pulled up the sheet, covering myself. "What's wrong?"

"Is something wrong there?" he asked, tipping his chin.

"What, with me? No."

"You sure about that?"

"Yes." Mostly.

He knelt at the end of the mattress, watching me. "We need to talk."

"Okay."

"You won't need this." He grabbed the sheet, pulling it down, exposing me.

Right, fine. I started to sit up, needing to be in more of a position of power. The big ape grabbed my ankles, dragging me down. My back bounced on the bed, teeth clattering.

"Hey!" I squeaked.

"Let me explain what I mean by 'talk.'"

His hands moved up my legs, spreading them wide. Cool as can be, he lay flat on his stomach, face level with my sex.

"Mal."

"I'm not talking to you," he said, fingers gently folding back the lips of my sex.

"You're not?"

"No. You had your chance to communicate with me and you chose not to. You let this relationship down. Feel bad, Anne." His breath tickled my still-sensitive pussy. It made feeling bad damn hard, frankly. Impossible when he flicked my clit with the tip of his tongue. My hips shot off the mattress but his hands were there, holding me down. "Hello, Anne's clitoris. It's me, Malcolm, your lord and master."

"Oh, god, no." I covered my face with my hands. "Please don't."

"Shh. This is a private conversation." He brushed hot, feverish kisses up and down the lips of my sex. My stomach tensed so hard it hurt. "Look at you all pretty, pink, and excited. Don't worry, I'll look after you."

"If you don't stop talking to my vagina I'm going to kill you." I put a hand down, trying to cover myself. The bastard slapped it. Hard too. I would get him back for that later.

"You're beautiful, Anne's pussy. Just beautiful. And I'm not mean like her. I'm on your side and I love you very much because you feel fucking amazing wrapped around my dick."

"Malcolm, I mean it. You're ruining oral sex for me forever. Cut it out."

"Bullshit. You're dripping wet. We'll never get these sheets clean."

"Oh, god." My back bowed as he dragged his tongue up the center of me, finishing with a flourish at the top. I saw stars. "Too much."

"Not even close."

I whimpered.

He laughed.

His mouth covered my clitoris and his tongue went to god damn town on me. I writhed, out of control, but it made no difference. Hands banded around my thighs, holding me to him. There was no escaping the terrible, all-consuming over-whelming pleasure. He sucked, flicked his tongue, and gener-ally unleashed an unsurpassed wealth of oral talent upon my unsuspecting sex.

The bastard.

Who even knew teeth could be used like that?

I came in under a minute, crying his name. My heartbeat thundered through my head and my whole body shook. I lay sprawled across the mattress, letting the aftershocks have their way with me. Endorphins had pickled my mind. Tears slid down my face, the orgasm had hit me so hard, so fast. That had never happened before. Hurriedly, I brushed them away. My heart seemed suddenly too big for my chest. The orgasm had engorged it somehow. It couldn't be healthy.

From next door came banging on the wall. "I already knew Mal's name, Anne. But thanks for the reminder."

I used the last of my energy reserves to give the wall the finger. "Morning, Lauren."

Distantly, there was laughter, male and female both. Our neigh-bors sucked.

"We need to kill them or move," I said. "I'm open to either option."

"You know, you talk tough," said Mal, "but inside, you're all soft and wet and really quite tasty."

I choked back a laugh. "Glad you approve."

Mal crawled up, pausing to wipe his mouth on the sheet. He laid his head on my shoulder, snuggling into me. That was good, I needed him near. The glut of emotions felt more manageable with him close, even if he was the cause of all the chaos.

"I think my legs are broken; they won't work." Not that I'd actually tried yet. My brain was too floaty for any movement.

He pressed a kiss to my cheek. "Next time, just tell me you need more."

"You're a monster," I whispered.

"Okay." He didn't even sound the slightest bit perturbed.

"I mean it."

"Mm-hm."

"But the worst part is, I feel something for you," I said, because fair was fair. Love was a stupid word. I'd heard it from various people and it rarely meant what you thought it did. Somewhere along the way, that word had turned into a pleasantry, not profound and weighty as it should have been. No, love wasn't what I felt. This was different, more complex. I couldn't even think of a word for it. "I only feel it a tiny bit . . . probably just because of the great orgasm, so it's not like it's a big deal or anything. It'll pass."

With a sigh, he went up on one elbow and put an arm around me, pulling me up against him. When he rolled onto his back, I went too. I lay sprawled across him. There was no better thing. Apart from what he'd just done to me, of course. One hand stroked my back, while the other lay behind his head.

"A miniscule amount, really." My thumb rubbed over his nipple, back and forth, back and forth. I seemed to have entered some stream-of-consciousness state and I didn't have the energy to fight it. "You probably couldn't even see it with a microscope."

Another sigh from the man.

"Well, maybe one of those lab ones, but not a kid's toy one. The magnification wouldn't be—"

All of a sudden we rolled again and I was on the bottom with the weight of Mal's body pushing me deep into the mattress.

"Hi," I said, just a bit discombobulated by the abrupt change in position. He'd barely given my head to time to stop spinning from the previous shift.

"Been thinking." He watched me, eyes intense. "Want you to do something for me."

"Okay."

"Need you to come on tour, least for a while. See what you can manage, okay?"

My engorged heart basically burst. My insides were officially a mess. "Need?"

"Yeah, need." His forehead furrowed. "Things are happening and I know you've got questions but I need you to not ask them right now. I just . . . I need you with me. I deal with stuff better when you're around."

"Stuff like the other reason why you wanted me around that you wouldn't admit to last night?"

Guilt slid across his face. "Yeah."

"We're going to have to talk about stuff eventually."

"Yeah, we are. Yours and mine both."

I froze beneath him, not answering. But he just patiently waited me out. The words were stuck inside my chest with the rest of the clutter. It was hard to find them. "You're right. I know. And I'll try and work something out about the tour."

Work would survive. Reece owed me. He wasn't going to like it, but he sure as hell owed me. Between Tara and the new guy, Alex, my shifts could be covered.

"Thanks." He nodded, gave me a small mile. "And it's okay about the feeling something thing. I get it."

"You do?" What a relief, because I still wasn't sure I did. I'd never even said anything close to resembling those words.

"Yeah. You don't need to keep babbling about it."

"I wasn't babbling."

"You were, but that's okay." His fingers toyed with my hair. "The timing isn't great for me, pumpkin. I didn't need shit getting any more complicated. But like I said last night, we see where this goes. Agreed?"

Sounded like a solid plan. "Yes."

"You're good for me. You take me any mood I come in. I don't have to be always happy or on around you. You roll with any shit I say and give as good as you get. You don't let me push you around if it doesn't suit you and you haven't asked me to buy you a fucking thing."

I arched my brows and "ooh"ed. "God, I'm so slow. It hadn't even occurred to me. Can I have a Porsche?"

"Sure. What color?"

Holy shit, he would too. If only to mess with me. I took a deep breath and let it out slowly, shook my head. "You never hesitate when I ask for something."

"You don't do it often. I figure if you're asking, it's something that matters."

My eyes did not tear up again. I had allergies or something, probably to feelings. And you had to know, this man, he made me feel *all* the things *all* the damn time. "I don't really need a sports car. But thanks."

"Let me know if you change your mind." He smirked, obviously having known full and well his agreeing would freak me out. Cunning man.

"Ev wants to organize a dinner tonight with the parents and everyone," he said. "You good with that?"

"Sure. They're nice and their place is beautiful."

He stilled, studying my face. "Yeah, it is nice. Glad you like it there. They mean a lot to me."

"They're great people." In my bedroom the alarm clock blared to life, belting out some long forgotten hit from the seventies. "I have to get moving."

"Your legs working yet?" Mischief danced in his eyes.

"I think so." I laughed.

"Call me today. I wanna know you're okay dealing with Reece and everything."

"I've been dealing with things for a long time." My jaw tightened. "I can deal with Reece."

"Hey, you were into him for over two years. I'm allowed to feel a little vulnerable and insecure about the fuckface. Stop trying to stunt my emotional growth, Anne."

"I thought you were going to try to be nice to him. And stunt your emotional growth? How do you even come up with this stuff?"

"*To* him, not *about* him. And it's a gift." Given what was making its presence known once more against my hip, love and understanding wasn't all he was searching for. "I have another gift for you."

"We don't have time for you to give me your gift. Plus, your good friend, my vagina, needs a rest."

His mouth turned down at the edges and he rose up on his arms, sitting back on the mattress. He stood and offered me a hand. "Call me. I'm not trying to mess with your boundaries or anything. Just want to know you're okay."

Easily, he pulled me up onto my feet. "Alright, I'll call."

"Thanks."

I cocked my head. "You going to call me if things aren't okay with you regarding stuff?"

The little line appeared between his brows. Now maybe he appreciated how hard it could be letting someone into certain places. He looked away, jerked his chin.

What a pair we were. Sometimes it seemed we'd need a miracle to make this work. But my usually cautious heart had already committed.

"Thanks." I placed my hand on his chest. "You don't need to worry about Reece."

"I know, I know. He's nothing compared to my magnificence." His fingers stroked mine and his eyes softened. "But just out of curiosity, how do you feel about getting my name tattooed on your forehead?"

CHAPTER NINETEEN

I was two blocks from work when I saw Reece walking toward me through the early morning crowd. His face was set in hard lines. Five minutes late. Five. Okay, seven (max) and he came looking for me? I'd even skipped my morning coffee fix to hurry things along. Excuses ran through my mind, backed up by all the times I'd stayed late to close because he had a date. I should have kept actual figures. They would have been so helpful right now.

"Reece, I—"

"About-face." He hooked my arm with his and spun me around to face the way I'd come. "Keep walking. You don't want to go to the shop."

"What's going on?" My cell buzzed in my handbag. Mal's name flashed up on screen. "Mal?"

"Ah, hey. Got good news and bad news. What do you want first?"

"Does this have to do with Reece keeping me from my place of employment?"

"Yeah, he called here a few minutes ago." He made a pained noise. "Listen, photos of us at the restaurant last night got around. Someone recognized you and told a reporter who is currently hanging around the shop waiting to get the inside scoop on our *lurve*."

"Right." Mind officially boggled. Reece rushed me across a road and down another block. "What's the good news?"

"Everyone knows about us now. We don't have to hide."

"We weren't hiding anyway."

"Good point. Sorry, pumpkin, there is no good news. Things are going to be painful for a while."

"You're lucky I'm extremely fond of you. What happens next?" We turned into the entry of a café. A table was available in the corner and Reece and I walked toward it.

"Reporters will probably just scrounge whatever information they can on you or make shit up, enough to have a story to run with. They'll wanna get it out fast, news'll spread, and there'll be more people digging into your life. It shouldn't be anything like what happened with Ev 'cause we haven't done anything crazy stupid like getting married in Vegas." He took a breath. "You don't do anything else too newsworthy, they'll lose interest. Meanwhile, how do you feel about us staying at a hotel?"

"What about work?" I asked him, then shook my head and turned to Reece. It was really a question for the boss. I turned to Reece. "What about work?"

Reece raised his eyebrows in question while Mal cleared his throat. "Well, I figured you'd want to talk to him about that," said Mal.

"Yes, I do."

"But, Anne, for once don't worry about the money, okay? I've got you covered."

Hmm. I didn't know about that. Realistically, though, if I was with Mal, I'd be crashing in his hotel room. My rent was paid up. Apart from the occasional meal, I shouldn't need much.

"Okay. Just give me a minute please, Mal." I moved the cell back a bit. "Sorry. Reece?"

"We talked," Reece said. "He said it'll probably be crazy for the next week or so, but then it should calm down."

"I'm sorry about the reporter. But I was hoping to ask if I could take some time off anyway? I realize this is short notice, but given the circumstances . . ."

Reece flinched and panic rose up like a tidal wave. He didn't seem angry last night, but that didn't mean he wasn't holding a grudge, or he might well decide he'd had enough and fire me. Things could get screwed up pretty fast here.

But he sighed and relaxed once more. "You're going on tour with him?"

"I'd like to. Just for a while. It would give this a chance to blow over."

"I guess it makes sense. Though if you stick with him, this shit could be ongoing. Have you thought of that?"

"Are you asking for my resignation?"

"Of course not."

"I'm not giving him up, Reece."

He looked away. "I can cover you for a week, Anne. With such short notice, I don't think I can do more."

"No, a week would be great. Thank you."

"You're overdue for vacation. And I can't have reporters hanging around, scaring the customers. I'll rearrange the shifts with Tara and Alex."

"I really appreciate it."

He grimaced.

"You're an awesome friend."

"I'm awesome," said Mal in my ear. "I'm so much more awesome than him, I can't even . . . there's no comparison. Why would you even use that word in reference to him?"

"Hush," I told him.

"Be back in time for your birthday, okay?" asked Reece with a hesitant smile. "We're still going to dinner, right?"

"God, I hadn't even thought about it. I'll be back then." We always went out to dinner on each other's birthdays. It was our tradition. Mal would still be on the road, so I could celebrate with him early. This would be a nice chance to mend bridges with Reece, going out as just friends. "I'd like that."

"What?" asked Mal. "When's your birthday? Pumpkin?"

"Take care," said Reece. "You need anything, call me."

"Thanks. Really, I . . . you're a great friend."

"A great friend . . . right," he said dryly. Then he leaned in, kissing me on the cheek. "Bye."

"Did he just kiss you?" Mal yelled in my ear, making it ring. I winced, pulling the cell back. "Whoa. Noise levels, buddy."

Reece moved through the crowd and out the door. Maybe we were going to survive this after all. Last night, I hadn't been so sure.

"When is your birthday?" Mal asked.

"Twenty-eighth of October."

"A week and a half away. I'll have to get something sorted for you."

"Just you will do. We'll have to celebrate it early, though. I've only got a week and I was probably damn lucky to get that what with the giving five minutes' notice."

"Can't believe he kissed you. Ballsy, but still, he's dead." He mumbled some more of what I presumed to be idle threats. "Don't come back here, just in case. I'll ask Lauren to help me pack a couple of bags for you. You head to The Benson, okay? There'll be a room ready by the time you get there."

"Thanks."

"You're not mad about me turning your life upside down?"

"I'm a big girl, Mal. I knew who you were going into this and I saw what went down with Ev. There was always a chance this could happen."

"And if it keeps happening, you gonna get sick of it and leave me?"

My heart rebelled at the thought. "No. We'll work something out."

"Yeah, we will," he agreed. "You're pretty mellow after a night of hot sex. I'm keeping a note of that."

"You do that, my friend."

He chuckled. "See you in an hour or two. We'll break in the hotel mattress, order some room service, and hang out, okay?"

"Sounds great." With a grin, I slumped down in the chair. I was officially on vacation. The last vacation I went on was to Florida with Mom, Dad, and Lizzy. I'd been fourteen years old, the year before everything went to shit. And no way did I need to be dwelling on the past.

Life here and now with Mal was a roller coaster. Scary and elating. No matter how strange the circumstances, I was going to enjoy this time.

The dinner with the band and his parents was lovely.

Afterward, we headed for a dive bar on the edge of China-town. It was located down a narrow staircase, underground. Not too clean but not too dirty. There were pinball machines and a pool table, a jukebox blasting out Joy Division. The crowd had the market on slacker-hipster style cornered. Apart from a few double takes, nobody got excited when we came in. I guess they were all too cool to freak out over some boring old rock stars.

Though Sam the body guard was along, just in case.

My cell had been ringing on and off due to my newfound

fame. Plenty of messages had been received, but I'd checked in with Lizzy and she was fine. There wasn't really anyone else I needed to talk to. Ev had given me a pep talk about dealing with all the attention. To keep my head down and not feed the monster. Eventually, they'd lose interest and move on.

At the hotel, Mal and I had watched movies and taken it easy. It'd been great. Lori had invited me down to the lobby bar for a drink before dinner. She seemed more concerned about the media attention than I was. Though I'd managed to pretty successfully hide from it so far. I assured her that her son and I were doing fine. Real fine.

It had, all in all, been a great day. And this dive bar was cool and relaxed and all that it should be. We'd spread out around a table against the far wall. With a nod to one of the bartenders, Ben had ordered pitchers of beer (water for Jimmy and Lena).

"Owner's a friend. We come here to play pool sometimes during the day," Mal said, pulling my chair closer to his. He seemed wired, beating out a rhythm on the tabletop with the palm of his hand. The mood was infectious, keeping me on edge too.

I don't think I'd understood how tight-knit the band and their families were. During the dinner, David and Jimmy had doted on Lori. They pretty much treated her as if she were their own mother out for a visit. Even Ben had demonstrated a subdued sort of affection. And they all seemed to respect the mostly silent Neil, Mal's dad. Father and son had kept a close eye on Lori again throughout the evening. They practically hovered at her side. Lori had gotten tired again and Neil had taken her back to the hotel.

Yes, I had suspicions aplenty about what was stressing Mal out and keeping him up at night. But we were getting along so well. He'd asked me not to question him. Not yet. And I wasn't ready to provide him with answers on my issues either. So I kept my concerns to myself for the time being. But judgment day was coming for both of us. I could feel it.

Only a few days out from the start of the tour, everyone seemed too restless to call it a night once Lori and Neil left. It was too early, only just past nine.

Strange looks were being passed between David and Jimmy. They'd give Mal curious glances and then talk amongst themselves. I had a feeling Mal was very much aware of it, the way he was turned away, giving the pair the cold shoulder.

"Hey," Mal said, his smile twitchy. "Let's go back to the hotel and break another bed."

"We just got here."

"Yeah, I changed my mind. I wanna be alone with you." His foot started tapping out a hyper beat against the ground. "What do you say? We'll just get naked and see what happens after that."

"Sounds like a great experiment. Can I just finish this drink and then we'll go? Be rude to take off right away."

"Pfft. How often do Davie and Ev disappear at things?"

"I'll drink fast," I promised, before proceeding to gulp half of my glass of beer. Only a little dribbled down my chin and wet my tight green sweater. Rushing might not have been lady-like, it's true. But with Mal wanting to get naked and dirty, can you blame me?

Hell no.

With all the whispering of wicked things stirring up my hormones, I hadn't noticed the Ferris brother's heated conversation. Down the other end of the table, they were all but growling at each other.

Jimmy thumped the table, making the beer glasses shake and drawing the attention of surrounding patrons. "Fuck's sake, Dave. Just ask him."

"I said leave it for now," his brother answered.

Ben sat back in his chair and crossed his thick arms, saying nothing, watching everything. A new song came on, the opening chords ear-shatteringly loud.

"Yeah!" yelled one of the long-haired, heavily tattooed men behind the bar. Glad someone was having a good time. The atmosphere around the table had turned decidedly dark.

A muscle started ticking in Mal's neck. He looked back at the Ferris brothers, his face like thunder. "What?"

"You know what," said Jimmy, yelling to be heard over the music.

Mal spread his hands expansively. "Jimbo, I'm a man of many, many talents, but reading your fucking mind ain't one of them."

"What's going on with Lori?"

Ev's gaze darted to mine. I didn't know any more than she did. Still.

"You on something, Jimbo?" asked Mal, sitting forward in his seat. "Tell the truth now."

"Don't be an asshole." David leaned his elbows on the table, staring furiously at Mal. "We care about her. She's lost a shit-load of weight. Looks like a breeze could blow her away. You and Neil never take your eyes off her. You know exactly what Jimmy's talking about."

I could almost hear Mal grinding his teeth.

"We have a right to know," said Jimmy.

David sucked in his cheeks. "C'mon, man. Just tell us."

Shit. Mal went rigid in his seat beside me and then he started rocking. We needed to leave.

I placed my hand on his arm. He vibrated with tension. I didn't know how to comfort him, but I had to try. "Mal?"

He shook me off without so much as a glance.

"She had a flu or something," said Mal. "That's all. Don't make a big deal out of it."

Jimmy shot forward in his seat. "It's more than that. Don't you fucking lie."

"This is what's been messing with your head, isn't it?" asked David. "Lori's sick. Real sick."

"I don't know what you two are talking about." Mal's laughter was a horrible thing. "This is ridiculous. Jimmy here's probably back to fucking freebasing, but what's your excuse, Davie?"

Lena pushed out of her seat. She grabbed the remaining half-full pitcher of beer and threw it in Mal's face. Foamy cold liquid splashed me, and Mal snapped back in surprise.

"What the fuck?" he roared, rising quickly out of the chair.

Across from him, Jimmy shot to his feet as well, shoving a belligerent Lena behind him. Everyone stopped, all conversation in the bar falling silent. The few quiet drinks plan had clearly fallen to shit.

"Don't you yell at her," said Jimmy, hands curled into fists.

Mal's shoulders heaved. The two men faced off across the table, both clearly furious. Slowly, Ben and David got to their feet. This was all going to hell in a handbasket.

"Mal, let's go," I said. "Give everyone a chance to cool off."

Again, he ignored me.

"Walk away, bro," said Ben, voice eerily calm.

Beer dripped from Mal's hair. The front of his shirt was soaked. From behind us came a flash of light. A guy stood with his phone, taking pictures. Asshole.

Without another word, Mal turned and bolted for the stairs, almost sending a girl carrying a bottle of something flying. I just stood there stunned for a moment, useless and stinking of beer. Ben and Sam took off after him.

"Anne, let us handle it," said David.

David and Jimmy both left too, jogging up the small, dark stairwell. Like hell I was doing as I was told.

Mal had left his jacket over the back of his seat. He'd freeze out there. I picked it up and a hand grabbed my wrist. Ev's hand.

"Please, give them a chance to talk," she said, getting in my face. "Those guys have been together a long time."

I picked up my purse and held his jacket to my chest. "No."

"But—"

I didn't have time for this shit. What I needed to do was to find Mal and see if he was all right.

I rushed up the stairs, past the ground-floor bar and out the door. The cold night air chilled me, courtesy of the wet patches on my sweater and jeans. My heart beat double-time. Shit. There was no sign of any of them in either direction. His black Jeep was gone from across the street. They could be fucking anywhere by now.

"Shit."

What to do? Where to go? Maybe he'd headed back to the hotel. Yes, of course. A cab cruised by and I held out my arm. Far too damn slowly, it pulled to a stop.

I threw open the back door and climbed in. "The Benson, please."

I'd find him.

CHAPTER TWENTY

The text from Ev came at quarter to eleven. I'd been wide awake, staring at the ceiling because staring at the walls had gotten old. He hadn't come back to the hotel. I'd been waiting for over half an hour.

> Ev: Lauren gave me your number. The guys talked things out with Mal then he took off again. They don't know where to.
> Anne: Ok
> Ev: Do you know where he might be?
> Anne: If I find him I'll let you know
> Ev: Thanks

He might have been driving around town. But far more likely, if he was still worked up, he'd want to take it out on his drum kit.

I took a cab. Money might be tight, but I wouldn't be waiting for him to come to me any longer. Hopefully David and co. had talked him down, calmed him. Now it was time to play my part, whatever that might be. I sat in the backseat, trying to think up speeches. All in all, I was out of wise words.

A hazy drizzle began to fall from the sky as I arrived at the practice hall. My breath misted in the cold. Ah, Portland. It never disappointed. Best weather ever. Mal's Jeep sat parked next to the building. Thank god, he was here.

The frenetic beat of drums hammered through the building's walls, shaking it to its foundation. A few brave bugs circled the dim light above the metal door. He'd left the door unlocked, thankfully. I stepped inside, bracing myself for the noise. Up on the stage, Mal, sitting in a pool of light, was creating an almighty storm of noise.

Closer to him, broken drum sticks littered the area. Mal had snapped an impressive amount in such a short time.

I climbed up onto the stage, making my way around to him. He sat, poised at the drum kit with eyes closed, hands moving so fast they were almost a blur. Sweat shone, already covering his upper body. Blond hair stuck to the sides of his face. A quarter-empty bottle of Johnny Walker Black Label sat beside him on the floor. The lines of his muscles and the angles of his cheekbones were stark beneath the harsh lighting.

He seemed lost in his own world, totally unaware. I hesitated for a moment then sank down, sitting cross-legged. I covered my ears but it made little difference to the deafening thunder of the drums. No matter. The clash of the cymbals cut through me. The heavy thud of the bass hit my heart. He played on and on, moving between rhythms but never slowing down. Not even to drink. He'd pick up the bottle and just hold it, one-handed, his other hand and both feet never missing a beat.

After the second slug of scotch, though, he didn't get the bottle all the way to the floor before letting go. It tipped over, liquid pouring out. I slid over and set it upright, replacing it in its spot beside him. For the first time he seemed to register my presence, tilting his chin in greeting or appreciation or I don't know what. Maybe I just imagined it. Then he was back to the music, powering on.

I pulled out my phone then hesitated. Ev had pissed me off, holding me up, but these people were also his family. They deserved to know he was still in one piece.

Anne: He's at the practice hall
Ev: Thank you

David Ferris strode in not fifteen minutes later. He nodded to me, then picked up a guitar and plugged it in. As the first strains of noise rang out Mal opened one eye and saw David standing opposite him. Nothing was said. Time moved by, both sluggish and swift at once. The two of them played for hours. I fell into some sort of daze. It took me a moment to realize when they finally stopped.

"Hey," he croaked, the words muted as if we were underwater. The noise might have broken my ears.

"Hi."

He put the almost empty bottle of scotch to his lips and tossed some back. His gaze stayed on me. Carefully, he screwed the lid back on. It took him a couple of tries. "I'm a little bit fucked-up, pumpkin."

"That's okay. I'll help get you back to the hotel."

He nodded, sniffed his armpits. "And I stink."

"I'll help you shower too." I walked over and knelt between his legs. "Not a problem."

His hands curved over my cheeks, molding my face. Slowly, he pressed his lips to mine. "Mm, I feel something for you, Anne. Which is pretty fucking impressive given how numb I am right now."

"It's huge," I agreed.

"I'm not normally like this . . . drinking this much. Want you to know that. It's just . . ." A muscle spasmed in his jaw and he stared off into the distance.

"I know, Mal. It's okay."

No response.

"We'll get through this."

"Anne—" In a flurry of motion, he fell back off the stool. I grabbed at his jeans, trying to keep him upright. Not the best idea. One of Mal's big-ass Chucks bumped the side of my head, which hurt. His other foot upset the cymbal stands and they clattered to the floor.

"Shit." Footsteps rushed closer.

Mal lay on his back, laughing.

I sat back on my heels, rubbing at the tender spot on my skull. What a night.

"You alright?" asked David, crouching beside me.

"Fine!" called Mal, still laughing like a loon.

"Not talking to you, asswipe. You kicked Anne."

"What?" Mal rolled over, grabbed the stool, and threw it out of the way. He rushed to my side, pushing David away. "Pumpkin, you okay?"

"Yes, you only clipped me. No damage done."

"Fuck. Oh, shit, Anne." His arms went around me, hugging me so tight he nearly throttled me. "I'm so sorry. We have to get her to a hospital and get a brains can. Brain scan. Fuck, one of those."

"I don't need a hospital or a scan. It's just a bump."

"You sure?" asked David, checking out my eyes.

"Yes," I said. "It was an accident, Mal. Calm down."

"I'm the worst boyfriend ever."

"I sure as hell wouldn't date you," said David.

"Fuck off, Davie."

"Party's over. Time for everyone to go home." David wrestled him off of me and onto his feet.

Mal seemed perplexed to find himself there. He just sort of stood and swayed, frowning down at me. "You okay?"

"Yep."

"I'm really fucking sorry, pumpkin. Wanna kick me in the head? Will that make you feel better?"

"Um, no. But thanks."

David got Mal's arm over his shoulders, dragging or carrying Mal toward the short set of stairs leading down off the stage. It was hard to tell which.

"Wait, where's his shirt? He'll freeze out there."

"Serve him fucking right."

"Shut up, Ferris. You're a whiny little bitch."

"Yeah, and you're loaded."

I rushed ahead and held the door open for them. Mal stumbled and they almost fell. But David got them moving forward again instead of face-planting. Just. "I'm fine, man," Mal said, pushing away from him to teeter precariously on his own. I grabbed his hand to support him and he pulled me in under his shoulder, steadying himself. "See, it's all good."

David just nodded, staying close.

"Gave my Ludwig kit a workout tonight. Broke a lot of drum sticks too." Mal threw his other arm around me, holding me close. He really did need a wash. "American hickory. Zildjian. Made to take a beating but I must have broken eight, maybe ten. Happens in concert often but you don't hear it. I just pick up the next one, keep going, never miss a beat. That's how we roll. Shit gets broken, no matter, play on."

He sighed, shifting his weight against me. I moved my feet farther apart, keeping my arms tight around his middle. The man was not light.

"I'm missing a beat, Anne. I can feel it. Shit ain't right."

I looked up into his beautiful face. My heart breaking for him. "I know. But it's okay. We've got you."

He just frowned down at me.

"I've got you," I said.

"You sure?"

"Very."

He nodded slowly. "Okay. Thanks, pumpkin."

"Let's get you back to the hotel room."

The rain had stopped, thankfully. David stepped in again, helping Mal over to the Jeep, leaning him up against it. One of the shiny black Escalades was parked nearby.

"Man, where are your keys?" asked David, digging through Mal's jeans pockets.

"Geez, Davie. I was saving that especially for Anne."

"I'm not interested in your dick. Where's the keys to your car?"

"Don't get me wrong, man. I love you, just not in that way."

"Uh, got 'em." David dangled the keys from a finger. "Anne, you good to drive him? I'll follow you back, help you get him up to your room."

"Sounds good. Thanks."

"Awesome," Mal mumbled. He let his head fall back and closed his eyes. His mouth, on the other hand, he opened wide. "I LOVE YOU, ANNE!"

I jumped, somewhat startled by the noise. "Holy shit."

"I LOVE YOU."

David just looked at me with one eyebrow raised.

"Huh. He is really drunk," I said, and David half-smiled. Best just to ignore my mini heart attack over Mal saying those words.

"I FUCKING LOVE YOU, ANNE."

"Yeah, okay. Shut up now." David tried to slap a hand over Mal's mouth.

"AAAAAAANNNNNE!" My name was a long, drawn-out howling kind of noise, muffled at the last when David managed to cover his mouth. Muted grunts and snarling came next.

"God damn it," swore David. "He just fucking bit me."

"My love shall not be silenced!"

I did my best not to laugh. "Mal? I've got a headache from you accidentally kicking me in the head. Do you mind being quiet?"

"Oh, shit, fuck, okay. Sorry, pumpkin. So sorry." He stared up at the sky. "Look, Anne, stars and shit. It's beautiful, right?"

I looked up and sure enough the clouds had parted, allowing a couple of brave stars to shine through. "Right. Let's go back to the hotel now."

"Mm, yeah, let's go. I have something in my pants I want to show you." His clumsy fingers started in on the waist of his jeans. "Look, it's real important."

I grabbed his fingers, squeezed them tight. "That's great. Show me back at our hotel room, okay?"

"Okay." Mal happy sighed. The air around him consisted solidly of scotch fumes.

"Thanks for texting Ev." David pulled open the passenger side door, grabbed Mal's arm, and proceeded to shove him into the car. "You think tonight was fun, wait till we go on tour. Then things'll get interesting. First time ever there's been girlfriends or wives along."

"The way you say that . . . should I be afraid?"

Mal hammered on the passenger side window. "Anne, my pants itch. I think I'm allergic to them. Come help me take 'em off."

We both ignored him.

David scratched his head. "Think it'll be a learning curve for all of us, yeah?"

"Yeah." The future was a big, ripe ball of I had no damn clue what would happen. And for once, that was okay.

CHAPTER TWENTY-ONE

There was groaning, loud, long, and explicitly painful. Most closely it resembled a wounded animal. Though with an animal, there would have been less swearing. These noises coming from behind me didn't speak of fun times. No, what these noises referred to was a special particular level of hell called The Morning After a mother truckload of booze.

"Pumpkin." Mal buried his face in the back of my neck, pressing his hot skin against me. "Fuck."

"Hmm?"

"Hurts."

"Mm."

The hand stuffed down the front of my pants flexed and curled. It pressed down on all sorts of interesting places, making me squirm.

"Why'd you put my hand down your panties while I was asleep? What's that about?" he mumbled. "Christ, woman. You're out of control. I feel violated."

"I didn't do that, sweetheart. That was all you."

He groaned again.

"You were most insistent about having your hand there. I figured after you fell asleep I'd be able to move you. But it didn't happen." I rubbed my cheek into my pillow, his bicep.

"This pussy is mine." His fingers stretched, pushing against the material of my underwear, stroking accidentally over the insides of my thighs. So not the time to get turned on. We had talking to do.

"Yes, that's what you said. Repeatedly."

He grunted and yawned, then rubbed his hips against me. Morning wood pressed into my butt cheek. "You shouldn't have made me drink so much. That was very irresponsible of you."

"I'm afraid that was all you too." I tried to sit up but his arm held me down.

"Don't move yet."

"You need water and Advil, Mal."

"'Kay."

His hand withdrew from my crotch and he rolled onto his back with much huffing and puffing. I hadn't managed to get him into the shower last night. Accordingly, this morning, we both stank of sweat and scotch.

I got him a bottle of water and a couple of pills and sat back on the side of the bed. "Up. Swallow."

He opened one bleary eye. "I'll swallow if you will."

"You got it."

"You better mean that. A man doesn't like to be lied to about that sort of thing." Ever so slowly he sat up, his lank, blond hair hanging in his face. He stuck out his tongue and I dropped the pills on it, then handed him the water. For a while he's just there, sipping the water and watching me. I had no idea what came next, what I should say. It was so much easier to just crack stupid jokes than to actually attempt to be deep and meaningful. To help him.

"I'm sorry," I said, just to break the silence.

"Why? What'd you do?" he asked softly.

"I mean about Lori."

He drew up his legs, braced his elbows on his knees, and hung his head. There was nothing but the noise of the air conditioner clicking on, the clink of silverware or something from the room next door. When he finally looked up at me, his eyes were red rimmed and liquid. Mine immediately did the same in empathy. There wasn't a part of me that didn't hurt for him.

"I don't know what it feels like so I'm not going to pretend I do," I said.

His lips stayed shut.

"But I'm so sorry, Mal. And I know that doesn't help, not really. It doesn't change anything."

Still nothing.

"I can't help you and I hate that."

Fact was, a part of wanting to soothe another person was making yourself feel useful. But nothing I could say would take away his pain. I could turn myself inside out, give him everything, and it still wouldn't stop whatever was wrong with Lori.

"I don't even have a functioning relationship with my mother, so I have no idea. Truth is, I used to wish her dead all the time. Now I just wish she'd leave me alone," I blurted out, then stopped, reeling at my own stupidity. "Shit. That's the worst thing to be telling you."

"Keep going."

Crap, he was serious.

I opened my mouth and my throat closed up. The words were dragged out kicking and screaming. "She, um . . . she checked out on us, Lizzy and me. Dad left and she went to bed. That was her great solution to the problem of our family falling apart. No trying to get help, no doctors, just lying in the dark doing nothing. She pretty much stayed in her room for three years. Apart from the time Child Protection Services came by. We managed to persuade them she wasn't a complete waste of space. What a joke."

He stared at me, his lips thin and white.

"I came home one day and she was sitting on the side of her bed with all these little colored pills lined up on her bedside table. She was holding this big glass of water. Her hand was shaking so bad it splashed everywhere, her nightie was all wet. I didn't do anything, not at first." That one moment was horrendously clear in my head. Hovering by the bedroom door, torn over what to do. It had to be manslaughter, to stand by and let it happen. Something like that had to stain you.

"I mean, it was so tempting," I said, my voice cracking. "The thought of not having to deal with her anymore . . . but then Lizzy and I would have gone into the foster-care system and probably gotten separated. I couldn't risk that. She was better off at home with me."

His gaze was stark, his face pale.

"So I stayed home to watch her. She tried to kill herself a couple more times, then gave up on that too, like even dying was too much effort. Some days, I would just wish I'd been five minutes too late. That she'd managed to finish it. Then I'd feel guilty for even thinking that way."

He didn't even blink.

"I hate her so much for putting us through that. I get that depression happens and it's a serious, terrible illness, but she didn't even try to find help. I would make her appointments with doctors, try to get brochures and information and she just . . . you know, she had kids, she didn't have the fucking luxury of just disappearing up her own ass." Tears slid down my face unchecked. "Dad wasn't much better, though he did send money. I guess I should be grateful he didn't forget us entirely. I asked him 'why' when he was leaving and he said he just couldn't do it anymore. He was really quite apologetic about it. Like he'd ticked the wrong box on a form or something and now sorry, but he was opting out. Family? No. Oh shit, did I say yes? Oops! Fucking asshole. As if saying sorry changes anything when you're walking out the door.

"You don't appreciate how much time it takes, running a house, paying the bills, doing all the cooking and cleaning until it's all down to you. My boyfriend stuck with me for a couple of months but then he became resentful because I couldn't go out Saturday nights to games and parties and things. He was young, he wanted to go out and have fun, not stay in to look after a manic-depressive and a thirteen-year-old kid. Who could blame him?"

I ducked my head, trying to line up the important details in my mind. It wasn't easy, considering how much time I'd spent trying to forget. "Then Lizzy rebelled and that just made everything so much worse. She hated the whole world, and who could blame her? At least when she behaved like a selfish, immature kid there was an actual reason behind it, what with her being one. She got busted stealing from this store. I managed to talk the owner into not pressing charges. The scare seemed to snap her out of it. She settled down, got back into her schoolwork. One of us had to make it to college because I tried, but there was no way I was keeping up with school on my own."

What a fucking scene I was making. I blinked furiously and scrubbed away the tears. "You know, I actually wanted to cheer you up or something. Anything."

His silence was killing me.

"So that's my tale of woe." I gave him a smile. Doubtless it looked as shitty as it felt.

"Mom's got ovarian cancer," he said, his voice rough. "They're giving her a couple of months at best . . ."

It felt like my heart stopped. Time stopped. Everything.

"Oh, Mal."

He pushed back his hair, lacing his fingers behind his head. "She's so fucking happy you're around. Kept going on about you at dinner, how wonderful you were. You're her dream come true for me. She's been wanting me to settle down for a while now."

I nodded, trying for a better smile. "She's really great."

"Yeah."

"Fuck, Anne. That's not the only reason why, though . . . I mean . . . at first that was a big part of the reason." He gripped the back of his neck, muscles flexing. "There's more to it now than making her happy before she'd—" He paused, his lips twisting, unable to say the word. "You know there's more, right? We're not pretend anymore. You know that, don't you?"

"I know that." This time I totally aced the smile. "It's okay."

So our start had been dubious. It didn't change where we were now.

"Come have a shower with me?" He held out his hand.

"I'd love to."

He gave me a gallant attempt at a smile.

The bathroom was spacious, white marble with gold trim. We even had a grand piano out in the living room, should the mood strike. Apparently his parents were up in the presidential suite so we'd had to make do with second best. Second best was pretty fine.

He stripped off his boxer briefs. I got the water running at the right temperature, letting the room slowly fill up with steam. Hands slid over me from behind, tugging down my panties, drawing up my old Stage Dive T-shirt. It was the only thing he'd okayed me wearing to bed last night in his drunken wisdom. We were our own small, perfect world in the warmth of the shower cubicle. Mal stepped under the water and it soaked his hair, ran down over his beautiful body. I slid my arms around his waist, resting my head on his chest. The arms he put around me made everything right.

We could deal with things alone. Of course we could. But it was so much better together.

"Worst fucking thing is the morning," he said, resting his chin on the top of my head. "For a few seconds, everything's alright. Then I remember she's sick, and . . . it's just . . . I don't even know how to describe it."

I held him tighter, hanging on for dear life.

"She's always been there. Used to drive us to shows, help us set up. She's always been our biggest fan. When we went platinum she got a Stage Dive tattoo to celebrate. At the age of sixty, the woman got inked. And now she's sick. I can't get my head around it." His chest moved against me as he breathed deep, let it out slow.

I stroked his back, the length of his spine, up and down, smoothing my hands over the curves of his ass, drifting my fingers over the ridges of his rib cage. We stood beneath the hot water and I soothed him as much as I could.

Let him know he was loved.

I picked up the bar of soap, running it over him, washing him like a child. First his top half, from the lines of his shoulder blades to the muscles in his arms, every inch of his chest and back. Washing his hair was tricky due to the differences in height.

"Lean down." I poured some shampoo into my hand then rubbed it in, massaging his scalp, taking my time. "Let me rinse it."

He did as asked without comment, hanging his head beneath the showerhead. Next came the conditioner. Carefully, I finger-combed it through.

"You're not allowed to cut your hair," I informed him.

"Okay."

"Ever."

He gave me an almost smile. It was definitely getting closer.

Once his top half was done I knelt on hard stone tiles, soaping up his feet and ankles. Spray from the shower drifted down over me, keeping me warm. Face to face with it or not, I ignored his thickening cock. It wasn't time yet. The muscles in his long, lean legs were so nice. I really needed to look up their names. He flinched when I did the back of his knees.

"Ticklish?" I asked, grinning up at him.

"I'm too manly to be ticklish."

"Ah." I dragged the soap over the hard length of his thighs, back and forth. Damned if he wouldn't be the cleanest, sparkliest rock 'n' roll drummer in the whole wide world. Water slid over his body, highlighting all the ridges and dips, the curve of his pecs and the satin of his skin. I should just call him cake and eat him with a spoon.

"You going higher?" Desire deepened his voice.

"Eventually." I soaped up my hands and put the bar of soap aside. "Why?"

"No reason."

The "no reason" was pointing right at me all large and demanding. I held it aside with one hand, slipping the other between his legs. His hard dick warmed the palm of my hand. A woman with more patience wouldn't have curved her fingers around it, squeezed tight. I was so crap at waiting.

Mal sucked in a breath, his six-pack contracting sharply.

"I love your ass." I said, tracing soapy fingers along the crack before cradling his balls. Every part of him was sublime, body and soul. The good and the bad and the difficult. The times I wanted him to be serious and the times I didn't have a fucking clue where he was at. He always made me want more while making me profoundly thankful for what I had at the same time.

Because I had him, it was right there in his eyes.

"No idea how I got so lucky." I nuzzled his hip bone, sliding my fingers over the smooth skin of his cock.

"You love my ass that much?"

"No, it's more of an all-of-you kind of thing."

I gave his cock another squeeze and his eyes went hazy in the way I liked so much. Things had definitely woken up between my legs, but this was all about him. The tips of his fingers drifted over the sides of my face, his touch gentle, reverent.

Enough playing around.

I guided the head of his cock into my mouth and sucked hard. Hands dug into my wet hair, holding on tight. My tongue flicked over the top of him, teasing the sensitive rim before dipping below to rub against his sweet spot. I took him in deeper, sucking hard, again and again. His hips shifted, pressing him farther into my mouth. I'd never perfected the art of deep throating, sorry. Mal made me want to learn. Something told me he wouldn't be averse to some practice time. With one hand I cradled his balls, massaging. The other stayed wrapped tight around the root of his penis, stopping him from going too far and gagging me. But I took him as far as I could, pulling back to lavish him with attention from my tongue. Tracing the thick veins and toying with the slit.

The fingers in my hair drew tight, stinging ever so slightly. But it was fine. It was all good. I fucking loved being able to do this to him.

I drew him in deep and sucked hard, working him. He came with a shout, pumping into my mouth as far as my hand would let him. I swallowed.

And they said romance was dead.

He stood, panting, arms hanging slack and eyes closed. Fuck, he was perfect. I slowly stood, my numb knees shaky. After oral, there always seemed to be this moment of shyness. Maybe I should have been smug, thrown in some swagger. There wasn't really the space for it in the shower, however.

Mal opened his eyes and stared at me, his arms going around my shoulders. He drew me in, placing soft kisses on my face.

"Thanks," he said, the word muffled against my skin.

"You're welcome."

"I'm sorry about your parents, pumpkin. So fucking sorry."

My fingers tightened on his hips, involuntarily. One day, I'd stop reacting like that and I'd let it go. "I'm sorry about your mom."

"Yeah." He rubbed my arms briskly, smooched the top of my head. "We need to think happy thoughts. And order a shitload of bacon and eggs. And waffles too. You like waffles?"

"Who doesn't like waffles?"

"Exactly. Anyone who doesn't like waffles should be put in the fucking penal system. Lock 'em up and throw away the key."

"Absolutely."

"No more sad stuff today," he said, voice gruff.

He picked up the soap and started washing me, paying particular attention to my breasts.

"There's just one more thing I think we should talk about," I said, as he worked hard at rubbing some imaginary spot from my left nipple. It felt rather nice, truth be told.

"What's that?" he asked.

"Well, about what you said last night when we got back here. About starting a family."

His hand paused, covering my right breast. "Starting a family?"

"Yes. You said you were really serious about it. You even threw all the condoms out the window and flushed my pill down the toilet."

"That's pretty damn serious. Did we fuck?"

I batted my eyelashes at him and gave him an innocent, if somewhat evil, look. "No. Of course not."

The whites of his eyes blazed bright. "God . . . you nearly gave me a heart attack."

"Sorry." I kissed his chest. "You did throw all of your condoms out the window. You couldn't find where I kept my pills, though. Then you lay down and proceeded to name all of our children."

"All of them?"

"I take it we're no longer having a brood of lucky thirteen?"

His brows arched up. "Shit. Um, maybe not, huh?"

"Probably for the best. You were going to name three of them David. It would've gotten confusing."

"How much crap did I speak last night, just out of interest?"

"Not too much. You fell off the bed a couple of times, trying to lick my toes, and then you went to sleep."

He washed the soap off his hands and reached for the shampoo, massaging it into my hair.

"Ouch," I gasped. "Gentle."

"What's wrong?"

"You don't remember?"

He turned his face slightly and gave me side eyes. "What now?"

"You might've accidentally kicked me in the head ever so slightly when you fell off your drumming stool."

"Oh, no. Fuck. Anne . . ."

"You didn't hurt me. It's just a little bump."

Face drawn, he carefully washed the shampoo from my hair,

starting in on the conditioner. He kept shaking his head, frowning hard.

"Hey," I said, grabbing his chin. "It's okay. Really."

"I'll make it up to you."

"You already did." I placed my hand over his heart, feeling it beat against my palm. "You listened to my story without judging me. You told me what was up with you. Those two things are huge, Mal. They really are. We're good."

"I'll make it up to you more. That won't fucking happen again."

"Okay."

"I mean it."

"I know you do."

He gave me cranky eyes and then suddenly smiled. "I know what I'll get you. Been thinking about it for a while now."

"You don't need to get me anything. Though waffles really would be good, I'm starving." I finished washing off my hair, ready to get out.

"You're getting more than waffles." His arms came around me from behind, a hand sliding down between my legs. Lightly, he started stroking his fingers back and forth along the lips of my sex. "First, you need to come too."

"Okay."

He chuckled in my ear. "So obliging about your orgasms. I like that."

I wound my arms up around his neck and held on tight. He raised his hand to his mouth, wetting some fingers. Then one finger slipped through the seam of my sex, tantalizing me. I tingled from top to toe. Slowly he pressed a little inside, then drew back to trace my entrance, spreading the wetness around. He worked me up in no time, my breathing coming fast and shallow. I writhed against his hand.

"You have to stand still, Anne," he chided me, laying a hand flat against my stomach. Two fingers slid up into me, rubbing at something that felt amazing inside. "C'mon, you're not even trying."

"I can't."

"You have to. I can't do this right if you don't stay still."

"Oh," I gasped as his thumb slid over my clit, sending lightning up my spine.

"See? You made me slip."

The way he loved to tease me was both a blessing and a curse. Fingers drew out, leaving me empty, and all of his attention turned to my clit. He rubbed both sides at once, making me moan.

"Stay still."

"I'm trying."

"Try harder." Lightly, he slapped the top of my sex. The reaction was immediate, my hips kicking forward. No one had ever done that before. Every nerve ending in me felt about ready to explode.

"Like that percussion?" he asked.

"Fuck." It was the only word I had.

He hummed in my ear and went back to working my clit even faster. The pressure just kept building. So close.

"Mal. Please."

He slapped me again and I broke. I cried out, my body caving in. If he hadn't been there to hold me up I'd have hit the floor. The man probably needed to be locked away for the safety of women everywhere.

The water stopped. He wrapped me up in a towel and placed me like a limp rag doll on the bathroom counter.

"Hey, look at me," he said, standing bent before me.

"Hi."

He carefully tucked my wet hair behind my ears.

"I feel like we should touch base about this relationship stuff. And I should probably say something profound here. But I'm not really up to it. Especially not this morning." He exhaled hard. "You're an awesome lay, a great girl, I fucking hate it when you're sad, and I don't like it when you're not around. I'm even getting used to the fighting and drama now and then, because the make-up sex is rockin'. And besides, you're worth it to me."

The tip of his tongue rubbed over his top lip. "That's basically it. Not necessarily in that order, though. Okay?"

"Okay." I laughed, but only a little. He was, after all, being sincere.

"You're my girl. You gotta know that." He grinned and put his hands on my knees. "Need anything else from me?"

I paused, gave it some thought. "We're monogamous?"

"Yep."

"We're seeing where this goes?"

"Mm-hm."

"Then yeah, I'm good."

He nodded, gave my knees a squeeze. "You need anything from me, I expect you to let me know."

"Same goes for you. Anything."

"Thanks, pumpkin." He smiled, leaned in, and kissed me. "Ready to go on tour, Miss Rollins?"

"Absolutely."

CHAPTER TWENTY-TWO

The first day of our official vacation/tour time together, we spent mostly in bed. Waffles were ordered and consumed. In the evening, we left the sanctity of our hotel room to have dinner with his parents up in their suite. Once more, Neil was stalwart and silent, staying close to Lori's side at all times. Lori was the life of the party. The stories she told about Mal as a kid annoyed him and had me howling with laughter.

My favorite was the time an eleven-year-old Mal and his dad had built a small skate ramp in the backyard and he'd broken an arm, two fingers, and a leg within the first two and a half months. Lori made Neil turn the ramp into kindling. Mal staged a hunger strike that lasted approximately two and a half hours.

To make up for the loss of the ramp, his mom promised him a drum kit.

And so the legend began.

It was a great night. His mom didn't mention her illness, so neither did we. If Lori weren't so thin and fragile, and the men so on edge, you could've almost imagined nothing was wrong. The more time I spent with her, the more I understood Mal's devastation. Skate-ramp destroyer or not, Lori Ericson was great. Now that I knew, the quiet despair in Neil's eyes seemed obvious. He was dying inside, going through this with her.

That was the problem with love, it didn't last. One way or another, everything came to an end. People got hurt.

When we returned to our room Mal was withdrawn, silent. I put on an action film full of explosions. We watched it together, his head in my lap. When the movie ended was when the night really began. The sex was slow and intense. It went on and on until I barely remembered my own name. He stared into my eyes, moving above and inside me like time didn't matter.

Like we could do this forever.

The second day, all of their equipment and instruments had been moved from the practice hall to the venue. Mal had a sound check, then a business meeting to attend. I had my own plans. Lizzy came over to keep me and my low profile company. Apparently a couple of reporters were staking out the bookshop and my apartment, still hoping for the inside scoop. An old, fuzzy high school photo of me was the best they'd been able to do. It'd run in the local paper yesterday to no particular acclaim.

Fortunately, given her fascination with Ben, Lizzy already had a date lined up for tonight and couldn't make the concert.

That night, the tour kicked off.

I had barely a week before I had to return to work.

We hung out backstage with the guys until Adrian, their manager, came in, clapping his hands loudly. "Five minutes, guys. We good to go?"

He was followed by a man with a headset and a clipboard or computer of some description. I'd seen quite a few people outfitted this way around. Exactly how much was involved in bringing Stage Dive to town, I had no idea.

Ev and I were watching the concert from the side of the stage beside a collection of massive amps. Holy fucking hell, the roar of the crowd and the energy filling the massive space was amazing. I wasn't particularly deep or spiritual, but standing there, looking out over so many thousands of people, was an impressive thing. There was a definite vibe.

Stage Dive had sold out the largest concert venue in Portland in record time. Their tour was nine cities stateside, then on to Asia. They'd be hitting several festivals in Europe next spring and summer along with doing more concerts. Somehow during all of this, they'd also spend time in the recording studio. David had apparently been busy writing more songs about the glory of doing his wife.

Ah, true love and stuff.

The music was amazing up this close and personal. I enjoyed myself immensely until I noticed a woman in the front row had my boyfriend's name written on her tits in big red letters. Kind of hard not to notice when she kept insisting on flashing them.

"Suck it up and smile," said Ev, her teeth on show.

"Screw her." I turned my attention back to the drummer, going hard at it. He was flinging his head about, blond hair wild and sweat flying off him. My heart went thump. Let's not even go into what my loins did.

After an hour and a half or so, Lori and Neil joined us. Both were sporting earplugs and smiles. The looks of pride they gave their son made my eyes mist up ever so slightly. Lori must have noticed, because she slipped her arm around my waist, leaning into me. I put my arm around her shoulder as the band played another song, and then another. Gradually she gave me more of her weight. She didn't weigh much, but when she started to sway on her feet I gave Neil a nervous look.

He put a hand beneath her elbow, leaning down in front of her with his subtle smile. Lori perked up, waving him away, standing taller. Then her knees buckled and gave out. Both Neil and I grabbed for her, keeping her off the ground. Unfortunately, all of this happened between songs. Jimmy was smooth talking the screaming audience up front of the stage. And despite all of the bright lights, Mal saw Lori stagger. He rose from his stool, standing, watching us. Anxiety lined his face.

Without further ado, Neil swung Lori up into his arms and carried her off. I held my hand up to Mal and nodded, hoping he'd get the message that I'd follow them and do what I could. He must have, because he nodded back at me and then sat down again.

"Come on," said Ev, grabbing my hand. We ran after Mal's parents, ducking and weaving around people and equipment. Lena met us just outside the room we'd been in before, backstage. Beside her stood an unhappy Adrian, but then I doubted I'd ever see a happy one.

"Let me know if you want me to call a doctor," she said.

"Thanks."

Neil had lain Lori down on a couch and was holding a glass of juice to her lips. A bird would have drunk more than she seemed to. Her skin was pale and paper thin, her eyes dazed.

"There's no need to fuss," she said chidingly to Neil. When she saw me, her mouth fell open in obvious dismay. "Oh, Anne, you didn't need to come. You were enjoying the show."

"They must be nearly finished. And Mal would want me to come and check on you, I'm sure."

"Well, you've checked. I'm fine. Go on back now."

Fuck. I knew all about *fine*. Care of my mom's early example, I was the Queen of fucking fine. I perched on the edge of the couch while Neil squatted near the end. Up this close, her face was tinged gray.

"I know you're sick, Lori. Mal told me."

The air hissed out of her. "I told him I didn't want everyone knowing and carrying on. Its life, sweetie, we all have to go sometime."

"He said you had a month or two," I said. Lori and Neil shared a look I did not like one tiny bit. "Is there something you need to tell your son?"

"It might be less than that now. We saw the doctor in Spokane before we left to come here." Her chin hiked high. "But it makes no difference. I'm not spending my final days in a hospital."

Something stuck in my throat. "Your final days?"

"Weeks," she amended. "They think another week or two at best. We'll head home tomorrow afternoon. I'd like to be there . . ."

Neil inhaled hard and turned away. His hand slid over his wife's, fingers intermeshing.

"You have to tell him," I said. There were razor blades in my throat, barbed wire, nails, assorted hardware, and sharp implements. It was wildly uncomfortable.

"I suppose you're right."

With a grunt, Neil gave her fingers a final squeeze and rose to his feet. "I'll let him know when he comes offstage. Can't ask Anne to keep it from him."

"No," agreed Lori. "Just, help me sit up. Everyone will come in and I'll be lying here like a fool."

This wasn't happening. Shit.

Carefully, Neil and I helped Lori to sit upright. Then he went off to wait for his son. I took over juice duties. At least holding the glass gave me something to do.

"I'm glad he has you," said Lori, straightening the skirt of her pale green dress. "I know I've said it before. But my going will hit him hard. He acts all loud and tough, but he's got a soft underbelly, my son has. He's going to need you, Anne."

She took my spare hand in hers. Mine was sweaty, hers was not.

"I really like your son," I said. Because I had to say something. So, of course it was woefully inadequate as per the ordinary when it came to feelings.

"I know you do, sweetie. I've seen the way you look at him."

"Crazy eyes?"

"Yes." She laughed softly. "Crazy eyes."

Out front, the crowd roared and the stamping of feet almost shook the building. Funny, back here, the music was a mild thrumming sort of noise at most. Negligible. Or maybe it was care of the pounding in my skull. I could feel a headache coming on. This whole situation was beyond heavy, the weight of it crippling. There was no making this right or fixing it.

People started flowing into the room. A long table full of drinks and food had been set up. Apparently an after party was planned for right here. Adrian stood by the door, shaking hands and laughing loudly at the shit people said. It was all so surreal. Somewhere out there, Neil was probably telling Mal, right now.

"Everything will be fine." Lori patted my hand. Funny, the way she clung to my favorite word. Perhaps there was something to the belief of finding a partner who reflected your parent. Which was fantastically creepy and wrong. I really didn't want to think about it after all. Mal was nothing like my father.

Then he stormed in. Mal, not my dad. A T-shirt was wrapped around his right hand, blood dripped from his fingers.

"What the hell happened?" I jumped out of my seat, running toward him.

Neil returned to Lori's side. Jimmy headed straight for the table laden with booze and gourmet goodies. He dug into the big bucket filled with foreign beers with a single-minded dedication.

"Jimmy. What are you doing?" Lena grabbed at his arm.

With a look of pure annoyance, Jimmy leaned down, whispered in her ear. Lena's gaze darted to Mal and then dropped to his hand. She looked up and down the table, searching for something.

"Mal?" The scent of him was a kick to my gut, same as always. But what the hell was going on?

"Hey, pumpkin. No big deal." He didn't meet my eyes. He also studiously avoided his mom's concerned gaze.

Jimmy returned with his hands full. He and Lena had turned a linen table cloth into an ice pack. "Here."

"Thanks." Slowly, Mal unwound the bloody T-shirt. Beneath it, his knuckles were raw, open wounds. His jaw clenched as he held the ice to his hand.

The managerial jerk, Adrian, elbowed his way into our circle. "Mal, buddy. I hear there was an incident upstairs?"

"Ah, yeah, Adrian, you mind getting that straightened out? Mal accidentally put a hole in the wall. Just one of those things, yeah?" David put a hand to the man's shoulder, leading him away.

I highly fucking doubted it was an accident, given the timing.

"We need to get someone in to look at his hand," said Adrian.

They kept talking but I tuned them out. I put my hand to Mal's face, willing him to look at me. "Hey."

His eyes were going to give me nightmares, the misery in them. He leaned forward, caught my mouth with his, kissing me fully, frantically. His tongue invaded my mouth, demanding everything. And I gave it to him. Of course I did.

At last he calmed, resting his forehead against mine. " 'S'all fucked."

"I know."

"She's only got a week or two at most."

There was nothing I could say.

He squeezed his eyes shut. Sweat from his face dampened my skin. He was bare from the waist up and the room was cold, the air-conditioning working overtime for some reason. Not so necessary this time of year.

"Let's get you hydrated," I said, grateful for anything I could do for him. "Find another T-shirt for you to put on. Okay? You're going to cool off fast in here."

" 'Kay."

"Stay with him," said Ev, her hand on my shoulder. "I'll go."

"Evvie." Mal looped his arms over my head in an awkward hug, still holding the ice to his hand. "Hard stuff."

Her forehead creased.

"Scotch or something," said Mal. "Please."

With a sigh, she turned away, headed off into the growing crowd. Worst damn timing for a party ever.

"We better go over," said Mal, turning to face his parents.

Neil perched on the arm of the couch, an arm around his wife. Lori's lips were pinched with worry.

"Hey, Mom," said Mal, keeping me tight against him. "Glad you guys could make it. Had a little accident with my hand."

"Are you alright?"

"Oh, yeah. No worries. "

The guys stood nearby, holding back spectators, keeping industry and other types at bay from our corner of the room. Soon, Sam arrived with another black-suited guy and took over this duty. Ben and Jimmy kept close, talking to people, doing their job, and socializing. But their gazes kept returning to Mal.

Ev must have run, because she returned with a Stage Dive Tour shirt for him to wear, a bottle of Smirnoff vodka and another of Gatorade. "They didn't have scotch."

"It'll do." He handed me the sopping wet ice pack while he pulled on the shirt. It had a big candy skull on the front. "Thanks, Evvie."

"Son," said Neil. There was a lot communicated through just the one word.

"Dad, all good," crowed Mal, suddenly switching mood to exuberant. It didn't give me a good feeling. "This is how we roll after the show. You know that!"

Neil said nothing. The latest Stage Dive record and the chatter of a hundred or so party people filled the air instead. Mal downed half of the bottle of green Gatorade. Then he passed it to me to hold and downed big mouthfuls of vodka.

Ah, shit. This was going to be like watching a car wreck.

"Baby," I said, slipping my arms around his waist, drawing him closer. "Just stop and breathe for a minute."

"You called me baby." He smiled.

"Yes."

"You called me sweetheart the other day."

"You're the one that wanted a stupid romantic nickname."

"Yeah. My Anne." He rubbed his cheek against mine like he was marking me. Stubble scratched my skin and my whole body glowed like embers. The emotion was too much, completely overwhelming.

"Mal."

"Don't frown, there's no need to worry. Do me a favor and go talk to Mom okay?" he asked. "Keep her happy. I can't, ah . . . I can't talk to her right now. Not yet."

He put the bottle to his lips again, tipped his head back and drank, while I swallowed hard. The booze was him self-medicating regarding this situation. But I'd be lying if I said it didn't scare me just the same. His eyes popped wide open and he exhaled. "That's better. That's fucking better."

"I think Adrian's going to get someone to come check your hand," said David, sidling up next to us.

"No need."

I tried to clear my sore throat. "Let him look at your hand, Mal."

"Pumpkin—"

Enough of this shit. "You want me not to worry? You get your hand looked at. That's the deal."

His gaze ever so slowly sized me up. "I love it when you get all hard assed on me. Okay. If it'll make you happy, I'll let them look at it."

"Thank you."

Another big swig from the bottle.

Ev situated herself beneath David's arm, both of them watching him with anxious eyes. There was strain and stress on everyone's faces and Mal just kept right on drinking. Bottom of the bottle, here he came. For some reason, it just made me mad.

"That's enough." I tugged the bottle out of his hand. He obviously hadn't been expecting it because he didn't put up a fight. Big green eyes blinked at me, then narrowed into anger.

"What the fuck?" he said in a low voice.

"Find another way to deal with this."

"That's not your call."

"You really want one of her last memories of you to be watching you get drunk?"

"Oh, please. Mom's been around since the beginning. She knows what parties are like backstage, Anne. She wants normal? I'm giving her normal."

"I'm serious, stop this."

He gave me more of the angry stare. No problem. If he wanted to do glaring competitions all night, fine by me. I'd said I had his back. It meant protecting him even from himself if need be.

"Look around you," I said. "They all just watched Jimmy go through this. They're scared shitless for you, Mal."

"It's not like that," he growled.

"Not yet."

"Not your job to tell me what to do, pumpkin. Not even remotely."

"Mal—"

"We've been together what, a week? And you know best now, huh?" He looked down at me, his jaw shifting from side to side. "Yeah, Anne's in charge."

"Ah, for fuck's sake," said David, stepping forward. "Shut up, you dickhead, before you say something you really regret. She's right. I got no interest in watching you go through rehab too."

"Oh give me a break," said Mal. "Rehab? A bit overdramatic there, Davie."

"Really?" asked David, getting right up in his face. "You're getting so drunk you're accidentally kicking your girlfriend in the head. So mad you're putting your fist through walls. How's that sound to you, hmm? Sound like someone who's got it all under control?"

Mal flinched. "Stuff is happening."

"I get that. We all get that. But Anne's right, you fucking yourself up every other night isn't the answer."

Mal's shoulders dropped, the fight leaving him. "Fuck you, Ferris."

"Whatever. Say sorry to your girlfriend and mean it."

His sad-eyed gaze turned to me. "Sorry, pumpkin."

I nodded, tried for a smile.

"Come on, you need a breather." David grabbed Mal by the back of the neck and towed him off into the crowd. Fortunately, Mal didn't fight him. I watched them go with relative calm. Sure, everything would be alright. Whatever happened, however, I didn't want to turn around. I could feel the weight of Lori's stare burning a hole in the middle of my back. Her and Neil had to have heard and seen it all. What could I possibly say?

I was so terrible at this family and relationship stuff. I wish Lizzy were here. She'd know what to do. She was so much better with people than me.

"It'll be okay," said Ev, taking my hand in hers.

A nice sentiment, but I highly doubted it.

CHAPTER TWENTY-THREE

"PARTY!" An hour later, Mal was in loud, manic mode.

He only had a bottle of water in his hand. Our words had gotten through to him at least. Just like the first night I met him, he stood on top of a coffee table, doing his groove thing. There were a lot of women willing to heed his party call. Plenty of slick, shiny women watching my man with avarice in their eyes. It was something I'd have to get used to. I couldn't kill all of them. I mean, where on earth would I hide so many bodies?

This dating rock stars business was harder than it looked.

One such young lady tried to climb up onto the table with him and no. Not even a little.

I grabbed her arm. "Not happening."

"Get your hand off me," she spat.

"PUMPKIN!" shouted my drumming delight from above.

Holy hell, my ears. They were ringing.

The woman gazed up and gave Mal a foxy grin. Her facial expression when she turned back to me was not as warm.

"Sorry," I said (blatant lie there). "He's taken."

"Who the hell are you?"

"I'm pumpkin." The "ha, bitch" was silent, but make no mistake, it was most definitely there.

She did some strange squinty-eyed thing and then about-faced, disappearing into the crowd. There was a flash of shiny silver stilettos and she was gone. Awesome shoes. I'd worn my usual boots and a skirt, denim this time, a black long-sleeve shirt and some chunky resin jewelry finished me off. Deep down inside, I had no idea how a rock star's girlfriend was supposed to dress, but for comfort would do. Those shoes though, I'd really like to know where she got them. Chances of her telling me now had to be somewhere between nil and none.

Lori and Neil were still stationed on the couch in the corner. David and Ev kept them company while I guarded my man from other women. Or something like that. Honestly, I wasn't having a very good time. The argument earlier had left me on edge and I didn't fit with this crowd. There were music reporters and industry types, a mixed assortment of the rich and famous all gathered together to kick off the tour.

"Pumpkin?" Mal called again.

I turned to face him.

"Oh, there you are. Hey. I have an announcement to make," hollered Mal. "Everyone. Yo!"

The crowd quieted, all heads turning his way. I didn't have a good feeling about this.

"Lot of shit's been happening lately. Got me thinking about things." He gazed over at his parents. "Life's short and you gotta make it count, take the time to be with the people you love. Keep 'em close to you. So I, ah . . . I've come to a decision. Right here, right now."

He stared down at me, his brows nearly meeting above the straight line of his nose. And then, he sank down on one knee, on top of the coffee table. His hand reached out for mine and I took it, fingers numb with surprise.

"Marry me, Anne."

My heart stopped. Holy fucking hell. He couldn't be serious. "What?"

"Yeah, marry me tonight," he said, his voice clear to one and all. "We'll fly down to Vegas on the red-eye. Be back in time for breakfast."

Flashes went off around us, blinding me. But nothing else existed. There was only his beautiful, hopeful face, fading in and out of view.

". . . So romantic," whispered someone nearby.

"We can take the guys with us," he said. "Go pick up Lizzy on the way. Even bring Reece if you want."

I couldn't breathe.

"I'll buy you the biggest fucking ring you've ever seen."

No, really, was there no oxygen in this room?

"I know this is soon. And I know you've got some issues with marriage, but this is you and me. We're solid."

No, we weren't. We'd just had a fight. We were always having fights and it'd only been . . . fuck, how many days? Yes, we could be good together. But we were only beginning; no way were we ready for this.

"C'mon, Anne."

"It's only been a week . . ."

"I need you to do this for me."

"I'll marry you, Mal!" Some bitch at the back of the room shouted. Others muttered their agreement.

"Why?" I searched his face, my heart beating overtime.

"Lots of reasons."

I shook my head, stupefied.

"Please," he said, staring into my eyes.

Neil was supporting Lori, they were standing right there, not four feet away, watching the whole thing. My stomach turned upside down. There was such hope on Lori's face. She had her hands clutched to her chest, her eyes shining with unshed tears. Ev stood just past her with David and her lips were drawn, but her eyes . . . Fuck, they all actually thought this insane idea might work. Well, I guess Ev would, she'd done some crazy stuff in Vegas herself.

But this wasn't romance. This was insanity.

"I need you to do this for me," he repeated. "Take a chance, Anne."

Take a chance on heartbreak and abandonment. All the pain and suffering I knew so well. I barely had a grip on being in a relationship and he wanted to make it legal and binding forever and ever until someone up and decided they'd had enough.

My shoulders curved in. "Mal . . . don't."

His gaze darted over my face. "You and me in Vegas. C'mon, it'll be fun."

I stepped closer to him, trying for privacy. "I can't marry you just to make your mom happy."

"It's more than that."

"It's not. If it weren't for her being sick, there's no way you'd be asking me this right now."

"But—"

"I'm sorry. No."

"Anne . . ."

I could see the exact moment he realized he wasn't going to talk me into it. That he wasn't going to get his way. His jaw hardened and he dropped my hand. In one smooth move he jumped off the coffee table and headed for the door. Any possible words stuck in my throat, choking me.

There he went. Going, going, gone.

He was gone.

Every eye in the room was on me. David followed Mal, and Ev appeared at my elbow. They really did have this shit down by now, managing drama the Stage Dive way. Jimmy and Ben stopped Adrian from following David and Mal. The manager gave me a look strongly encouraging me to curl up and die. I was so sick of this.

Something broke inside. The pain was excruciating.

It was really best just to get this dealt with.

Lori's look was hesitant, sad. "Oh, Anne . . ."

"I'm sorry," I said, and then I got the fuck out of there.

Mal didn't return to our hotel room that night. There was no message from him the next day either. I went home.

CHAPTER TWENTY-FOUR

I spent the remaining days of my vacation spring cleaning the apartment. Lizzy and Lauren took turns sitting on the love seat, watching me go berserk. Berserk being their word, not mine. I was fully functioning and fine given my heartbroken status. No way had I crawled into bed like Mom and refused to come out. I was stronger than that and my apartment was very, very clean.

"Look at that bowl," I said, gesturing toward the bathroom with my pink, rubber-gloved hand and toilet brush. "You could eat out of it."

"Babe, all power to you, but I am not inspecting your toilet." Lauren crossed her legs, swung her foot back and forth.

"No shit, it's sparkling."

"I believe you."

The front door opened and Lizzy walked in. "She still at it?"

Yes, during particularly unlucky times, they'd both be there, commenting and getting in my face. So helpful. Friends and family were the worst. They were also the best, seeing me through this temporary insanity.

"Yes, she is. Please knock before you come in uninvited," I said.

Mal would be pissed. He hated people just waltzing in. Not that he would ever be here again or cared, so whatever. Maybe

I should scrub the kitchen one more time. Going back to work tomorrow would be good. It'd help keep me busy. Reece had dropped off a couple of new bottles of environmental all-surfaces cleanser and a scrubbing brush for me yesterday (I'd worn my old one out.). He got my drive to keep busy right now. Or, if he didn't get it, he at least had the sense to stay out of my way and not mention any famous drummers.

"And you didn't close the door properly, Lizzy."

My sister looked at me over the top of her sunglasses. "That's because you have another guest about to arrive. Hopefully you'll be nicer to this one."

"I'm nice to everyone."

Lauren winced. "No. Not really. You're kind of pretty fucking painful lately. But we love you and we get that you're hurting, so here we are."

My frown did feel permanently pressed into my face. Perhaps they had a point. It might be time to move on. If I'd only been with him a week, then mourning him for half a week was probably about right. Too bad my heart disagreed.

"Helllooooo!" cried Ev, appearing around the door frame. "Yeah, okay. Wow, Liz. She needs help."

"Told you," said Lauren, standing up to give Ev a hug.

"Um, Anne?" Ev approached me with extreme caution, slowly slipping out of her woolen jacket. "Take the gloves off and go put on clothes that don't have holes in them. You might want to shower first, wash your hair, maybe? Wouldn't that be nice?"

"I've been cleaning," I explained, holding the brush up as evidence. "You don't wear good clothes to clean in."

Lizzy turned me in the direction of the bathroom. "About the time you're waving a toilet brush around exclaiming about the beauty of your bowl, it's probably time to stop and rethink your life."

"Go back in there and clean you this time," directed Lauren. "I'll find you some clothes."

"Wait." I turned back to Ev. "Why are you here? Why aren't you on tour?"

She grimaced. "The tour's been cancelled. Put off until next year. It's for the best. They're saying Lori only has a couple of days left so the guys have all gone to Coeur d'Alene."

Oh, god. Poor Mal. My ribs squeezed breathtakingly tight.

"Why aren't you with them?" I asked.

"I'm flying there this afternoon." She spoke slowly, carefully. "But I wanted to be here for your intervention. And to ask if maybe you wanted to come with me."

I just stared at her blankly.

"I think he would really appreciate you being there, Anne. I know things got left in a bad place between you two. But I think he could really do with your support right now. Lori would probably like to say good-bye."

"I turned down her son's proposal of marriage, so I highly doubt that."

Ev gave a one-shoulder shrug. "She was sad, but . . . I don't think she was mad at you exactly."

"It doesn't matter anyway. I can't go." I wandered into the bathroom, put away the toilet brush, and peeled off the rubber gloves. Ev, Lauren, and Lizzy huddled in the doorway, watching me. I washed my hands, soaping them up super well. "Look, guys, I appreciate the intervention, not that I believe I needed it. I was just keeping busy before I had to go back to work."

"Sure you were," said Lizzy. "That's why you scoured the ceiling."

"It was dusty."

"Focus, ladies." Lauren clicked her tongue. "Anne, you need to go with Ev. Talk to him."

I dried my hands with a towel. The girl in the mirror was a bit of a mess, hair lank and skin greasy. They were right there, I had looked better.

"You two were good together," said Ev. "He got carried away with the wedding idea, but I think he gets that now."

"Oh, I don't know. I don't think there's so many good ways to take someone refusing to marry you." I huffed out a laugh. "Not sure there's any coming back from that one. Thanks for the thought, Ev. But he doesn't want me there."

She shook her head. "You don't know that—"

"Yes, I do." I put my hands on my hips. It didn't feel quite right so I swapped over to crossing them over my chest instead. "I texted him the other day, asked if there was anything I could do. If he wanted me there even just as a friend. He said no."

And yes, Mal's one-word, two-letter answer had pissed me off and hurt. The fact that I bought myself a new phone for my birthday was somewhat related. As was the mark I needed to paint over on my bedroom wall. Turns out I had a better throwing arm than I was aware of.

Ev, Lauren, and Lizzy just stared at me. Awesome. I could do without yet again having my heartbreak on display for one and all. And that was a shitty, stupid thought. "Seriously, thanks anyway, guys. For everything. I'm going to take your advice and have a shower."

"That took balls, reaching out to him," said Lizzy.

"I had to try."

Lauren frowned at the floor. "We need booze. Food."

"Yeah," sighed Lizzy.

My smile started twitching at the edges. I couldn't quite make it. "Sounds good."

Ev nodded somberly. Then she paused. "Anne, be smarter

than him. If he means something to you, if you get another chance . . . don't give up so easily."

I had nothing. I just stared at her, lost, not a clue how to react or what to do with myself. It was the same damn way I'd been feeling since the night Mal walked out on me.

"Go get cleaned up." Lizzy hugged me from behind, wrapping her arms around me and squeezing tight. "I'll organize some food and drinks."

"Oh, I can do that after I—"

"Anne, please. Let me look after you for a change."

I nodded slowly, on the verge of tears yet again. "Okay. Thanks."

Lizzy set her chin on my shoulder, not letting go. "You're my amazingly strong big sister and I love you. But you are allowed to need help now and then. You don't have to fix everything on your own anymore, you know?"

"I know." I didn't know it exactly, but I was beginning to feel it. And it was warm, wonderful, and everything it should have been. Not being alone in this, having them all here was a beautiful thing. "Thank you."

My birthday didn't feel like my birthday. The last two had been nice, shopping with Lizzy and going out to dinner with Reece. But this year's? Not so much. It was a lot like being back with Mom and pasting a smile on my face for Lizzy's sake. Making a cake and then getting sick after eating half of it because it was what you did.

I'd been back at work for three days now. The "intervention" had stuck. I hadn't indulged in anymore crazy cleaning marathons. To be fair, the apartment couldn't get any more hygienic if I tried. I hadn't heard from Mal again and I didn't expect I would. End of story.

My stripy jersey dress was definitely the go-to look for dinner with Reece. It made me happy. Heartbreak could be covered over by a million and one things including cake and happy stripy dresses.

Fucking rock stars with their fucking ridiculous marital demands and their fucking incredible smell, face, body, voice, sense of humor, mind, generous spirit, and all the rest (Not necessarily in that order.).

Fuck them all. But especially fuck Mal.

Reece was fifteen minutes late. I tapped my knee-high brown boots on the scuffed wooden floor, beating out a hectic rhythm. No need to mention whom I might have picked up the habit from. Maybe waiting outside was a better idea, out in the cold wind. I trudged down the stairs and out the door while firing off a text message to Reece making sure he hadn't broken down or anything.

He hadn't.

I knew this because he was rolling around on the small patch of front lawn with someone. Not in ecstasy so much as agony. Lots of agony, if the groans and grunts were any indication. A battered bouquet of roses lay tossed aside. What the hell?

"Reece?"

No response.

I blinked, double-checking my vision. Was that really . . . "Mal?"

Yes, Mal and Reece were fighting on the front lawn. Blood wept from a cut on Mal's brow and on Reece's lip. A dark mark covered Mal's cheek and Reece's shirt was ripped open. They wrestled on, throwing punches and making animalistic-sounding noises.

"Motherfucking little . . ." Mal's drove his fist hard into Reece's stomach.

Reece grunted and countered by attempting to kick him in the groin. He caught Mal's thigh instead. Given the way Mal's face twisted, it obviously stung.

"You're the asswipe that left her," sneered Reece.

They came clashing together again, fists and blood flying. Bile stung the back of my throat and I swallowed it back down. Shit, shit, shit. What to do? I fished out my cell phone, dialed Lauren's number.

"Hi, Anne."

"Are you guys here? I need Nate out front now, please. Hurry."

"What's going on?"

"Mal and Reece are trying to kill each other."

There was swearing and muttering. "On our way back. We'll be there in five minutes."

I hung up. Five minutes. They could hurt each other worse in five minutes and do some real damage if they hadn't already. I couldn't wait five minutes. I needed to do something now.

I cupped my hands over my mouth, standing on the front step. "Hey! What the fuck do you two idiots think you're doing?"

Reece looked my way and Mal clocked him on the chin. Beyond enraged, they fell on each other again.

Well, that didn't work.

Then Reece swung hard, catching Mal in the face, knocking him back a step. Mal stood, stunned for a moment. And no damn way could I stand there and watch him get hurt any more. It just wasn't in me. Reece pulled back his arm, his bloody lips drawn, baring his teeth.

"Reece, no!" I didn't stop and think. Instead, I made like a fool and rushed in, hell-bent on defending my man.

Mal turned. "Anne."

I ran straight for him. Reece's fist hit me in the eye and I dropped. Pain filled my world, blanking my mind. Fuck, did it hurt.

"Are you okay?" asked Mal.

"Ah . . ." was about the best I could do.

"Anne, oh fucking hell, I'm so sorry," Reece babbled.

"Easy," said Mal. My head was carefully lifted and placed upon a firm jeans-clad thigh.

"Hey. Hi," I said, somewhat dazed and confused. I covered my battered eye with both hands, breathing through the exquisite agony.

"Pumpkin, what the fuck were you thinking, running in like that?"

"I was saving you. Or something. You know . . ."

They had stopped fighting. It was sort of a success.

Excited whimpering came from the box beside me. A little head popped up, then disappeared. What the hell? To the whole scene basically, I couldn't restrict the question to any one thing happening tonight on the front lawn. The grass was cool and damp beneath me. I lay on my back, staring up at the night sky. My brain pounded. Mal stared down at me, his eyes tight with concern, his face a bloody mess.

"How you feeling?" he asked.

"Ouch."

"Anne, I'm so damn sorry," said Reece, looking about as contrite and torn up about it as possible. "Are you alright?"

"I'll live." Mostly. "Advil and ice would probably be good."

"Yep, let's get you upstairs." Mal carefully brushed the hair back from my face.

Panting this time came from the box, along with a high-pitched yelp.

"It's alright, Killer. Mommy's okay." Mal put a hand in the box and lifted out a wriggly little body covered in black-and-white fur. A fancy, studded collar sat around his neck, topped off by a big red bow. The bow was bigger than the dog. "Mommy was trying to save Daddy from evil Uncle Reecey, wasn't she? A nice thing to do, but Daddy is still going to spank Mommy for being so silly and jumping into a fight. Yes he is, because Daddy's the best."

"Oh for fuck's sake," mumbled Reece.

"Happy birthday; I got you a puppy." Mal held the puppy near my face and a wet, pink tongue darted out, licking my chin. He had the darkest, sweetest little eyes. "I named him Killer."

"Wow." God, he was cute—the man and the dog both. "Mal, you can't call something that small Killer."

"He earned it. Killed one of my Chucks right after I picked him up this afternoon. Chewed a hole right through it."

The puppy licked me again, nearly getting me on the lips this time.

"Gross, little dude." I smiled. "I know what you do with that tongue."

Mal smiled, then handed the puppy to Reece. "Here, carry him up. Don't drop him."

"I won't drop him."

"You better not."

More grumbling from Reece and some yips from Killer the puppy. Truly, this night was surreal.

"Wait, Mal. What about your mom?" I asked. "How is she?"

His mouth firmed and his brows descended. "Not good. She doesn't have long now."

"What are you doing here?"

His bloody face screwed up and gave me a pained look. "That's kind of a long story too. I'll tell it to you upstairs."

A car pulled to a screeching halt at the curb, and Nate and Lauren rushed out. I waved groggily at them. "It's okay. They stopped fighting."

"Ooh, look at the puppy!" cried Lauren.

"You two fucking idiots. What did you do to her?" Nate squatted down next to me, scowling, studying my rapidly swelling shut eye. The world was a blur on that side. "How's your head, Anne?"

He turned back to Lauren, who was still busy petting and cooing at Killer. "Lauren, leave the dog and call that nurse friend of yours. If we take Anne anywhere like this people will ask questions I'm assuming she won't want to answer."

"Sorry. Yes. Good idea." Lauren pulled her cell phone out of her purse.

"No, please don't," I said. "It's fine."

Lauren hesitated, looking between me, Mal, and Nate.

"Really," I insisted, trying to look perky. "I'm going to have a shiner, but I'm okay."

"I'll carry her," growled Mal when Nate tried to pick me up.

"I'll walk. Just help me up." I held up my hands and Nate gently pulled me to my feet. Behind me, Mal jumped up. He gripped my hips, holding me steady as the world slipped and slid.

"Whoa." My head spun round and round.

"Easy." Mal stood at my back, letting me lean against him until I found my feet. "Fuck, Anne. I'm so sorry."

"I've never had a black eye before."

"Could have lived without you getting one now because of me." His lips brushed against my ear. "Let me carry you."

"Okay." Fighting was dumb. Mal and Reece fighting, and me resisting being carried.

Mal picked me up in his big, strong arms while I swooned like a proper romance-novel heroine.

"I'm thinking my career as a prizefighter has come and gone." I rested my head on his shoulder, breathing in his familiar scent. Man, I'd missed that. Mal just shook his head. I don't think he was quite ready to see the humor in my getting hit just yet.

Nate opened the front door to our apartment building and the rest followed behind me and Mal, Reece carrying the puppy, and Lauren still trying to pat the puppy.

"You're back and you got me a puppy?" The concept still seemed strange. It might have been my recent brain injury. I looped an arm around his neck, taking liberties with him while I could. Who knew how long he'd stay this time. Or why he was even back.

"You never had one as a kid."

"I can't have pets in this building, Mal."

"Yeah, I know. I got you a new apartment too. No point doing things halfway, right?"

"Riiiight." I had the worst feeling he wasn't joking.

Up the stairs we went. Nate rummaged in my purse and pulled out my keys, opening the door.

"Just put me on the couch, thanks," I directed. "Ah, there's an ice pack in the freezer."

Without a word, Mal deposited me as told then went to find the ice. It didn't hurt too badly to let him go. Not in comparison to my eye. I kept one hand over it, shielding it from the too-bright overhead light.

"Thanks for coming back, guys," I said to Nate and Lauren. "Sorry to mess with your night."

They just looked at me, sort of stunned still. Lauren had on heels and jeans, clearly ready for a night on the town.

"I'm sorry I interrupted your date. And Reece, relax," I said, moving right along. "It was an accident."

He gave me eyes full of guilt.

Mal came bustling back in with an ice pack wrapped up in a towel, a bottle of water, and a bottle of Advil.

"Thanks." I swallowed two of those suckers straight down and held the ice pack over my eye. "Reece and Mal, you need to stop fighting. Can I have that for my birthday, please?"

Without delay, Mal stuck out his hand, ready for shaking.

"Yeah, okay." Reece moved the puppy to one arm and shook Mal's hand.

"Thank you."

"Here," he said, holding my new dog out to me. The big, red bow had flopped down over Killer's face and he was growling and tugging on it with his teeth. Cutest thing ever. I hadn't even realized I wanted a dog but despite my eye throbbing like a bitch, I couldn't stop smiling. Reece placed him in my lap. Immediately he tried to climb me and lick my chin. Out of the three males present, he was definitely my favorite, despite being the jumpiest.

"Chill, little guy." Mal sat beside me on the love seat, placing a restraining hand on Killer.

"You sure you're okay?" asked Lauren, reaching in to give Killer a final scratch behind the ears.

"Yeah, I'll be fine. Thanks."

"You want us to go so you can kick Mal's ass?"

"Please."

She nodded, grabbed a scowly faced Nate, and dragged him out the door. Because girls got it. Men, not so much.

"Listen, Anne," said Reece. "I'm sorry about the scene out front. About you getting hit and everything."

"I know you are, Reece. But right now, I need to yell at Mal. Can we do dinner another time?"

"You're not going to yell at me?"

"No. I'm going to yell at him, because I'm in love with him."

Mal stiffened beside me, the hand petting Killer missing a beat.

"Right," said Reece. "Which means you're definitely not in love with me, and I need to give up and back off."

"I'm sorry, Reece."

"All right." Reece gave me a sad smile, then leaned in and kissed me on the cheek. "I'll remember that next time. Just do me a favor? Don't come to work for a few days. Stay home and give your eye and my guilt time to heal."

"You got it."

"So damn sorry about that."

"I know. It was an accident, Reece. No hard feelings."

"Yeah, no hard feelings," he repeated softly. Then he gave me a halfhearted wave and left, closing the door behind him. And here we were, me, Mal, and Killer. The apartment was eerily silent apart from the snuffling, panting puppy. Mal picked him up and put him carefully on the floor.

"I want to yell at you for leaving me the way you did, for disappearing on me," I said, moving the ice pack from my face. "But I can't because the situation with your mom is terrible and I know you're hurting. And for some stupid reason I still feel guilty about not agreeing to marry you even though you asking me was an insane, ridiculous stunt that had next to nothing to do with me."

"That's not true. And keep the ice on your face."

I covered my war wound back up. "I can't see you clearly if you sit on that side."

He sighed and knelt before me, his hands on my knees. "Can you see me now?"

"Yes. Why aren't you with your mom? That's where you should be."

"She wanted me here with you on your birthday. I wanted me here with you on your birthday. Neither of us wanted some other guy taking you out. Just the thought of it drove me nuts." His face tensed up and his hands smoothed up and down my woolen-tight-covered thighs. "Mom and I talked . . . about you and about everything. She helped me figure a few things out."

"Such as?"

"You just told Reece you were in love with me."

"Yes. But what did your mom help you figure out?"

There was growling going on down by Mal's shoe. We both ignored it.

"I dunno, what a relationship is, what love is. Lots of things. Seeing her and Dad together these last few days . . ." He pressed my knees apart, getting closer. "You know, I'm in love with you too. I just, I pushed too hard on the wrong thing, at the wrong time, for the wrong reason. I was a whole lot of wrong, pumpkin."

"Yeah."

He nodded. "Right girl, wrong everything else."

My good eye teared up. My bad one had never really stopped, but that was something else altogether. "Thank you. But things went to shit and you disappeared on me again. You need to stop doing that. That's a boundary, Mal. It's not the sort of thing I can keep taking from you."

"I won't disappear on you again. I promise. We'll sort things out together."

"Okay." I sniffed and smiled. "You better get back to your mom."

"In the morning. I hired a jet to take us back. She, ah . . . they think in the next day or two." He shut his eyes tight and pressed his forehead into my lap. "Hardest fucking week of my life. Hardly gotten any sleep at all. Will you sleep with me, Anne? I really need you to sleep with me."

I placed my hand on his head, rubbing at the soft strands of hair. "Whatever you need."

Eleven-forty glowed green on my alarm clock when I woke. We'd turned out all the lights and lain down together on my bed (still a mattress on the floor). The Advil had knocked me out like it always did. Where Mal was now, I had no idea. Distantly, there were footsteps on the stairs, the door opened, and little nails were clicking across the floor. Next thing I knew, Killer was jumping all over me, being psycho energetic. Having greeted me properly, he then bounded over to my stripy jersey dress. I'd tossed it at the set of drawers but they'd failed to catch. It lay on the floor, a perfect puppy bed, apparently.

"Our son needed to take a leak," said Mal, stripping off his hoodie and toeing off his boots.

"You're a good father."

"I know, right? I'm the best." His jeans went next and there was nothing but him beneath. If only there was more than ambient light from the street to see him by. He crawled underneath the blanket next to me. "How you doing, pumpkin? Your eye's looking a little messed up."

"I know. I can't see out of that side at all. But you're supposed to tell me I'm beautiful, no matter what."

"You are beautiful no matter what. You also have an awesome black eye. In the future, no running into fights." He kissed me, soft and sweet. Then he kissed me deep and wet, sliding his tongue into my mouth. His taste was home, the feel of his hands cradling my head perfection. I ran my fingers over his rib cage and up over his thick shoulders, getting familiar with him once again. My thighs tensed, between my legs turning swollen and wet for him. His thickening cock nudged my hip bone. So damn nice not to be alone in this.

"Happy birthday," he whispered.

"It is now that you're here."

"Fuck, I missed you."

"Missed you too."

"You fell asleep so fast. What's under here?" He toyed with the hem of my sleep shirt.

"You've forgotten already?"

He dragged my T-shirt over my head and tossed it aside. "Oh, breasts. Best present ever. Thanks, pumpkin."

"You're very welcome. I'm all about the giving on my birthday." I sucked in a harsh breath as he licked across first one nipple, then the other. They hardened, aching in the best way possible. "Wait till you see what else I've got for you."

"In here? Show me." His fingers hooked in the waistband of my underwear, dragging them down and off. "Nice. I need a closer look."

He crawled between my legs, his fingers drifting up and down my thighs featherlight. Torturously slow, he licked a path from the top of my sex up to my sternum. Every part of me he touched tingled. His mouth covered mine and his hand massaged my pussy, a finger sliding deep inside with ease. "I think you like me."

"Shut up and kiss me."

He laughed. The finger inside me moved and he rubbed at some sweet spot that drove me out of my fucking head. I gasped.

My neck arched and my eyes opened wide, staring sightlessly up at the ceiling.

"Christ, Mal."

"That's it." His thumb circled my clit, making my leg muscles tremble. This was going to be fast and hard, no doubt about it. I might have somewhat neglected my orgasms during his absence. My libido had been on vacation. Now, it was back and then some. A hot mouth closed over one nipple, sucking hard, teasing with tongue.

I moaned and held him to me. "More."

A second finger joined the first, stretching me slightly, making the contact on my sweet spot so much more effective. My heels dug deep into the mattress. He might just kill me this time, but it would be worth it.

"Tell me you love me," he said, still toying with my nipple.

"I love you."

"No you don't. You're just saying that 'cause you want to come." He rose to look me in the eye with an evil grin. I was done for. "I don't believe you at all."

I grabbed his face, mashing our lips together, kissing him hard. Showing him how I felt. Between my legs, his hand never stopped working, driving me out of my mind. Fingers pumped into me again and again. It was almost enough, but not quite. God, the knot building inside of me. So close.

"Do you love me, Anne?" He sat back on his heels, sliding his fingers in and out of me, making the pressure grow.

"Yes."

From the edge of the bed he grabbed a condom wrapper, ripping it open with his teeth. "Lots?"

I nodded, fighting for breath.

"Like, lots and lots? Or just a little lots?"

"What?"

With a grin, he rolled on the condom. "How much do you love me? How many lots?"

"Mal . . ." I couldn't make sense of the question. My hands fisted in the pillow behind my head.

"See, this is what I mean." He set his arm beside my head and lowered himself over me. Slowly he slid his fingers out of my sex and lined up his cock. I tried to keep my eyes open, but it was a losing battle. My eyelids drifted down. I was lost to the sensation of his thick length pushing into me, making a permanent place for himself. We fit just right.

"I love you more," he said. Then his fingers slid around my clit, giving me what I needed, applying the perfect pressure to set me alight. I exploded. The fire inside of me burning out of control. But so long as I held on to him, it was okay. My legs held him tight, my hands anchoring him to me, bound around his neck. The muscles in my pussy grabbed at his cock, greedy and needing.

And he groaned, pressing his cheek into mine.

I drifted back to reality, awareness returning ever so gradually. Mal started moving, slowly at first, sliding in and out. Little shudders wracked me with each stroke.

"Liar," I whispered, remembering what he'd said. "I love you more."

He smiled, thrusting into me. "Prove it."

I wrapped him up in my legs and arms, bringing his mouth to mine, giving him everything. Trusting him with everything. Because I'd finally found someone who could take both the good and the bad, the sad and the happy. I wanted to do the same for him.

He was being so careful, but there was so much emotion built up inside of him. I could feel it, coursing beneath his skin, raging behind his eyes.

"Harder," I urged him.

He picked up the pace.

"Stop holding back."

"Anne . . ." His jaw was tensed, his green eyes ablaze.

"Do it. Give it to me. I can take it."

Mal didn't need any more prompting. He gathered me up against him, our skin slapping as he pounded into me. Our hips hit hard, his cock driving deep into the heart of me. It was like standing in a storm, frightening and beautiful both. I'd never trusted anyone to be this rough before, to take things this far. He hammered into me. His teeth fixed on my neck, marking me, as his hand gripped my ass cheek, holding me to him. The whole of him shuddered against me as he buried himself deep and came. He shouted my name, his mouth still pressed against my skin.

I kept my arms and legs tight around him, making him collapse on top of me. The heavy weight of him pinned me to the bed. I could hold on to him forever.

We lay there in silence. My face was wet where he pressed his cheek against it. His sweat or tears, I don't know, but he shook for a long time. I petted his hair and stroked his back, running my fingers up and down his spine.

"I love you," I said. "So much I can't say."

He trailed his lips against my jaw. "I believe you."

EPILOGUE

"I'm not sure about this." I sat on the side of our bed, cuddling Killer. He'd tolerate it for short periods, but the way his butt was wriggling my time was nearly up. Puppies tended to only have two speeds in my limited experience. Stop and go. It wasn't unusual to find him fast asleep face down in his food bowl now and then after a hard day's playing.

"What do you want to do?" asked Mal.

"I don't know."

He looked around our bedroom, leaning a hip against the end of our brand-new gigantic four-poster bed. Mal had insisted we needed it and gone into great detail regarding plans for its usage. Apparently I was to play the part of the sacrificial lamb, regularly tied down and offered up to the gods of oral sex. As a fate, I found this to be not even remotely dire. Also, the bed was a far sturdier structure than the one from my apartment. If and when we decided to do more bed jumping, he assured me this one wouldn't die on us.

Mal made living fun. But today was a different matter entirely.

"They'll start arriving soon," he said. "You've been working your ass off. The food's all ready. Everything's organized and you wanted to do this. This was your idea. But if you really think turning tail and running away like a cowardly little lion is best, then that's okay with me too. I'll even help you live with the shame and regret for the rest of your life."

I slumped. "Oh god, you bastard."

"I love you, pumpkin."

"I love you too. I'm just not very good at this stuff." I set Killer down and he immediately chased down the empty Diet Coke bottle. It was his favorite toy since being forced to give up eating Mal's Chucks. His unofficial aunts, Lizzy, Ev, and Lauren bought him every dog treat and toy under the sun, but he would not be swayed from his redneck ways. Best dog ever.

Someone knocked on the door out in the living room area.

Killer might have been my first birthday present. But the real one was the condo opposite David and Ev's, where Mal and I now lived together. Pets were allowed there. What did you say to a guy who bought a condo so you could have the dog you missed out on as a child? Actually, I didn't say anything. I gave him a blow job once I stopped crying. He seemed to appreciate it. Besides, he already knew I loved him. I pretty much told him constantly.

Someone knocked on the door, again.

My shoulders jumped.

"Ready?" he asked.

I nodded. He held his hand out to me and I took it, letting him lead me through the hallway, into the living room.

"You won't leave?" I asked, hating the way my knees were knocking.

"I won't leave. I'll be at your side the whole time."

"Okay." I smiled. "Not that I'm some pathetic weakling using you for a crutch or a safety blanket or anything."

"Hey," he said, grasping my chin gently. "You've been my crutch for the last month and a half. Given me whatever I needed whenever you could. We lean on each other, pumpkin. It's all good."

"Thank you."

He sketched a bow. "Thank *you*."

It was ridiculous really, what a monster I'd made of this situation in my head. But I could slay dragons with him at my side. Without a doubt. I stood up straight, took a deep breath. "I'm fine."

"Yeah, you are. All of our friends are coming. Everyone's got your back, Anne," he said. "This will be the best day before Thanksgiving dinner ever."

We were spending the actual Thanksgiving at his eldest sister's place in Idaho. Lori had died not long after we flew back to Coeur d'Alene, the day after our reunion. It had hit Mal hard. It still hit him hard, but there'd been no more slamming his fist into walls or wiping out a bottle of Jack Daniel's every other night. He did get quiet and withdrawn sometimes. He always came back to me, though.

"You can do this," he said. And I believed him.

He opened the door and there stood Lizzy and Mom. Mom gave me a cautious smile. Her carrot-colored hair had more gray in it than I remembered and lines softened her face. If anything, she seemed more nervous than me, the way her fingers were clasped tight in front of her.

"Hi, Mom." I stepped forward, almost kissing her cheek but not quite. It was a really close call. Maybe next time. "Mom, this is Mal. Mal, this my mother, Jan."

"Hey, Jan. Nice to meet you." Mal moved forward to greet her, all smiles. But his hand never left mine.

Worry lined Mom's face further at the sight of Mal. Her words were nice enough, however, as they exchanged pleasantries. Everything would be fine. We'd get through this. Because the fact was, my life here was good. It had been before Mal came along. And now it was even better. Astronomically so. If my mom and I could move forward and have some sort of functioning relationship, then that was great. If not, I'd survive.

"Come see their place, Mom. It's gorgeous. Mal bought it for Anne for her birthday." Lizzy winked at me, ushering Mom past us and into the condo. Giving me a moment to catch my breath, bless her.

I was extremely fortunate because our home was, indeed, gorgeous. The floor was covered in a very cool, slightly sparkly, black Italian tile. Our walls were pristine white and the furniture gray with splashes of turquoise. Despite the layout being the same, it had a different feel to it than Ev and David's place. Speaking of which, they made excellent neighbors. They loved puppysitting Killer. Or at least Ev did. David still bore some resentment over my dog's chewing of a leather guitar strap or two and peeing on their rug. Some people were so judgy.

Mal and David hung out often, with Ben and Jimmy drifting between their own places and the two condos. The Stage Dive Family never blinked at my inclusion. Something I was profoundly grateful for. They'd even made sure Lizzy felt welcome. Though her continuing crush on Ben still gave me pause.

"Check out the size of their bathtub, Mom." Lizzy's voice drifted down the hall along with Mom's answering words of admiration. It was a big tub. And Mal and I made full use of it. I hardly missed the old claw foot tub from the apartment at all.

"All good?" he asked me quietly, ignoring Killer's scratching at his jeans-clad leg.

"Yes." I turned my face up to his and slipped my hand around his neck. Without a word, he leaned in, fitting his mouth to mine and giving me everything and then some. By the time he finished I was breathing heavy, feeling flushed.

"Break it up." Ben groaned, swinging a bouquet of bright flowers in one hand. "You've got guests, for fuck's sake."

"Aw, that's sweet. You bring me flowers, Benny?" Mal asked, rubbing a hand up and down my back.

"Hell no. I bought your hot girlfriend flowers." He handed the heavy bunch over to my waiting arms.

"Thank you, Ben." I smiled, charmed.

"Well, your hot girlfriend and her equally hot little sister."

I narrowed my eyes at him.

The big man smiled. Such a shit stirrer.

"Where's the rest of them?" asked Ben. He scooped up Killer and then settled himself in the corner of the couch, turning on the TV. With one hand he flicked through channels, with the other he proceeded to rile up my puppy. Soon crazed baby-sized barks, snapping, and growling filled the air. Killer adored Mal, but Ben wasn't too far behind in his doggy affections.

"They'll be here soon," said Mal.

"You heard Lena quit?"

I just about jumped. "What? No. When?"

"Couple of days ago. Jimmy is not pleased."

Mal gave a low whistle but otherwise didn't comment. His gaze went to the hallway, where Mom and Lizzy were winding up their tour on account of them running out of places to look.

"Quick," Mal said, bringing his face close to mine.

"What?"

"This." He covered my mouth with his, sliding his tongue into my mouth. Generally kissing me stupid. Whatever mocking statement Ben made, I missed it. Only kissing Mal mattered. His hands cupped my ass, fingers kneading. My toes curled and my senses went wild. By the time he pulled back, my lips were wet and most definitely so were things downstairs. It took a long minute for me to catch my breath.

"Can't make out in front of your mom," he explained. "Oops. I kinda fucked up your lipstick. More than last time even. Sorry."

"It was worth it."

"Was it?" he asked, heat and affection and a hundred other things shining in his beautiful green eyes.

"Oh, yeah. You're the best." I grinned back at him.

"Pumpkin, hello. Of course I am!"